TIMOTHY R. BALDWIN

Dynasty of Deceit

A Cassie Maddox Mystery, Book 2

INDIES UNITED PUBLISHING HOUSE, LLC

Also by Timothy R. Baldwin

A Shot at Mercy (2019, 2021)
A Crock of Sundries, Volume 1 (2021)
Chemical Burns (2022)
The Unwanted Guest and Other Short Thrillers (2024)

A Kahale and Claude Mystery Series
Book 1: Camp Lenape (2019)
Book 2: Shadows of Doubt (2020)
Book 2.5: A Bazaar Christmas (2020)
Book 3: Operation Varsity Blues (2020)
Book 4: Turkey Trot Troubles (2025)

These and more at
https://www.indiesunited.net/timothy-baldwin

Welcome to Lenape City

Lenape City remembers everything.

The streets keep their secrets, the skyline watches in silence, and behind the polished doors of power, the past is never as buried as people hope.

Private investigator Cassie Maddox has already learned that truth in Lenape City rarely comes easy. What begins as a routine investigation soon pulls her into a web of old money, political influence, and carefully guarded family legacies. The deeper she digs, the clearer it becomes: some names carry power—and some secrets are worth killing to protect.

In Dynasty of Deceit, Cassie moves beyond the shadows of her first case and into the halls where Lenape City's most powerful families built their empires. But in a city built on reputation and inheritance, exposing the truth may cost more than she ever expected.

Coming Soon to the Series

Book 3: Behind the Ivy

Book 4: The Tarnished Band

1

Paper Trail

The spreadsheet on my laptop had outlived its original purpose. It began as a handful of transactions—fractured into tabs, notes, color-coded cells. Now the page won't fit on my screen without compressing the truth into something unreadable.

I push back from the desk.

February snow slants past the window in heavy flakes. Across from me, Rafi scrolls in silence, the soft click of his mouse the only sound in the office. We weren't hunting surprises anymore. We needed confirmation. Patterns don't materialize. They wait until you've stared at them long enough to admit they were never coincidences.

"Anything?" I ask, unable to keep the frustration from my voice.

Rafi glances up, his warm eyes meeting mine. "Not yet. But the variance is tightening. There's a pattern here."

I sigh, rubbing my temples. "We've been at this for weeks, Rafi."

He sets down his pen, giving me his full attention. "Cassie, these things take time. Your uncle's smart—if he is involved, he's covered his tracks well."

My uncle—Alfred Maddox. Not close. Never close. Just present in the way money is present, especially at his establishment, The Genesee Country Club. His polished smile. The flash of his cuff links, a set paired with every three-piece suit he owned. The way he called me "kiddo," though he was as much of a stranger to me as I was to him. During my last investigation, his eyes never quite met mine when I attempted to bait him. It's like trying to catch smoke—there one moment, gone the next.

"I know, I know," I mutter, more to myself than to Rafi. "It's just…"

Rafi leans forward, his voice low and steady. "Trust your instincts, Cassie. They've never led you astray before. If you think there's something here, there probably is."

My eyes drift back to the laptop screen, determination renewed. "You're right. Let's keep digging."

As we return to our respective tasks, I can't help but steal glances at Rafi. His presence is a balm to my frayed nerves, even as it stirs up other, more complicated feelings. I push those thoughts aside, focusing on the numbers before me. There's too much at stake to get distracted now.

The silence stretches between us, broken only by the rustle of paper and the soft tapping of keys. I lose myself in the financial records. But Rafi's right. We're close to creating a clear picture of the college admission scheme Mel Albright has herself tangled up in because of my uncle. I only hope we can gather enough evidence to get Mel, one of many likely victims, out of their financial obligations and pin it all on the one who is truly responsible, or so we suspect.

I rub my temples, the dull ache behind my eyes intensifying. The implications of what we're uncovering hit me like a freight train. A thought I hate, and one I don't earn with evidence, flares anyway. What if Dad knew what my uncle has been up to?

"Cassie?" Rafi's voice pulls me back to the present. "You okay?"

I force a smile. My gaze drifts to the window, the cold glass a stark contrast to my warm skin. Outside, a fresh blanket of snow, pristine white, covers the Lenape City skyline, the familiar buildings silhouetted against the darkening, bruised-purple sky. "Do you ever think about what happens after? If we're right about this, it's not just Uncle Alfred who goes down. It could be my whole family."

The words taste bitter in my mouth. I'd seen what Alfred does to obstacles.

They don't just lose; they disappear—jobs, reputations, sometimes whole lives. There's no predicting what my uncle would do to family.

Rafi's chair creaks as he leans in. "This is odd." His finger traces a line on the spreadsheet. "A transfer from Ignite Global to Genesee."

I snap to attention, previous thoughts momentarily forgotten. "Let me see that." I scan the numbers, my heart racing. "You're right. This could be how they're hiding it."

We lock eyes, the excitement of a potential breakthrough palpable. "We need to dig deeper into the Country Club's finances," I say, already reaching for my laptop.

Rafi's gaze sharpens. "I'll see what I can find on their digital trail."

As we dive back in, part of me wants to pull back, to protect my father and mother from the storm that's coming. To do so would make me just as complicit with my uncle's schemes. I chew my lower lip as my eyes hover over the lines of numbers before me. Ignite Global just may be the lead we need to follow a dangerous road to taking my uncle down.

With dramatic flair, the door swings open, and Lila bursts in like a whirlwind of color and energy. "Coffee delivery for the world's most dedicated private eyes!" she announces, her blue-streaked pixie cut bobbing as she sets down a tray laden with steaming mugs.

I can't help but smile at her entrance. "Lila, you're a lifesaver."

"Don't I know it," she winks, passing me a mug. The rich aroma of freshly brewed coffee fills the air, momentarily drowning out the musty scent of old papers.

Lila's eyes narrow as she takes in the cluttered desk and our haggard appearances. "Seriously, Cass? When was the last time you slept? This case is eating you alive."

I take a sip of coffee, savoring the bitter warmth. "We're close to something big, Lil."

"Uh-huh," she says, unconvinced. With an exaggerated eye roll that would put a teenage drama queen to shame, she declares, "That's it. We're going to Phantom Beats tonight. No arguments."

"Lila, I can't just—"

"Nope!" She cuts me off. "You need a break before you turn into one of these dusty old files."

I turn to Rafi for support, but he raises his hands in surrender. "Don't drag me into this. You know clubs aren't my scene."

Traitor.

Lila's grin is triumphant. "See? Even Rafi agrees you need a night off."

I sigh, knowing I'm outnumbered. "Fine, fine. One night out."

"Yes!" Lila pumps her fist. "But one condition—absolutely no work talk. I mean it, Cassie. Leave the case files at home."

As she sashays out of the room, I can't help but chuckle. Maybe one night of normalcy is exactly what I need to face whatever comes next.

I take a sip of the coffee Lila brought, savoring the rich flavor. It's a stark contrast to the bitter dregs I've been nursing for hours. Rafi catches my eye, a hint of amusement playing at the corners of his mouth.

"She's got a point, you know," he says, leaning back in his chair. "Even brilliant minds need a recharge sometimes."

I roll my eyes, but there's no real annoyance behind it. "I thought you were on my side."

He shrugs, his expression softening. "I'm always on your side, Cassie. That's why I agree with Lila. You've been pushing yourself too hard."

The sincerity in his voice catches me off guard. My chest tightens with a mix of gratitude and something else I can't quite name. To cover the moment, I gesture at the piles of documents surrounding us.

"And what about all this? The trail could go cold if we take our eyes off it for even a second."

Rafi's response is calm, measured. "The documents will still be here tomorrow. Your health and sanity, on the other hand..."

I can't help but laugh. "Are you implying I'm going insane, Alvi?"

"I'm implying that even the most dedicated investigator needs balance," he counters, his tone gentle. "And Lila has a gift for bringing that balance into our lives, doesn't she?"

As if on cue, Lila's laughter echoes from somewhere in the building. It's infectious, lightening the atmosphere even from a distance. I smile despite the weight of our investigation.

"She has that effect," I admit, taking another sip of coffee. The warmth spreads through me, releasing the tension I've been carrying. "I don't know what I'd do without her. Or you, for that matter."

Rafi's eyes widen slightly at my admission. He clears his throat, suddenly very interested in the spreadsheet in front of him. "Well, um, that's what friends are for, right?"

Deep in a case, it's easy to lose sight of the support system I have.

"You're right," I say finally. "Both of you. A night out is exactly what I need."

Rafi lifts his head. Relief softens his features. "Good. Because if you didn't agree, I'm pretty sure Lila was planning a kidnapping."

We share a laugh, the tension of the investigation momentarily dissolving. I turn back to my laptop with renewed purpose. The path ahead is still murky, fraught with potential danger, but I'm not walking it alone. And sometimes that makes all the difference.

As Lila's footsteps fade down the hallway, Rafi leans forward, his eyes bright with newfound energy. "Cassie, I've got something here," he says, tapping his finger on a column of numbers. "These transfers between the Genesee Country Club and your uncle's foundation. The timing is... interesting."

I lean in, my heart quickening as I scan the data. "You're right," I murmur, my mind racing. "It's like clockwork, always right after a major donation to the university. But why route it through the country club?"

Rafi's fingers fly across his keyboard. "Could be a way to obscure the paper trail. Let's cross-reference these dates with the club's event calendar."

We fall into a familiar rhythm, the quiet hum of computers and rustling papers punctuated by our focused exchanges.

"Here," I say, pointing to a series of entries. "Check out these 'private events' at the club. They line up perfectly with the transfers."

Rafi's brow furrows. "And the guest lists for these events?"

"Conveniently missing," I reply, frustration creeping into my voice. "Of course."

As we dig deeper, I find my thoughts drifting to my uncle—Alfred Maddox, a name that keeps resurfacing on financial records from a case file we couldn't let rest. At this point, we're acting on speculation, hoping to find that solid shred of evidence on which to hang Mel's case.

"Cassie?" Rafi's voice breaks through my reverie. "Where'd you go just now?"

I blink, forcing myself back to the present. "This goes way beyond just my uncle, doesn't it?"

Rafi's expression softens. "It does. But we're doing the right thing here. You know that, right?"

I swallow hard. "I do. It's just... messy."

"Life usually is," Rafi says with a wry smile. "But hey, that's why they pay us the big bucks, right?"

I snort. "Oh yeah, I'm rolling in it. All those long nights and cold coffee? Totally worth it for my nonexistent fortune."

We share a laugh; the tension easing slightly. As we turn back to our work, I scan the document in front of me, and suddenly, my heart leaps into my throat. "Rafi," I whisper, my voice barely audible over the hum of the office. "Did you see this?"

I slide the paper across the desk, my hand trembling slightly. Rafi leans in, his brow furrowing as he reads. The document is a financial statement from The Genesee's Scholarship Fund, and there, clear as day, is a transaction with Alfred Maddox's personal account.

"Holy shit," Rafi breathes, his eyes widening. "This could be it, Cassie. The smoking gun?"

My mind races, thoughts colliding like pinballs. This is the break we've been waiting for, but the implications...

"We need to verify this," I finally manage, my voice hoarse. "Cross-reference it with the other accounts; see if there's a pattern."

Rafi's already pulling up spreadsheets on his laptop. "On it. But Cassie, if this checks out..."

"I know," I cut him off, not ready to hear it spoken aloud. Pence's rooftop allegations press in—my father's reputation not as spotless as I once believed, my grandfather's potential mishandling of funds at the old Lenape Savings and Loans. I didn't have the guts to verify these allegations. So, why now? Conducting a deep dive into my uncle's affairs seems somehow safer, easier. But if we do find something, what does that say about the whole of the Maddox name?

We work in tense silence for a few minutes, the only sounds the clicking of keyboards and shuffling of papers. My heart pounds so loud I'm sure Rafi can hear it.

"Cassie," Rafi says softly, breaking the silence. "We've got multiple corroborating transactions. This... this could be the lead we need."

I close my eyes, taking a deep breath. When I open them, I meet Rafi's gaze. "We have to pursue this," I say.

Rafi meets my eyes, his jaw tightening just a fraction. "Are you sure? This could have serious consequences, not just for your uncle, but for you and your family."

I picture my father's face when he finds out. I remember the family dinners. The holidays.Though he was ever elusive, I wanted to believe the image—successful and a part of my family. That is until he offered me the opportunity to go on a guaranteed scholarship to Dartmouth. Something felt off about my uncle's offer, and that's when I followed my parents' lead. I distanced myself from him. That's also why I took on Mel Albright's case. She and countless other students had their futures manipulated, and their hard work undermined by this scheme.

"I'm sure," I say, my resolve solidifies. "We owe it to the truth, and to everyone affected by this scandal. We can't back down now."

Rafi reaches across the desk, squeezing my hand briefly. "Alright then. Let's do this."

As we dive back into our work, the weight of what's coming settles on my shoulders.

"We need to follow the money trail," I say, tapping my pen against a notepad. "These transactions through Ignite Global—they're our best lead."

Rafi's fingers fly over his laptop keyboard. "I can set up an algorithm to track similar patterns across other accounts. If we can establish a consistent flow of funds..."

"...we might just nail him," I finish, a mix of excitement and dread coursing through me.

We work in tandem, the familiar rhythm of our partnership falling into place. Rafi's tech savvy complements my investigative instincts. For a moment, I'm grateful for his unwavering support as we outline our next steps—subpoenas to prepare, interviews to conduct. This is what I've trained for, what I've built Maddox Investigative Services to do.

But as the adrenaline of the moment fades, reality sets in. I lean back in my chair, the weight of what we're about to undertake settling over me like a heavy blanket.

"This could tear my family apart." I whisper, more to myself than to him.

Rafi places a warm, grounding hand on my shoulder. "You're doing what's right, Cassie. It's who you are."

I take a deep breath. The path ahead is fraught with danger—legal, personal, emotional. I reach for my phone and send a message to my uncle.

Tomorrow. At his house.

If I'm going to dismantle a member of my own family, I'll do it to his face.

2

Pressure Points

The imposing structure of Alfred's mansion looms before me. I take a deep breath, straighten my jacket, and approach the entrance. The doorman nods with recognition as if I'm expected—which, of course, I am—and I step into the hushed opulence of the lobby.

My footsteps echo on the polished marble as I make my way toward Alfred's office. With each step feeling heavier than the last, the weight of my suspicions press down through my ribs. I pause outside his door.

"You can do this, Cassie," I mutter, then knock.

"Come in," Alfred's voice calls out, smooth as ever.

I push open the door, plastering on a smile. "Uncle Alfred. Hope I'm not interrupting."

From behind his desk surprise flickers across his face for half a breath before it's replaced by his usual charm. "Cassie. Punctual as usual. What can I do for you?"

I settle into the chair across from him. He closes his laptop and clears a few papers to the side, as if making space for me in his world. On the desk, a framed photo catches my eye—Alfred with another man around his age, both sharply dressed, posed in front of a symmetrical brick building with a distinctive belt course of raised stonework.

I reach for the photograph.

"Is this—"

"Penamore College," Uncle Alfred says with pride. "And that's Dean Harold Stratford, PhD.D." His smile turns faintly amused. "You of course know the other handsome devil."

I return the smile, polite enough to pass, not enough to hide the quickened rhythm in my pulse. "I didn't know you had ties with the college."

"The Genesee set up the Genesee-Penamore Action Fund in partnership with the college," he says. "But that's as far as the partnership goes."

I cross one leg over the other, rest my elbow on the arm of the chair, and let my smile sharpen into something deliberate. "Funny you should bring that up. I'm working on a case right now involving financial records. Lots of transactions between educational institutions and private foundations. It's fascinating how money moves in those circles."

I wait for a flicker of recognition or discomfort.

Nothing.

Alfred's expression remains impassive, posture relaxed. Too relaxed.

"Is that so?" he asks with an easy smile. "I'm pleased to offer whatever advice I can. As you already know, the world of finance can be quite complex—especially for large institutions and charitable organizations."

"Absolutely," I say. "It's amazing how intricate some of these transactions can be. I've seen some patterns that are... intriguing, to say the least."

Alfred's eyebrow rises slightly. "Intriguing? How so?"

"Oh, you know," I say, aiming for casual. "Unusual patterns of donations. Scholarships that don't quite add up. That sort of thing."

As I speak, I concentrate on micro-expressions, shifts in body language—anything.

Nothing.

His composure is infuriating. And I have to admit, impressive.

"Well, Cassie," he says, leaning back, "I'm sure there are perfectly reasonable explanations for whatever you're seeing. The world of high-level finance and philanthropy can seem opaque from the outside."

I bite back a retort. Stay calm. Stay smart. This man is a master of deflection with a facade that won't easily crack.

I knew that coming in.

I uncross my legs and set the photograph back down—slightly off-kilter. "You're right, Uncle Alfred. But sometimes what seems opaque can become painfully clear under scrutiny. Especially when subpoenas start landing."

His fingers tighten almost imperceptibly on the armrest. His face doesn't change.

"Subpoenas?" he chuckles, practiced and hollow. "My dear, you're letting your imagination run wild. Unless I misunderstood you, you just started working on your little financial case against..." He tilts his head. "Who did you say?"

"I didn't." I lean forward, my voice lowering. "But some transactions I'm seeing tell a familiar story. One about a teenage girl receiving a full-ride scholarship in crew even though she never applied for it—never touched a paddle in her life." I laugh once, sharp. "Imagine that. And when she dropped out, even getting into community college was a bitch."

For a split second, something flickers behind his eyes—anger, annoyance, a spark of something human.

Then it's gone.

"Cassie," he says, tone gentle but firm, "I can assure you I had nothing to do with your poor decisions so many years ago."

My jaw tightens.

I reach for the Newton's Cradle nestled on his desk and give a gentle tug on one ball, setting the steel in motion, watching it swing back and forth with mesmerizing precision.

Maybe I do it because I need something in this room to admit cause and effect.

"Maybe not," I say, voice low and even. "But engaging in bribery and financial fraud raises red flags for an auditor. And that often leads to conviction. Prison time."

I let the words hang there. Clean. Sharp. Final.

Alfred never lets his eyes settle on the cradle.

He leans forward and adjusts the photograph, straightening it with careful fingers.

"So can libel, my dear niece," he says. "I do hope you avoid another costly mistake. Especially one that drags your colleague down with you." His smile is almost kind. "How's Rafi, by the way?"

The air shifts.

I bite my lip. For the first time, I'm at a loss for words.

I came in with two of a kind. A pair at best.

He's holding a royal flush and smiling like he's doing me a favor.

"I assure you," he continues, voice soothing, "there's nothing to worry about. Perhaps you're simply seeing shadows where there are none."

I force myself to breathe.

He's good. I'll give him that.

But his composure only fuels my determination.

"Maybe you're right," I concede, forcing a smile that doesn't reach my eyes. "I suppose I can get carried away sometimes."

I stand.

As I turn toward the door, my mind is already racing, plotting my next move. This conversation didn't crack Alfred's façade—but he freely admitted ties to Penamore.

And he volunteered a name I didn't ask for.

That's something I can use.

Outside, the crisp February air nips at my cheeks as I descend the marble steps, but I barely notice. My thoughts replay every nuance of the exchange like a recording I can't shut off.

His composure was impeccable—almost too perfect. He didn't flinch at subpoenas. He didn't blink at Penamore. But when he said Rafi's name, he said it like a password.

When I get into my car, I pull out my phone and fire off a text to Dad.

2 Beans Café.

His reply comes almost instantly:

See you there.

* * *

I push open the door to 2 Beans Café, the familiar rush of warmth and coffee wrapping around me. Dad's already seated in the back corner, jacket still on, hands cupped around a mug like he's been waiting longer than he'll admit.

"Hey, kiddo," he says, sliding the coffee toward me before I sit. "You've got the face of someone who picked a fight with someone who fights back."

I huff a quiet laugh and take the cup. "That obvious?"

He studies me over the rim. "You've got the Maddox set to your jaw. The one where you learned something you didn't want to be right about."

I don't answer right away. Steam curls between us. Finally, I say, "I talked to someone today. Someone careful. Someone who knows how to stay clean while other people get dirty."

Dad's mouth tightens a fraction. "And?"

"And I couldn't crack him," I admit. "But I rattled him."

"That's not the same thing," he says evenly.

"No," I agree. "It's worse."

He leans back, eyes never leaving mine. "Tell me what he did, not what you think it means."

I consider how much to give him. Then I choose one clean thread.

"He volunteered the name of a fund. One I didn't ask about." I take a sip, buying steadiness. "And he warned me about libel before I accused him of anything."

Dad nods once. "Defensive move. Means he thinks you're close enough to matter."

"Or close enough to crush," I say.

"Same thing," he replies. "Depends on who gets there first."

I trace a finger along the rim of my mug. "He also knew my partner's name."

That gets his attention. Dad's gaze sharpens. "Without you offering it?"

"Yes."

"That's not coincidence," he says. "That's reconnaissance."

The word lands heavy.

I let it settle. "So what do I do?"

He doesn't answer right away. Instead, he asks, "Did you threaten him?"

"I implied scrutiny. Auditors. Paper trails."

Dad exhales slowly. "Then you've done all the talking you're going to do with him for now."

"Dad—"

"Cassie." Gentle. Firm. "If he's as careful as you say, the next move isn't conversation. It's containment."

I sit back, listening.

"You don't confront people like that," he continues. "You box them in. You figure out who touches the money, who files the paperwork, who signs without understanding what they're signing. You make it impossible for them to keep their hands clean."

My pulse slows, replaced by something steadier.

A plan.

Dad takes a sip, then adds, quieter, "And you don't do it alone."

I hesitate. "I wasn't planning to bring you in. Not yet."

A corner of his mouth lifts. "Good. You shouldn't. Not until you've got something that doesn't disappear the second someone makes a call."

There it is—the line between us. Still intact. Still tense.

"I'm running into the same thing on my end," he goes on. "Roadblocks. Missing files. Orders that don't come in writing."

"From Burgess?" I ask carefully.

His jaw tightens. "From people who answer to him."

That's all he gives me.

And it's enough.

Dad sets his mug down. "Here's my advice, Cass. Don't focus on the man. Focus on the system he's hiding behind. Institutions get sloppy. People like him don't."

It locks into place—the fund name, the threat, the polish, the way he said Rafi like he already owned a file on him.

"Thanks," I say. "That's exactly what I needed."

He studies me for a moment, then nods. "Be careful."

"I will."

We stand. There's an awkward beat—the space where things could be said and aren't. Then he gives my shoulder a brief squeeze.

As I step back onto the street, the cold air clears my head.

Alfred didn't lie to me.

He didn't have to.

He showed me which threads not to pull.

I pull out my phone and text Rafi:

Genesee–Penamore Action Fund. Need filings, admin names, and event calendars. No more conversations. We build the box.

His reply comes seconds later.

On it.

I slip the phone into my pocket and start walking.

This time, I'm not chasing Alfred.

I'm chasing the paper he thought no one would follow.

3

Recruiting Allies

I burst through the door of my office, purpose hot on my tail. "Did you find anything on Genesee–Penamore Action Fund? Stratford?"

Rafi's eyes flicker to meet mine. "Good morning to you, too, Cass."

"Good morning, Rafi," I say, my eyes shifting away from his gaze and onto a stack of documents. "What's all this?"

"Dead ends."

"Shit!"

"Exactly," Rafi says. He shifts the monitor toward me.

"Nothing there, either?" I ask.

Rafi taps the stack of papers next to him. "Listen, Cassie," he says. "Setbacks are just part of the investigative process."

I square my shoulders and suck in a breath. Focus on the institution, not the man, my father had advised. "Let's table Alfred, the Action Fund and Dean Stratford."

Rafi's eyes widen. "Who are you and what did you do with my friend?"

I smile. "Ignite Global. That's our focus. Secondary is The Genesee. Let's assume, just for a moment my uncle is clean."

Rafi's fingers fly with rapid precision over the keyboard, his skin an amber warmth, his deep brown eyes aglow in the monitor's light. He catches my gaze. "What?"

Heat radiates to my cheeks. "It's... warm in here." I undo my jacket and loosen my scarf, and lean in. "What've you got?"

"We focus on what we've got," Rafi replies, gesturing to the documents. "These financial records are from Ignite Global. We've already found some interesting discrepancies. From there, we cross-reference what we have electronically. We build a solid case, one that points to… whoever… is running Ignite Global."

I'm about to respond when the office door flies open, bringing with it a whirlwind of blonde hair, flakes of snow, and nervous energy. Mel Albright bursts in, her usually graceful movements now sharp with urgency.

"Cassie!" she exclaims, slightly out of breath. "We've got a problem."

I straighten in my chair, my senses on high alert. "What's going on, Mel?"

She paces the small space, her athletic frame taut with tension.

"I just got back from The Genesee. Mr. Maddox—he said my acceptance to Penamore could disappear overnight if I didn't do what he wanted."

My stomach drops. "What? How can he do that?"

Mel runs a hand through her hair, her voice trembling slightly. "I don't know, but he seemed pretty confident. And with the Gala coming up… Cassie, this could ruin everything I've worked for."

I stand up, moving to place a steadying hand on Mel's shoulder.

"Tell me exactly what he said."

"He asked me how excited I was about Penamore. Told me it was a fine institution—very particular about its standards."

She swallows.

"Then he said admissions files don't really close when people think they do. That they stay… flexible. Especially when funding is involved."

I don't interrupt.

"He asked whether I'd ever had reason to look closely at the source of my scholarship money. Whether I was confident everything attached to my application would hold up to a second look."

Her voice drops.

"And then he said, 'I'd hate for something administrative to interfere with your fall plans.'"

She meets my eyes.

"He never used the word revoke. He didn't have to."

My mind races, trying to piece together this new development. Is this Alfred striking back? The thought retreats.

"Did he say why?" I ask.

Mel shrinks back. "You know why."

I exchange a glance with Rafi. "We're already backing off of my uncle."

Mel takes a deep breath, her eyes darting between Rafi and me. "There's more," she says, her voice dropping to a near whisper. "The Super Sleuths followed us."

My eyebrows shoot up. "The Super Sleuths? You mean those high school kids?"

Mel nods, her fingers fidgeting with the strap of her bag. "Abby and I were getting into Mr. Maddox's car, and I swear I saw Alissa and Janice sneaking out of the building after us. They tailed us, but not very well."

I lean against my desk, processing this information. The Super Sleuths— teenage amateur detectives who'd already caused more trouble than they knew. What are they doing mixed up in all this?

"Did they follow you all the way to The Genesee?" I ask, my investigator's instincts kicking into overdrive.

"I kept catching glimpses of them," Mel replies. "It wasn't until we got to the club that I lost track."

My mind races with possibilities. Are these kids onto something, or are they just causing trouble? Either way, it's a complication we don't need, especially not with Alfred hanging Mel's acceptance to Penamore over her head..

"Tell me exactly what happened at The Genesee," I press, leaning forward. "Every detail."

Mel's expression tightens. "Well, that's the thing. Our meeting with Mr. Maddox and Ms. Calhoun was cut short. We were discussing my 'scholarship,'"—she makes air quotes—"when suddenly Mr. Maddox went rigid. He excused himself, saying he had urgent business. But Cassie," her voice drops even lower, "I'm pretty sure someone was caught listening in on us."

My heart rate picks up. "Listening in? Are you certain?"

"Not 100%, but…" Mel bites her lip. "I heard a commotion outside the room. Raised voices, like someone was being chased down. And Mr. Maddox was… scared. I've never seen him like that before."

I exchange a glance with Rafi. This could be the break we've been waiting for. But it also means the stakes just got a whole lot higher.

"Mel," I say carefully, "I need you to walk me through everything you remember. Every word, every reaction. This could be important."

As Mel recounts the details, my mind whirs with possibilities. Who was listening in? What did they hear? And most importantly—how can we use this to apply leverage our investigation?

Mel's eyes light up as she finishes recounting the events at The Genesee. "You know what?" she says, leaning in conspiratorially. "You should meet the others. They hang at Slice's practically every day after school. Maybe they picked up on something I missed."

I raise an eyebrow. "The others?"

"Yeah, you know—Marcus, Nate, Janice, and Alissa. The Super Sleuths," Mel explains, a hint of pride in her voice. "They're sharp, Cassie. They might have crucial information."

"They may be a liability—legally," I say, and turn to Rafi. "What do you think?"

"Agreed," he says. "Hear them out, but they need to understand they are acting as witnesses in your case, not as investigators."

"Understood," Mel says. "Texting them now."

* * *

My fingers drum against the steering wheel as I pull into Slice's parking lot. The neon pizza slice in the window flickers, casting an intermittent glow across the asphalt. I kill the engine but don't immediately get out, lost in thought.

"What am I doing?" I mutter to myself, leaning back in the seat. Images of my teenage years flash through my mind—the thrill of investigation, the rush of uncovering secrets. But also the consequences. The juvenile record that still haunts me.

Mel catches my eye and waves. I give a slight nod in return and climb out of the car. As I approach the group, Mel tilts her head.

"You okay?" she asks quietly.

I plaster on a smile. "Just thinking. Let's do this."

We enter Slice's together, the smell of melting cheese and tomato sauce enveloping us. As we settle into a large corner booth, I study each teen's face. Their eagerness is palpable, but there's also an undercurrent of nervousness.

"Alright," I say, leaning forward. "Before we start, I need you all to understand something. This investigation—it's not a game. There could be serious consequences if we're not careful. Are you sure you want to be involved?"

There's a moment of silence as they exchange glances. Then Marcus speaks up, his voice steady. "Ms. Maddox, we know the risks. But this affects our future, our school. We want to help."

I take it in—the way they hold their ground, the way no one breaks eye-contact. I recognize the expression because I've worn it before. Back when no one bothered to show me how to aim it.

"Okay," I say finally, feeling a weight lift from my shoulders. "Let's hear what you've found out."

As the four of them compare notes, the picture sharpens fast. As they talk over each other—dates, donations, whispered warnings—I start fitting the pieces together. Applications reopening. Scholarships as leverage. Reviews quietly re-triggered when money changed hands.

As their recap comes to a close, one question comes to my mind. "Exactly how did you come by all this information?"

Marcus begins. "My—"

Alissa cuts him off. "Someone inside the administration recruited us."

"To find out what our classmates know," Marcus adds.

"And do nothing illegal," Janice says, elbowing Nate in the ribs.

He grimaces. "Yeah. They stressed that one."

I take a sip of my soda, more to buy time than because I need it. The teens are watching me closely, waiting for a reaction. It's a delicate balance—I need to be open enough to earn their trust, but professional enough to keep the room from tipping into panic.

"It's... interesting," I say carefully. "And what exactly did you see and hear at The Genesee?"

As Mel starts to answer, my attention drifts to the others. Nate's fingers drum a nervous rhythm against the tabletop. Alissa nods along, her expression intent, like she's matching Mel's words to something already filed away. Janice, though, keeps scanning the pizzeria, shoulders tight, like she's half-expecting someone to recognize her.

I lift a hand. "Hold on a second. Janice—are you okay?"

She hesitates, then shakes her head. "We didn't mean to eavesdrop," she says quickly. "But we were there. Alissa and me."

Alissa straightens. "They were in one of the private rooms," she says. "Mr. Maddox, Mel, and Abby Jenkins. We were in the hallway. We didn't hear everything."

"But enough," Janice adds. "Mr. Maddox kept saying things were 'administrative.' Like admissions decisions weren't really final. Like they could be reopened."

"And he talked about scholarships like they were leverage," Alissa says. "Like funding and acceptance were the same thing."

Janice swallows. "He mentioned Ignite. Said they don't like loose ends."

The table goes quiet.

"Mel told him her future wasn't a transaction," Alissa says. "And he said it was. Just not one she controlled."

Janice hesitates, searching my face. "We left right after. We don't know if we heard it right—or if it even matters."

"It matters," I say. "And you did the right thing telling me."

I turn back to Mel. "Is this an accurate picture of what my uncle told you?"

Mel nods.

Janice startles, her eyes snapping back to me. "Are we really onto something."

Protectiveness hits hard. They're smart, but they're still just that—kids.

Am I doing the right thing by involving them? The weight of it settles on my shoulders anyway.

"It might be," I concede. "But remember, our priority is staying safe. If at any point you feel uncomfortable or threatened, you tell me immediately. Understood?"

They nod solemnly. Whatever comes next, it's on me. This investigation is about to enter a new phase, and I'm not sure any of us are ready for what it's going to demand.

Marcus leans forward, his hazel eyes intense. "Ms. Maddox, you should know about the scholarship applications we saw. Ms. Calhoun, our guidance counselor, dropped a folder, and... well, something didn't add up."

I lean in, my curiosity piqued. "What do you mean, Marcus?"

He exchanges a glance with Nate before continuing. "The applications were filled with inconsistencies. GPAs that didn't match the transcripts, extracurriculars that seemed made up. And the weird part? All the applicants had connections to Ignite Global."

My mind races, connecting dots. Ignite Global. Maybe even The Genesee - Penamore Action fund. Provided we can find a connection.

"That's... concerning," I say, careful to keep my tone neutral. "Nate, did you notice anything else?"

Nate nods, his bravado subdued. "Yeah, there were notes in the margins. Things like 'priority admission' and 'special consideration.' It felt... off."

A familiar tightness settles in my chest—the kind that comes with a lead and everything attached to it. "Alissa, Janice, you mentioned Principal Moss and some photos?"

Alissa leans forward, her voice low but intense. "Principal Moss has been acting weird lately. Secretive phone calls, closed-door meetings. And then there's what we found at the Genesee."

Janice pulls out her phone, her fingers trembling slightly as she swipes through photos. "We stumbled onto this hidden room. It was like something out of a movie, all dark wood and plush red velvet chairs. But this is what you need to see."

She hands me the phone, and I find myself staring at a placard: "Our Legacy and Our Future." Below it, a sea of names. I recognize some—prominent families, business leaders, politicians.

"My God," I breathe, my mind whirling. Every name a thread begging to be pulled.

Eager faces around me await my reply, their expressions a mix of excitement and apprehension. They've done good work, but they have no idea of the hornets' nest they've just kicked.

"You've all been incredibly helpful," I say, choosing my words carefully. "But from this point forward, you don't go snooping around on your own. But if something crosses your path, you bring it to me, or to your administrator. That's not a suggestion."

Soon after we wrap up, the teens promise to stay at a safe distance and share what they uncover. I promise to share what I can to keep them safe. They file out of Slices, their heads bent together in excited conversation. A knot forms in my stomach. I pray I haven't made a terrible mistake.

For now, they'd keep on eye on Principal Moss, Ms. Calhoun, and their classmates. Meanwhile, another idea comes to mind.

Picking up my phone, I dial Rafi. The familiar sound of his voice answers on the first ring, bringing a smile to my face.

"How did it go with the Super Sleuths?" He asks, his tone laced with laughter.

I recount the details of our conversation, then pause before adding. "How would you like to go undercover with me tomorrow?"

Rafi lets out a playful scoff. "Usually, I don't agree to anything unless I know what it is," Rafi says. "But sure, fill me in on the plan when you get back."

The idea of working shoulder-to-shoulder in the field with Rafi sends a charge through me—excitement and anticipation. That's how I know it matters.

4

Undercover Connections

Waxed floors and teenage angst hit me the moment Rafi and I step through Lenape High's front doors. I'm in a blazer meant to read concerned parent. Rafi catches my glance—almond-brown eyes, the faintest sparkle of amusement—then keeps moving like he belongs here. We don't need words. Years of friendship have turned silence into shorthand.

"Ready, dear?" He grins. "Scott's future rests in this very moment."

Suppressing a smirk at the mention of our imaginary prodigy, I say. "Let's hope our acting skills are up to par."

The student body—a torrent of backpacks and nervous energy—flows around us. Two security cameras monitor the hallway. A group of girls huddles by a set of lockers. One glances at a group of tall, athletic boys and turns to whisper to her friends. They laugh. Two teachers brush past another group of students, breaking up the traffic jam in the hallway.

My shoulders tense, and I can't decide if I'm reacting to memories from my high school days or whether there's something else lingering beneath the typical high school chaos.

"See anything?" I ask Rafi.

He tilts his head. "Other than looking only a few years older than most kids here. Nothing's standing out to me."

I relax my shoulders as we navigate through the crowd toward the administrative offices. Should the question of our age come up in conversation, Rafi and I have our cover story. Hopefully, it'll convince our audience.

Rafi tips his chin toward the bulletin board outside the main office. A full-color display celebrates hundreds of honor roll and high honor roll recipients from the previous quarter.

"Impressive," I say. "I'm sure Scott will soar to the top of that list."

Without missing a beat, Rafi responds. "I was thinking the same thing, dear. The academic rigor here is what Scott needs to thrive."

We are greeted by a smiling receptionist, reading glasses affixed to a chain around her neck, in the administrative offices. "How can I help you?"

I open my mouth to respond, though Rafi beats me to it. "Mr. and Mrs. Alvi. Here to see the principal."

"We're hoping to understand the admissions process," I add smoothly, stepping forward before the woman can ask anything else.

While the woman hits a few keys, my jaw tenses. Rafi glances at me, a playful glint in his eyes, but I don't return the smile; a knot of tension tightens in my chest.

"Now," the woman says. "Why don't you lovely folks take a seat? Mr. Moss should be out in just a moment."

We sit. Rafi nudges my knee. "Too much?"

"Fine." I say, but my pulse won't settle. If he keeps driving, I'll keep reacting—and that isn't why I built my own agency. Next question is mine.

A moment later, Principal Moss emerges from his office. The broad smile and wire-rimmed glasses don't soften his presence.

With an extended hand, he approaches us. "Mr. and Mrs. Alvi. Welcome to Lenape High School. What can I do for you?"

I step forward, taking Moss's hand into mine. Together, Rafi and I follow him into his office. Awards decorate the walls, boasting of the school's supposed excellence and Mr. Moss's stellar leadership within the school district. How many of these accolades did he legitimately earn and how many resulted from the alleged corruption the Super Sleuths claim hides behind these walls?

"We've heard wonderful things about Lenape High," I begin, settling into a plush chair. "We're impressed by your admissions process. It appears very selective, especially for a public school."

Moss's smile doesn't waver, though I notice his fingers tighten on the leather portfolio he holds before him. "We pride ourselves on maintaining high standards," he replies. "Our focus on academic and athletic standards ensures our admissions process is rigorous, though fair."

Rafi glances at me and nods. A green light for me to take the lead. "Principal Moss—"

"Please call me Wayne."

I smile. "Wayne, could you walk us through the admission process? We want to ensure Scott has the best chance at getting into this high school."

The leather office chair creaks as Moss leans back with a smile. "Though I must admit, you both seem quite young to have a high school-aged son."

"Quite young," Rafi replies. "My wife and I opted to adopt. When we went to the agency, we connected with Scott."

Moss's already broad smile expanded further. "Ah! Philanthropists. Well, you are both in for a treat."

At that, Moss launches into a well-rehearsed spiel, becoming animated as he highlights the pride of Lenape High—their legacy of academic excellence, community service, and ten-year championship streak in eighty percent of the school's sports.

"Impressive," Rafi interjects, keeping his tone casual and neutral. "But, what my wife and I are concerned about are services for students who might need additional support."

Moss appears to deflate. "Are you referring to special education services?"

"For starters," I say. "But we're also interested in the school's partnerships with colleges and universities."

Moss averts his attention to flipping through the portfolio in front of him. "We have several programs available," he says at last. "But without official enrollment and transcripts, I can't discuss the details of the school's relationship with local or national colleges and universities."

I lean forward, my heart pounding. We're close to something; I can feel it.

"Of course, we understand," I say, forcing a note of disappointment into my voice. "It's just that we've heard rumors about arrangements for families with the right connections."

Moss's eyes narrow almost imperceptibly. "I can assure you, Mrs. Alvi, that all our admissions decisions are based on merit."

Moss clears his throat. "Admissions decisions are—" He stops, adjusts the portfolio. "They're guided by policy. Consistently." He smiles again, but it doesn't reach his eyes. "If Lenape High admits Scott, we'll take good care of him."

I take Rafi's hand and squeeze. "That's reassuring to hear, Mr. Moss... er... Wayne. We will keep Lenape High School as an option for our child's future."

"Speaking of options," Rafi adds. "Those are some impressive trophies. What's the ratio of academic and athletic scholarships offered to your students?"

Once again, leather creaks as Moss shifts in his seat. The principal pulls out a brochure and hands it to Rafi. "On average, community colleges accept just about anyone holding at least a 2.0. However, the most well-rounded students are the ones who get a second look by the most prestigious universities."

"Such as Penamore?" I ask.

Moss nods toward the brochure. "Among others. I believe the brochure your husband holds will provide sufficient details about college admissions. As any educated adult would know, athletic achievement is only a minor factor."

Rafi hands me the brochure, and I feign interest as I flip through it. Setting the brochure aside, I lean in. "And other factors? We have connections through the Genesee Country Club. We've heard such connections can be quite influential when applying to universities and receiving scholarships."

For a split second, Moss's broad smile fades. His eyes shift from me to Rafi, who raises his eyebrows in baited anticipation of Moss's response.

"What any well-established and well-endowed institution does with its finances is its business," Moss says, choosing his words with calculation. "But I can assure you, admission into this institution and beyond is a fair and above-board process."

When our time is up, I stand and extend my hand. "Your time is very much appreciated."

"You've given us a lot to think about," Rafi says as he shakes hands with Moss.

"The pleasure is mine," Moss says. "Schedule a meeting with the counseling office if you have additional questions."

Taking our leave of Principal Moss, I catch Rafi's eye. Understanding passes between us as our conversation with Moss has confirmed the Super Slueths' suspicions. Something is up with Lenape High School.

The school bell rings, and my shoulders tense. Rafi smiles at me and says, "Relax, dear. Our need to rush to AP Bio is way behind us."

I laugh as a stream of chattering students rushes around us. "Check it out," I say, nodding toward a woman rushing down the hallway. Her brow furrows, her loose bun falls over her shoulders, and she clutches a stack of papers. Just as she reaches a corner, she collides with a group of teens, sending her papers scattering everywhere.

I rush to her aid with Rafi in tow.

"Thank you," she says, as I hand her a stack of papers—file folders to be exact. My eyes catch the heading. A student's name. Records.

Rafi hands her a stack of papers. "Can we help you carry this stuff to your office? You seem—"

"Overworked?" the woman asks. "This is the busiest time of year for the counseling office. Debbie Calhoun." She extends a hand from beneath her papers.

"Cassie," I say, taking her hand. "And this is my... husband... Rafi. We'd like to enroll our son, Scott."

Debbie's smile comes fast—professional, practiced—but her grip is tight, like she's bracing for the next crisis.

"Follow me. We have four full-time guidance counselors employed at the high school. So, we can support all of our students. Did you have a specific concern in mind?"

As I walk beside her, I keep my tone casual. "How does your office support students as they apply to schools? It is such a stressful process."

Debbie nods. "Tell me about it! Though we average close to four hundred students in our graduating classes, all our students receive the one-to-one support they need. Students can schedule with us anytime, and we follow up with those who don't schedule with us on their own anyway."

"That's wonderful!" I say, then steer the conversation. "Are there a lot of extracurricular activities like chess or National Honor Society? Do these help with college admissions?"

She nods with a slight tightening around her eyes. "Chess club? Maybe. But every student's journey is unique. At Lenape High, we encourage our students to pursue their interests and discover their strengths. What works for one kid doesn't work for another. College admissions aren't one-size-fits-all."

I offer an understanding smile. "I remember how difficult it was for me, so Rafi and I want to ensure Scott has the best chance.

We reach the counseling office just as Debbie launches into a rehearsed description of the school's most rigorous academic programs, from the high international baccalaureate program to the array of advanced placement and honors courses.

Debbie places the load she was carrying onto the secretary's counter. "Thank you for your help with these. When you're ready to enroll your son, please call us." She hands each of us a business card.

"We appreciate your time, Debbie." I offer my hand. "You've given us a lot to think about."

As she offers her hand to Rafi, a flicker of relief catches her eye. Thankfulness for the help—yes. Something else weighing on her—to be determined. In the future, I'll have to catch up with her in a less formal setting.

Rafi and I head towards the exit, our footsteps echoing in the now-quiet hallway. The bell must have rung while we were talking; a few stragglers hurry past us to their classes.

"Well, that was interesting," Rafi murmurs, his voice low. "Did you notice how she—"

I spot a familiar face further down the corridor. Mr. Kahale, Marcus's father, steps out of a classroom and closes the door behind him.

"Hold that thought," I whisper to Rafi. "We should speak with Mr. Kahale."

"Mr. Kahale?" I call out, keeping my voice casual. "Do you have a moment?"

He turns, surprise flickering across his face. "Of course," he says, glancing at his watch. "But I only have a few minutes before my next class."

"I understand," I say, offering him my card.

Upon taking the card, Mr. Kahale studies it for a moment, then asks with stiffness in his voice. "What's this about, Ms. Maddox?"

"I've been in contact with Marcus and his friends."

Mr. Kahale folds the business card into his pocket and leads Rafi and me toward an alcove at the end of the hallway. "Is this about the... unusual activity at the school?"

My eyebrows shoot up. "So you're aware that—"

He hushes me. "Of course. I asked them to keep their ears tuned to a few things. I've had suspicions about the scholarship practices for a while now. With Marcus' previous success, I thought he and his friends could confirm them without anyone noticing."

Admiration washes over me. This man risked his career to expose the truth, and his loyal son backed him up. "Can you tell me more about your suspicions?" I ask, trying to keep the eagerness out of my voice.

He glances at his watch, then down the hall. "Ms. Maddox, I wish to protect my son and expose this corruption. If you're on this case, as you appear to be, you'll know some students don't meet the criteria for these full rides, and other more deserving students are being passed over."

"Thank you for your honesty, Mr. Kahale. This could be helpful in the next part of our investigation."

His eyes narrow. "Just how deep into this investigation are Marcus and his friends?"

I give him a small smile. "I advised them to keep a distance and follow your lead. Today, Rafi and I came to get a sense of the school. Should we need further help, what Marcus and his friends have already found will prove valuable."

Mr. Kahale's shoulders ease. "Thank you," he breathes, and pulls out the card I gave him. "You should know, though, I've been working with a detective as well. You might know him."

My heart tightens. "A detective?"

He nods. "Detective Dylan Maddox. Your namesake?"

My shoulders slump. "My father."

Mr. Kahale's eyes light up; his voice exudes enthusiasm. "Your father? He's a good man, and very determined to see justice done. I'm sure your partnership with him will be just what we need for this case."

"It will be," I say, forcing cheer into my voice, while masking my frustration over my father's unintentional involvement. I resign myself to the inevitable—my father and I will work together on this case.

As Mr. Kahale concludes his talk about my father, I thank him for his time. "It's been wonderful meeting you. We'll keep you updated as the investigation progresses."

"I appreciate that," he replies, gripping my hand, then Rafi's. "And please, if there's anything you or Detective Maddox needs, ask."

* * *

I squint into the bright afternoon sun as Rafi and I step outside. "Your father's involvement complicates things."

"Yeah," I say, when we're strapped into the car. "He probably knows more than we do, and I don't know how to feel about it."

Rafi's eyebrows shoot up, but he doesn't interrupt. Instead, he waits, giving me space to continue.

"Part of me is angry he didn't tell me, but another part... I don't know, maybe I should have expected it? Dad should've known I would continue digging into my uncle's finances."

A group of students files out of the school, their laughter contrasting with my frustration. I wipe my palms onto my jeans.

"What if..." I start, then pause, almost afraid to voice my deepest fear. "What if he knew my uncle's financial affairs would lead to this connection with college admissions? Or worse, what if my dad doesn't think I can handle this case?"

Rafi unbuckles his seat belt. "Cassie," he says. I turn to meet his gaze. "Your dad's involvement has no bearing on your abilities as a PI. If anything, your dad understands the complexities of the situation and is pulling in all the resources he can."

"I know," though without conviction.

Rafi reaches an arm around me. "I get where you're coming from, Cass. But we can't lose sight of why you've taken up this investigation. You've been a victim once, now your friend, and who knows how many other kids are being cheated out of their futures. We need to stay focused."

"Well, Raf," I say. "You'd better buckle up."

His seat belt clicks. I turn the key. The old Cadillac coughs once—hesitates—then catches. I pull into traffic without checking the rearview. Not unlike this case.

5

Containment

Garlic and oregano greet me the second I open the apartment door, warm air spilling into the hallway like a promise I don't deserve. For one beat, I let it fool me.

Then the case slips right back under my skin.

Does Alfred really have his claws in Lenape High? Or is he just the clean face in front of a dirty system?

"Hey, girl!" Lila's voice cuts through my thoughts.

I peek into the kitchen. She's at the stove with a wooden spoon in hand, sleeves pushed up, purple-streaked pixie cut tucked behind one ear. She is home — a life with edges that don't cut.

"Smells amazing," I manage, dropping my bag on the dining room table.

Lila's cheer dims the moment she meets my eyes. "Cassie? What's wrong?"

"It's not that anything's wrong," I say, collapsing into one of our mismatched chairs.

She turns off the stove, sets the spoon down, and leans her hip against the counter. "The case."

"Always the case," I admit, eyeing the bottle of Chardonnay waiting like a bribe. I glance up at her. "One glass?"

"One glass," she agrees, and pulls two stems from the cabinet.

As she pours, my phone buzzes in my coat pocket. Instinct jerks my hand toward it.

33

Lila lifts one brow. Just one. It's enough.

I stop myself, wrap both hands around the wine glass instead. "Fine. I'm present."

"Miracles happen," she says, sliding into the chair across from me. We clink glasses in a mock toast and drink.

I tell her about going undercover with Rafi—husband and wife, concerned parents, imaginary son with an imaginary transcript. I keep my tone light. I talk about Moss's rehearsed smiles and the way the school offices smelled like lemon cleaner and old paper.

"Our findings," I conclude, "left us feeling like something is definitely going down at the high school, but—"

"But nothing," Lila says. "Skip back to the part you glossed over."

I blink. "Which part?"

"The Rafi part," she says, grin widening as she takes another sip. "You always sound like you're narrating a documentary when you talk about him. Like you're afraid the camera might catch your face."

Heat rises to my cheeks. "Nothing happened."

"Mm-hmm."

"It was a work thing," I insist. "A case thing."

"It's always a case thing with you," she says, setting her glass down with a soft click. "Other than Phantom Beats, when was the last time you actually took a break?"

I open my mouth to protest.

Lila holds up a finger. "Passing out on the couch with your laptop on your lap is not a break."

A laugh slips out of me before I can stop it. "Okay. Fair."

She softens, but her gaze stays sharp. "Cass, you can't keep this pace forever. It's unhealthy."

"I know," I say, raking a hand through my hair and catching a tangle. "I just need a few more days. With my contacts inside the school—Marcus, Alissa, Janice, Nate—I can—"

Lila's expression shifts at the names. Not jealousy. Concern. The kind that has weight.

"You have kids doing your legwork?" she asks quietly.

"I'm not using them," I snap, too fast. "They volunteered. They're smart. And they're closer to the heat than anyone wants to admit."

"Which is exactly why you should be careful," she says, gentler now. "You're treating this like it's just chess moves, Cass. Like nobody's heart is on the board."

Her words hit harder than they should.

I stare at my wine. "I'm trying to do this right."

Lila reaches across the table and places her hand over mine—warm, grounding. "I know. But at what cost? I miss my best friend. And lately, it feels like I'm living with a case file."

Guilt twists in my gut. She's right, and I hate that she's right.

"I'm sorry, Li," I whisper. "I didn't realize how much I've been…"

"Obsessing?" she offers.

I wince. "Yeah. That."

She squeezes my hand. "I'm not asking you to quit. I'm asking you to stay human. Make time for Cassie and Lila. No work. Just dinner. Just… us."

The knot in my shoulders loosens a fraction. Maybe it's the wine. Maybe it's the way her voice sounds — like a door I can still walk through.

"You're right," I say, forcing a smile. "Dinner first. The case can wait."

Lila brightens instantly. "Deal. Come help before I burn the sauce."

I stand and move to the stove. She hands me the pasta spoon like it's a peace offering. I stir while the water threatens to bubble over.

For a few minutes, I almost make it.

Almost.

Even the smell of garlic and tomatoes can't keep my mind from sliding back to the same image: Alfred's smile, the way he said *Rafi* like it meant something. Like a password.

"Earth to Cassie," Lila says.

I blink. I've been stirring for way too long.

"Sorry," I murmur. "I was thinking about—"

"I know," she says, stepping closer. "You can't turn it off."

She pauses, then says the quiet part out loud. "When was the last time you slept through the night without waking up to scribble notes? Without running numbers in your head? Without chasing your dad's approval like it's a finish line?"

My stomach drops at the mention of him. "It's not about him."

But my voice betrays me. The uncertainty cracks through.

Lila leans against the counter, arms crossed. "Cass. Be honest. You're not just fighting your uncle. You're fighting the part of you that still wants your dad's approval."

I turn away before she can see the truth land.

My phone buzzes again. This time I pick it up.

Rafi: *Got something. But it can wait.*

A third buzz follows immediately.

Rafi: *Not about Alfred. About the system.*

My throat tightens.

I set the spoon down like it weighs too much. "I should go."

Lila's gaze doesn't waver. "Too personal?"

"I've got to meet Rafi at the office."

"Cassie—"

"I'll make it up to you," I say, grabbing my bag. "I promise."

Guilt and relief wrestle in my chest as I escape into the night.

* * *

The walk clears my head—somewhat. The cold air bites at my cheeks, steadies my pulse. By the time I push open the office door, I've already rehearsed the lie I'll tell myself later: *I didn't abandon her. I postponed.*

Rafi is hunched over his computer, the glow of the screen painting sharp planes across his face. He glances up, and the expression that hits me is half professional focus, half something warmer.

"Hey, Cass," he says. "I thought you weren't coming back."

"Change of plans," I say, dropping into the chair across from him. "What'd you find?"

His eyes search my face—too perceptive. "Everything okay?"

I force a smile. "Fine. Show me."

Rafi slides his chair closer. I lean in beside him, close enough to catch the scent of citrus and cedar. For a second, the tension from my conversation with Lila thins.

Rafi's fingers move across the keyboard. "Remember those folders Debbie dropped in the hallway?"

I lean closer.

"I caught a few labels when we helped her," he says. "Not names. Filing codes." He pulls up a directory listing. "I searched the district's server indexing—public-facing entries, nothing illegal. And the codes match this pattern."

I take the mouse and scroll.

ALB–REVIEW

ALB–APPROVED

MRC–REOPEN

MRC–DENIED

And more. A whole ribbon of initials. Two-letter prefixes. Status tags.

"What does this mean?" I ask.

"It's speculation," Rafi says, "but ALB likely refers to an applicant file, not a student name. Same with MRC. They're being reopened. Reviewed. Approved." He taps the timestamp column. "These dates."

My eyes narrow. "Those all cluster around—"

"Last year's gala," he confirms. "Same week. Same day in several cases. And a few of the reopenings happen after the 'final' decision window should've closed."

A cold line runs down my spine. "Admissions files don't really close," I murmur, hearing Alfred's voice through Mel's story. *They stay flexible.*

Rafi keeps going. "There's more. I pulled last year's Genesee vendor payments—legally. They list contractors, amounts, and descriptions." He clicks to a line item and highlights it.

Ignite Global: $250,000 — HVAC / sublevel / steam tunnel access.

My breath catches. "Steam tunnel access."

Rafi watches me carefully now. "You know something."

I sit back slowly. "When I worked at the Genesee in high school, I stumbled onto a hidden wall on the ground floor. It didn't belong there. Not in a building like that. Too clean. Too... intentional."

Rafi's brow furrows. "Cassie—"

"If I wanted to hide a paper trail," I say, the words coming faster as the idea takes shape, "I wouldn't keep it in an office. I'd put it somewhere nobody would find it. Somewhere people assume is sealed off. Somewhere that costs a quarter-million dollars to access."

Rafi's mouth tightens. "You're talking about tunnels."

"I'm talking about access," I correct. "To wherever those tunnels goes."

He exhales through his nose. "Risky. Possibly illegal."

"I know." My hands curl into fists. "But this isn't me chasing Alfred. This is me chasing what he's hiding behind."

Rafi holds my gaze. "Your dad said it, didn't he?"

The words hit like a shove—because they're true.

"Stop looking at the man," Rafi says quietly. "Start looking at the system."

I swallow hard. "Yeah."

"And Cass," he adds, voice careful now, "your dad also said you shouldn't move until you have something that doesn't disappear when someone makes a call."

I hate he remembers. I hate that he's right.

I pace once, then stop, a decision snapping into place like a lock.

"Okay," I say. "We don't touch tunnels blind. We map them first. We build the box."

Rafi's expression shifts—approval and worry braided together. "How?"

I pull out my phone.

"I've got four sets of eyes inside that school," I say, thumb already moving over the screen. "And a planning department full of public records."

Rafi's eyes widen slightly. "Cass—"

"I'm not sending them into danger," I cut in. "I'm sending them into a building with fluorescent lights and a front desk."

I open a group text: Marcus / Alissa / Janice / Nate.

Need a favor for a "school research project." Go to Lenape City Planning Dept and request maps/records of the underground steam tunnel system. Old infrastructure, public works, anything. Take pics/notes. Keep it legal. Keep it casual.

A beat. Then my phone buzzes.

Marcus: Nate and I are on it.

My chest tightens hard enough to make me pause.

Rafi lets out a slow breath. "Smart. That's smart."

"I'm trying," I say, though it comes out rough.

Rafi steps closer and sets his hands lightly on my shoulders. Not possessive. Steadying. Warm.

"You're doing it right," he murmurs.

His eyes are deep brown in the low light, softer than he lets the world see. His thumbs shift—barely—pressing into the tension at the base of my neck.

The office closes in. The air charged.

For one breath, I forget tunnels and funds and my father's shadow. I forget Lila's hurt.

There's nothing else to hold onto.

Rafi's gaze drops—briefly—to my mouth, then back to my eyes, like he's asking without asking.

I should step away.

Instead, I let the silence stretch.

And then my phone buzzes again—another thread yanking me back to reality.

I clear my throat, stepping out from under his hands before I do something I can't categorize as "work."

"That wasn't very professional," I say, forcing a thin smile.

Rafi's mouth quirks. "Neither is breaking into a country club."

"I haven't broken into anything," I say.

"Yet," he counters.

I shake my head, but I'm smiling despite myself.

Rafi sobers. "Now the hard part."

I already know what he means.

Looping my father in.

I fold my arms, more to protect myself than to prove a point. "We're not calling him yet."

"Of course not," he says. "But we do what he told you to do."

"Meaning?"

"We build the box," Rafi says. "We get maps. We get timelines. We get names. We get enough that if someone tries to make a call, the evidence doesn't vanish."

"And then?" I ask, though my voice gives away that I already know.

"And then," he says gently, "we decide whether we want to pursue this with him. Together."

The echo of Dad's words rises in my head: *You must be certain you want to pursue this together.*

My chest tightens.

"Cass," Rafi adds, softer, "this isn't surrender. It's containment. It's making sure you're the one steering when the storm hits."

I stare at the screen—at the file codes, the gala timestamps, the tunnel access line item—until the pieces are no longer separate threats but a single structure with pressure points.

A system.

Something that can be boxed in.

I exhale. "Okay."

Rafi's shoulders ease. "Okay?"

"Okay," I repeat, firmer. "We wait for Marcus. We follow the paper. We don't poke Alfred again. Not yet."

Rafi smiles—small, relieved. "That's my Cass."

I scoff. "Don't get sentimental."

"Too late," he says, and his hand brushes mine—light, quick, like he's leaving a reminder there.

My phone stays silent for two long minutes.

Then it buzzes.

My pulse quickens.

Not Marcus.

A reminder on my lock screen—*Dinner: Lila.* The one I set this morning, then skipped out on after half a glass of wine.

Guilt blooms hot in my throat.

Rafi sees it anyway. He always does.

"We'll make it right," he says quietly. "After we make it safe."

It's the only promise I can accept without lying.

My gaze drifts back to the screen. To the structure. To the box we're building. And to the one piece I've been avoiding because I already know what it costs.

I unlock my phone and scroll to his name.

Rafi stills. "You sure?"

"No," I say. Then, more honestly, "But I'm done pretending I can do this without him."

I step a few feet away, giving myself space—and him distance. The phone is heavier than it should be.

He answers on the second ring.

"Cassie."

I close my eyes. "I need to talk to you. Not as a courtesy. As part of the case."

There's a pause on the line. The kind that means he's listening, not bracing.

"Tonight?" he asks.

"Yes."

Another beat. "Where?"

"I'll text you," I say. "And Dad—" I stop myself, then finish, "I'm not handing this over. I'm looping you in."

His exhale is quiet, measured. "Good. That tells me you're ready."

I hang up before he can say anything else.

Rafi's watching me when I turn back. No judgment. Just steady presence.

"Come on," he says, grabbing his jacket. "If your dad's already circling this case, we don't want him building a box without us in it."

I follow him to the door.

And as we step out into the cold, the warmth of his touch lingers—long after it's gone.

6

Fault Lines

Road noise and the occasional attempt at casual conversation fill the car as we drive. My thoughts linger on the moment that passed between Rafi and I.

Lila was right. There is something more between us. I just don't want to make the first move.

By the time I pull into the lot outside the old diner, the heater's cranked all the way up. It still isn't enough. The cold cuts through me the second I step out, sharp and unforgiving. Neon buzzes overhead. The windows are fogged, the inside glowing dim and yellow, like a place that exists outside the rest of the city.

Rafi holds the door for me. My breath ghosts between us.

The place is empty except for a hunched man in a Carhartt jacket and a pair of line cooks at the counter, speaking to each other in hushed Spanish.

My father sits in a corner booth, coffee steaming in his grip, attention pinned to the window as if he's been tracking our approach since we parked across the street.

Rafi's fingers brush mine, then drop away. It's brief. Unintentional. Still, my pulse stutters.

"Didn't think you'd call tonight," he says.

"I didn't either," I answer.

That earns a faint shift in his expression—not a smile, but something that suggests he heard more than I said.

"You got the files?"

I pull the battered folder from my bag, set it on the table between us, and push it toward him. It's thick with color-printed PDFs and bank statements, the evidence we've been hoarding for weeks. Rafi's tabs are still in place, color-coded and precise. Dad thumbs through the documents with a care that says he's used to handling delicate things—crime scene photos, subpoenas, broken trust.

A waitress tries to drop menus at our table, but Dad waves her away with a polite but firm, "Not now." She retreats behind the dessert case, her mouth softening at the corners.

After a full minute of silence, Dad speaks. "This is good," he says, flipping a page so hard it nearly tears. "Better than what our financial guys strung together. You should have gone to Quantico."

I bite back a retort. "If I'd wanted to work for the government, I'd be in D.C. Maybe I'd get paid more, but I'd hate every moment."

He almost smiles, but catches himself. "The pattern's clear. Foundation money into Genesee. Withdrawals tied to donor events. Vendors that exist on paper and nowhere else." He taps the stack once. "But suspicion isn't a charge."

Rafi leans in. "We need intent."

Dad nods. "You need proof of what the money's buying."

"There's something else," I say.

He raises his eyebrows, and a smile plays at the corners of his mouth. I am twelve years old and thirty at the same time.

"When I worked at the Genesee in high school," I continue, "I found a sealed door in the basement. Hidden behind storage shelving. Uncle Alfred caught me near it and lost his mind."

Dad doesn't interrupt. He never does when he thinks the important part hasn't arrived yet.

"I didn't understand it then," I say. "But if someone wanted to keep something off the books—physical records, leverage—that's where I'd do it."

He considers that, gaze steady, jaw set.

"Undocumented access," he says.

"Or forgotten."

Rafi shifts beside me. "We're not planning to go in blind."

Dad turns to him. "Good."

He leans back, folds his arms. "If there's a tunnel, it'll show up somewhere. Old permits. Planning maps. Maintenance overlays."

"I've got people on that," I say.

That gets a pause.

"Who?"

"Students," I answer. "Smart ones. Careful."

Dad studies me for a moment longer, then nods—not approval, but acknowledgment. The kind that says *you're not wrong*, even if he's not ready to say *you're right*.

"You find proof it exists," he says. "You bring it to me. No trespassing. No shortcuts."

Rafi's shoulders drop a fraction, tension bleeding out of him in a slow, controlled way.

Dad stands and leaves cash on the table. "You're close, Cassie. Just don't outrun the work."

He hesitates, then adds, quieter, "And don't do it alone."

Then he's gone, coffee unfinished, already moving on to whatever comes next.

The diner settles around us again.

Rafi exhales, not all at once, but like he's letting the air out of something tightly wound. "He didn't shut you down."

"No," I say. "He narrowed the path."

We walk back to the car without speaking. The night presses in, watchful and sharp.

As I start the engine, my phone buzzes.

Marcus: Confirmed. Archives open at 8. Nate and I are on it.

I stare at the screen longer than necessary.

Rafi notices. He always does. "They good?"

"They're sharp," I say. "And they know when not to leave fingerprints."

"You're letting them handle it."

"For now."

He studies me. "That's growth."

"Don't get used to it."

* * *

Morning comes thin and gray.

I park half a block from the Lenape City Planning building and kill the engine. I don't get out.

From here, the place appears like it's supposed to—municipal beige, fluorescent-lit, unremarkable. A building where no one expects anything interesting to happen. Where secrets can sit untouched for decades because no one thinks to look.

At 8:11, Marcus crosses the street first—hands in his jacket pockets, posture loose, like he's late for homeroom. Nate trails him, already talking too fast, gesturing like he's halfway into a theory Marcus isn't ready to hear.

They're not investigators.

They're harmless.

That's the point.

They disappear inside the Lenape City Planning building, swallowed by glass doors and fluorescent light. I don't move. I don't text. I don't intervene.

Not yet.

Dad said paper first.

Rafi said slow down.

But neither of them were the ones standing in my uncle's basement all those years ago, staring at a wall that didn't belong.

I ease my hands off the steering wheel and flex my fingers, working out the stiffness. The city hums around me—delivery trucks, early commuters, the low, impatient rhythm of a weekday morning. Everything moving forward while I sit still.

Waiting is a choice.

And I've struggled with waiting.

My phone buzzes once, then again—updates from Marcus, rapid-fire. I don't open them. Not yet. I already know what they're going to say. If the tunnels exist on paper, it's only a matter of time before someone decides they exist in practice.

Including me.

I pull away from the curb, merging into traffic with more intent than caution. Rafi will want to talk this through. He always does. Lunch. Neutral ground. A sandwich and a reasonable discussion about risks and timelines.

I already know how that conversation is going to go.

He's going to tell me we need to wait.

I'm going to tell him I won't.

The thought tightens something in my chest—not fear but anticipation. A reckoning. Between the case and the partnership. Between what's safe and what's necessary.

I glance at the clock on the dash and make a mental note.

By lunch, I'll have enough to change the terms of the conversation.

Whether or not Rafi's ready for that.

7

Points of Entry

The blueprints of the Genesee and its interconnecting tunnel systems sit open on my desk, their edges curling like they've been waiting years to be unfolded again. I'm reminded of my teen years and the summer I worked on the ground floor and found the hidden chamber. I hadn't the time to explore the chamber. I barely had time to understand what I'd found.

Now, holding the maps Marcus delivered less than an hour ago—clean, public records pulled under the cover of a school research project—a flicker of triumph surfaces, one I don't quite trust.

Not because the tunnels exist—I always knew they did—but because I'm holding proof in my hands, and proof has weight.

Enough weight to pull people into places they shouldn't be. Including me.

If the Genesee hid anything physical, anything that couldn't be scrubbed from spreadsheets and shell companies, it's down there.

At quarter after twelve, my alarm chimes.

I shut the folder, roll the blueprints tight, and slide them into my bag between my phone and the battered legal pad that holds every version of this case I've tried to make sense of. I tell myself that getting to Renzulli's first—five whole minutes before Rafi—counts as a win.

It might also be a sign I'm already losing control.

I order a seltzer and take a seat by the window, scanning the sidewalk—not for the kids this time, but for anything out of place. A stranger lingering too long. A familiar face where it shouldn't be. The city has a way of warning you when you're being watched.

When Rafi arrives, it's with a blast of cold air and the faint smell of winter cologne. He slides into the booth across from me, sets his phone face down, and gives me that gaze—equal parts worry, pride, and resignation.

"You good?" he asks.

I shrug. Which means no. And yes. And maybe never again. "I've got the blueprints."

His eyebrows lift. "Already?"

I slide the folder across the table. He opens it, like he's afraid the maps might vanish if he moves too fast. The worn, stamped, and annotated pages reveal sublevels, utility lines, and crawlspaces, and there, a service tunnel sketched faintly in red pencil.

Rafi exhales. "Holy shit."

"Told you."

He traces the route with his finger. "Runs straight to the utility access on Green Street. That's past the back nine. You could get in without crossing the main grounds."

"Which means no cameras," I say. "And minimal staff."

He lifts his head. "You're really going to do this."

"Do you see another option?"

He leans back, arms crossed. "Yeah. Wait. Let the police get a warrant. Let your dad take the risk."

I huff. "You heard him. He doesn't move without airtight proof. And by the time that happens, whatever's down there is gone."

"You're not doing this alone," he says.

"I have to."

The words come out sharper than I mean them to. He notices. He always does.

"This is about your dad," he says.

I bristle, forcing myself still. "It's not just about him."

He doesn't blink. "Yeah. It is."

I stare out the window at the slush-stained curb. "He's not wrong," I admit. "But neither am I. I need something he can't ignore."

Rafi's voice drops. "Don't be reckless. If you get caught—"

"At least I tried."

The woman in the next booth glances over.

"Sorry," I say, lowering my voice..

"Let me help," Rafi says. "If you won't bring him in, fine. But I can run overwatch. Be on comms."

"He'll know," I say. "He'll find out if you're involved."

"So what?" Rafi says. "I'm not letting you crawl through tunnels alone. And Lila—"

"She's not an option." I don't hesitate. "I won't drag her into this."

He studies me. "You're not using her."

I study my hands. The faint line where a ring used to be. "She deserves better than being collateral."

There's a beat. He reaches across the table, covers my fist with his palm.

"I'm not just a tool," he whispers.

"I know."

"Good." He sits back. "Let's plan."

I outline it for him—not as a theory, but as a timeline.

"Late night. After midnight, before the cleaning crew switches over. The Genesee posts its private security shifts online—an insurance requirement. They rotate every ninety minutes, but there's a blind window between the handoff and the perimeter sweep."

Rafi doesn't interrupt. He goes still instead, jaw set, eyes fixed on the tabletop. He hates the plan already.

"The north maintenance hatch sits below grade," I continue. "Camera covers the driveway, not the retaining wall. I'll approach from the tree line, drop down, pop the latch. It's an old lock—mechanical, not keyed to the system."

I tap the table once, each word measured. "From there it's a crawlspace straight to the old wine cellar. Steam lines overhead, concrete floor, no Wi-Fi. You're invisible unless someone's actively looking for heat signatures."

"In and out," I finish. "Less than an hour."

Silence stretches between us.

Rafi exhales slowly. "That's not a plan," he says. "That's a liability report."

I don't smile.

"You're talking about trespass, thermal cameras, and confined space entry without an exit buffer," he goes on. "One wrong step and you're either trapped or charged."

"I know."

"And if the Genesee moved whatever you think is down there?"

"Proof my uncle panicked."

He shakes his head. "Or that he's smarter than you."

I meet his gaze. "More experienced, yes. But not smarter."

Rafi leans back, scrubbing a hand over his face. "I hate this."

"I'm not asking you to like it."

"No," he says flatly. "You're asking me to watch you walk into something you can't muscle your way out of."

"I'm asking you to be ready."

He studies me for a long beat, then reaches across the table and takes my hand. His grip is firm, grounding. Protective.

"I just want you safe," he says.

I pull my hand back.

I don't promise anything. We both know better.

The food arrives—burgers, fries, heat curling up into the air—but my appetite is gone. The noise of the place presses in, too loud, too normal.

I slide my plate away untouched.

Rafi doesn't comment. He just reaches over, folds the paper, and boxes my burger like it's muscle memory.

I stand. "I should go."

He nods once. "I'll call if I see anything."

"I know."

Outside, the cold bites hard, sharp enough to clear my head. I pause long enough to glance back through the window.

Rafi's already stacking plates, folding napkins, cleaning up the mess I left behind.

Like always.

I don't go back in.

* * *

I drive aimlessly until a red light stops me near the high school. It's 2:07. Early release.

Students flood the crosswalk in packs. Hoodies, backpacks, noise, Nate's battered Jeep at the curb. Marcus inside, phone in hand. Alissa and Janice emerge from the building, arguing as they walk.

I follow at a distance. Park near Slice's. Wait.

They spill out of the Jeep and disappear inside, already debating toppings.

I check my phone.

Janice: We need to meet. Tomorrow. Non-negotiable.

A voicemail from Rafi sits unopened. I don't listen.

Instead, I text back: *Tomorrow works. You bring the juice. I'll bring the donuts.*

I tuck the blueprints deeper into my bag and head inside.

The odor of grease and oregano hits me.

They're in the corner booth. Loud. Animated. Too confident.

I don't go to their table.

Not right away.

I take the booth behind them instead, angled enough to see without being seen. I order a black coffee I don't want and set my bag at my feet, the blueprints still tucked inside—already logged, already copied, already real.

"I'm telling you, it connects," Nate says, tapping the tabletop hard enough to rattle their sodas. "You don't pay two-fifty for 'sublevel steam access' unless there's something worth hiding."

I lean back, keeping my face neutral.

Janice laughs. "You sound like a conspiracy podcast."

"It's not a theory," Nate shoots back. "It's infrastructure."

Alissa lowers her voice, leaning in so her words don't travel past the edge of the table. "The tunnels aren't just under the club. They run municipal. That means access points."

My stomach tightens.

Marcus says nothing. He's watching Nate's hands.

A folded sheet of notebook paper. Pencil lines darkened and erased and redrawn. A crude but careful sketch—rectangles, arrows, labels. The Genesee's footprint, mirrored and simplified.

And underneath it, written smaller, tighter:

UTILITY ACCESS — GREEN ST.

Nate flips the page, jabbing at a corner. "If we don't go in through the club, we don't trip alarms. It's basically public infrastructure."

Not exactly.

Janice grins. "So... trespassing lite."

That's it.

I stand, grab my coffee, and slide into the empty seat at their table before any of them register what's happening.

Four reactions, as expected.

Marcus straightens.

Alissa's hands curl into fists.

Janice lights up, already thrilled.

Nate goes pale.

"You're about to do something idiotic," I say.

Janice blinks. "Wow. No hello?"

"Hello," I say. "Now stop talking."

Marcus recovers first. "We weren't—"

"You were," I cut in. "And you were doing it loudly."

I tap the paper. "That map. Who drew it?"

Nate hesitates, then lifts his chin. "I did."

"It's good," I say. "Which is the problem."

Alissa bristles. "You don't get to—"

"I do," I say, firm now. "Because the moment you step into a tunnel, marked municipal or not, you stop being curious students and start being trespassers."

Janice folds her arms. "We didn't say we were going tonight."

"You said 'access point,'" I reply. "And 'no alarms.' And 'basically public.' Those are justification words."

Marcus exhales. "We're trying to help Mel."

"So am I," I say. "Which is why I'm telling you this now instead of after someone gets arrested."

Nate examines his map. "It's not illegal to look."

"It is if you cross a restricted threshold," I say. "And tunnels count. Always."

Silence.

I soften my tone—not much, but enough. "Listen to me. You do not enter tunnels. No testing doors. No 'just checking'. You stay above ground. Research only."

Janice mutters, "That kills all the fun."

I meet her eyes. "This isn't fun."

Marcus nods. "Then what *can* we do?"

"You pull records," I say. "Permits. Infrastructure maps. Historical maintenance logs. All public. All clean."

Nate brow furrows. "We could get those through the planning department. Say it's for—"

"A school project," I finish. "Exactly."

Janice perks up. "Urban development. Civics tie-in."

"Correct," I say. "And you don't freelance beyond that."

Alissa studies me. "And if we find something... big?"

"You bring it to me," I say. "Not the tunnels. Not the club. Me."

Marcus folds the paper once, then again. "Okay."

I believe him.

I don't believe the rest of them.

They gather their things, standing one by one. Nate lingers, eyes still on his map.

"Hey," I say. "That map—don't lose it."

Nate straightens. "I won't."

They file out together, already whispering.

When the door closes behind them, the noise of Slice's rushes back in. Grease. Laughter. The jukebox coughing up something from the nineties.

I finish my coffee and sit there longer than necessary, staring at the empty booth.

They heard me.

They agreed.

And tomorrow night, someone is going to decide that municipal access doesn't count as breaking the rule.

That's how it always starts.

8

Beneath the Web

Rafi and I park two blocks distant, near enough to view, yet distant enough for us to avoid notice should anything turn bad. Rafi's sits in the driver's seat, tapping his fingers against the steering wheel, but he's not nervous—he's focused. His mouth says nothing, but his eyes do a little Morse code in the dark, flicking between me and the glowing dashboard clock. It's early enough for the neighborhood to be empty, late enough for anyone out walking to appear suspicious. He's already mapped every outcome.

"You sure about this, Cass?" Rafi asks.

It's a dumb question, but a sweet one, born out of concern for my safety. I double-check the black duffel at my feet—lock picks, headlamp, backup gloves, burner phone, the flash drive taped to the bottom of an old ChapStick. I left the taser and my concealed carry at home on purpose. I'm here for evidence, not escalation.

"I was born for this," I say, only half joking.

He gives a small, tight smile. "I'll be on comms. No heroics, okay?"

"I'd hate to upstage you," I say, and the grin he gives me is so real and fond it makes my stomach turn.

He helps me set the earpiece, his hands careful and gentle. We used to joke that he was my "Q" with gadgets, but right now, there's nothing funny about

56

how soft his fingers are or how quietly he says, "You got this."

He's worried, but he keeps it to himself.

I step out of the car, zip my jacket, and let the night swallow me. The old streetlights throw a sickly glow on the sidewalk, and every step toward the Genesee heavier than it should be. If I close my eyes, I can see all the times my uncle alienated me at country club functions, at charity galas, at my high school graduation brunch where he'd "accidentally" spilled juice on my dress and called it a teachable moment. Now I'm the one teaching.

I move through backyards and alleyways, cutting a diagonal across properties so the fewest security cameras catch me. Rafi's voice comes through the earpiece, low and calm:

"You've got about sixty seconds before shift change on the east side. Are you seeing the Jeep?"

"Affirmative," I whisper, and duck behind a lattice fence to get a better view.

Nate parked the Jeep at the far edge of the lot, under the only non-functioning lamp. Inside, I can see two silhouettes. Janice is in the passenger seat, waving her arms and talking a mile a minute. Even from here, I can hear the faint rhythm of her voice.

"It's so boring just sitting here," she's saying, loud enough for the next county. "Marcus and Alissa get to do something, and we just play lookout? I should have brought my Switch."

Nate's reply is quieter, and I only catch, "—comms only, Janice. Marcus said be cool—"

The teens shouldn't have been here. I told them not to be here. I count them anyway.

Two stayed where I said.

Two crossed the line.

If security observes, their focus is on the Jeep, not on the Genesee's rear.

This was the line I'd drawn for them. Observation only. No tunnels.

The maintenance hatch is where I remember it, tucked under an overhang by a trash compactor that hasn't been serviced since Clinton was president. The only light comes from a motion sensor flood, which, if I time it right, gives me twenty seconds of perfect shadow between blinding glares.

"Flood light cycle in three... two..." Rafi cues me.

I move on the count, low and fast, and the cold metal of the hatch stings my gloves. It's got a simple, older padlock, like the city records said. I let myself take a single second to enjoy the irony before I set the pick and tension wrench, listening for that sweet, feathery click.

"Don't take too long," Rafi says in my ear. I can hear the edge of nerves now. "You've got company in two minutes if the logins I spoofed are right.

"Copy," I say, focused. My hands aren't shaking. I pop the lock in five seconds flat.

Inside, it smells like every other forgotten tunnel in Lenape—mildew, wet concrete, the chemical sting of off-brand bleach. I close the hatch behind me, careful not to let it slam. Once inside, complete darkness envelops me.

"This is so much creepier in real life," I mutter.

Rafi's voice is an anchor. "You're good, Cass. Go fifteen feet, take a left at the first junction, and the wiring closet will be dead ahead. No cameras until you hit the utilities room."

I move, step by cautious step, the walls squeeze around me. It's not the tightest crawl I've ever done, but something about the air makes my lungs work harder. Every footstep echoes louder than I expect. The only comfort is the map on my phone, which Rafi updates in real time with my position. He's dropped a little red dot for the security patrol: they're still topside, but moving fast. If the kids were smart, they'd still be in the Jeep.

At the junction, I stop and listen. Through the pipes above, I hear a far-off clatter—someone dropping a mop bucket, maybe, or one of the night crew screwing up their nerve before a smoke break. Though built like a bunker, the maintenance tunnel's acoustics make every noise bounce in waves, making it impossible to tell what's real and what's memory.

I count my breaths and follow the route. The wiring closet door is ahead, painted a municipal beige that matches the cinderblock, but the lock is newer—digital, with a keycard swipe. I fish out my badge, a perfect dupe of the janitor's, and swipe. The reader blinks green. Rafi is a god.

"Thanks, Raf," I say, almost giddy.

"Don't thank me yet," he says. "You'll need to move fast. Security just checked in. They're on a sweep."

Inside the closet, it's wall-to-wall server racks and humming routers, each with a tangle of colored cables. The room is ten degrees warmer than the tunnel, and it hums with a weird, mechanical life. Nostalgia for my first IT job passes over me until I remember why I'm here.

"Go for the third rack, left side, second shelf up," Rafi says, reading my mind. "That's the node for internal financials. The login is the same one we prepped."

I kneel in front of the rack, pull the old laptop from my bag, and connect the ethernet cable. The club's security is robust, but nothing Rafi can't handle. He's tunneled me into the network, so all I have to do is follow the script.

I type in the access credentials, heart pounding a little faster now. Every click echoes, but the data flows: scholarship fund records, internal memos, charitable giving receipts. I sort by donor, set the filter for "Maddox" and "Genesee-Penamore Action Fund" and watch the hits roll in.

"Whoa," I whisper, watching the folders multiply. "How much evidence do you want?"

"All of it," Rafi says. I can hear the smile in his voice.

I start the download, the progress bar crawling like cold molasses. Every second, the whir of the server grows louder. It sounds like an alarm.

Anyone on the other side of the wall could hear it.

For a moment, the entire building breathes with me.

"Fifty percent," Rafi updates.

"That's not fast enough," I say, fingers flying across the keyboard, searching for a backdoor in the settings.

"Just watch the hallway," he says. "Security's stopped moving, but there's a new heat signature heading your way. Could be a janitor."

I freeze, but then remember I'm wearing the uniform. Worst case, I play dumb. At best, I'm invisible.

The download hits seventy. My palms sweat inside my gloves. I glance at the flash drive disguised as ChapStick—my nuclear option if the laptop gets confiscated.

Ninety.

There's a sound outside the door, a scuffle and then the soft slap of rubber soles. I kill the headlamp and hold still, the dim glow of the screen the only light. The doorknob turns.

I hold my breath.

The door creaks open, and a flashlight sweeps the room in a lazy arc. I duck behind the server rack, flattening myself against the cables. The beam dances across the far wall, then the ceiling, then back to the open laptop. My heart punches a hole through my chest.

"Who's there?" a voice says, bored but not suspicious. "Maintenance?"

I say nothing as the download ticks over to one hundred.

The flashlight pauses on the server, then the person grunts and leaves. As the door closes, footsteps fade. I wait a full thirty seconds before moving.

"Clear," I whisper.

Rafi's relief is palpable. "Get out now, Cass. Security's on the move again, and they're not far."

I pull the flash drive, close up the laptop, and back out of the wiring closet. Every footstep lands like a gunshot. I'm out in the tunnel when I hear the walkie chatter, distorted but urgent, echoing off the walls. They're close. I take the left at the junction, moving faster than before. I keep moving.

"Thirty meters to the exit," Rafi coaches. "You'll have one minute, tops."

I hit the hatch at a dead sprint, slam it behind me, and crouch in the space between the compactor and the wall. Above, I hear boots crunching on gravel.

"Cassie, freeze," Rafi whispers.

I stop breathing.

Through the crack in the wall, two guards come into view—one in Genesee's navy blazer, the other in street clothes, off-duty. They're arguing about the Jeep in the lot, which has turned its lights on. Janice is waving out the window, yelling something about needing to use the bathroom.

Classic.

The guards move off, distracted by the teen chaos. I take my chance, bolt for the corner, and duck into the line of pine trees that borders the property. I don't stop running until I'm three blocks away and can barely hear the noise of the club.

I'm back at Rafi's car in five minutes, lungs on fire, sweat freezing to my neck. He's standing outside, pacing, arms folded tight. When he sees me, he lets out a breath.

"You're insane," he says, but he hugs me anyway.

We collapse into the car, doors locked, windows fogged. I pull the flash drive from my glove and hold it up like a trophy.

"Got it," I say, voice trembling.

Rafi laughs, loud and free. "Let's go home."

The club shrinks in the rearview mirror until it's just a silhouette on the hill, its secrets in my pocket. But for every lock I pick, there's another waiting, just out of sight.

I'm barely down the block with Rafi before my phone vibrates with an alert. It's the burner, and the text, a string of numbers and a single word: "Problem."

I know it's Janice. She was supposed to be outside. That was the rule.

I pop the glove box and pull on a pair of blue nitrile gloves. I go nowhere near a scene without them. Especially not when minors are involved.

"Swing around the east," I say to Rafi, and he doesn't ask why.

He nods and guns it, doing a quick loop that puts us on the opposite side of the country club. We park behind the abandoned florist shop. This time I leave behind everything except my lock pick and headlamp. My hands shake, but not from fear. It's just the cold, I tell myself.

* * *

The hatch is still open, which means either the guards missed it or they're baiting me. I slip inside and let the tunnel swallow me, slower this time, listening. The only sounds are the faint hum of distant compressors and the soft slap of my sneakers on the concrete. Then, overlapping voices, echoing off the cinderblock.

I flatten myself against the wall and kill the headlamp. In the dark, the smell of cleaning solution is sharper now. But there's something else: the metallic tang of blood. Not a lot, just enough to wake up the old animal part of my brain.

The voices get louder. Two guards, one older, one young, both out of shape and using the walkie as a prop instead of a tool. They argue about whether to call for backup.

"Just some dumb kid, like the ones in the parking lot," says the older one.

"Or a meth head," says the younger. "You know how they get."

Their steps fade, and I wait fifty counts before following. I duck into a side tunnel, the one marked "UTILITY—NO ENTRY," and squeeze through the gap where the conduit meets the ceiling. I barely fit, but the blueprints said this led to a maintenance annex, and the blueprints have yet to let me down.

The annex is a room the size of a prison cell, jammed with janitorial carts and buckets. Through the crack in the opened door, and inside, under the harsh flicker of a fluorescent bulb, Marcus is slumped on his side. His hands are zip-tied behind him and a bloom of blood on his left temple. He's not moving. So this happens when rules get ignored.

I check the corridor. Clear. Then I'm at his side, whispering, "Marcus. It's Cassie. You in there?"

No response. I check for a pulse... There, fast and steady.

Thank God! He's breathing, but there's a cut over his brow, already swelling. I dig the knife from my pocket and work the ties loose. The plastic bites deep, but I don't care. It's just plastic. I get them off, then gently shake his shoulder.

His eyelid flickers, and he groans. "Did we win?"

I almost laugh. "Hold that thought," I say. I check his limbs. No obvious fractures, just a hell of a bruise.

He blinks at me. "Thought you were—"

"I know what you thought," I say, and help him sit up, slow. "Can you stand?"

He tries, but his knees buckle. I catch him and ease him back down. That's when I spot the leather folio propped against the wall, right where his head was. It's stamped "Genesee Country Club—Scholarship Committee" in gold letters, so tacky it hurts. I flip it open, half expecting to find blank forms, but there's a stack of folders and a thumb drive clipped to a hand-written note:

"To Alfred—per our arrangement, destroy after review."

I shove it all into my bag.

Marcus just sits there, blinking. "Alissa—she's still outside. Nate too."

"We'll get them," I say, but right now my first job is getting Marcus out. I crouch, sling his arm over my shoulder, and drag him up, trying not to let him see how hard it is. He's taller than I am and not a featherweight.

I stagger down the hall, counting every step, praying nobody else is on patrol. The return trip is a blur of concrete and darkness. Marcus's weight serves as a punishment for every time I thought this was just a game. He doesn't talk much, but he manages, "Sorry," like it's his fault for being human and in the wrong place.

"Not your job to be a hero," I say, angry they went off script and proud his efforts paid off.

Dragging Marcus through the last thirty meters of concrete corridor is a masterclass in suffering. He's dead weight, arms flopping and shoes scraping every uneven edge, but I keep him upright, one arm around his waist and the other gripping the wall when my legs threaten to give out.

Every few steps his head lolls, and I whisper, "Almost there," as if he can hear.

Maybe he does.

Maybe that's why he doesn't just let himself fall and leave me behind.

When we hit the far end, the tunnel opens into an electrical alcove half-filled with crates and some kind of rusty pump. I wedge Marcus behind the biggest crate and crouch down, listening: guard voices again, closer this time, their flashlights bouncing like anxious fireflies off the far wall. I hold my breath and pray they won't spot the scuff marks I've left in the dust, or the faint outline of two sets of footprints where there should only be one.

A guard says, "They're not down here. I told you they doubled back."

His partner sounds less certain, and for a moment their beams hesitate on the door I just left. But after a tense minute, they curse and keep moving, footsteps growing faint.

I wait until I'm sure they're gone. My quads tremble from the weight of Marcus and the miserable half-squat I've been holding. I lower him just enough to check his face. His color's better, but the swelling above his eyebrow has risen to the size of a walnut. I pat his shoulder. "Up and at 'em, big guy."

He gives a little groan but stays put.

It's time to move. I pop the hatch, peeking out into the freezing night. The only light is a single car's headlights, idling across the road. Not Rafi's. The Jeep. Nate's.

Janice stands outside the passenger door, pacing a tight, nervous circle, while Alissa leans against the hood, arms crossed, scanning the street.

I drag Marcus up the embankment and across the parking lot, using every ounce of leverage I can muster. At one point, his knee buckles and we both go down hard. I grit my teeth and think: If anyone deserves a medal for poor life decisions, it's me. Still, we make it to the Jeep,

* * *

Janice clocks me and sprints over, voice a trembling shout:

"Oh my god, what happened? Marcus! Are you—?"

I wave her off, lowering Marcus to the ground as gently as I can. "He's alive. He needs to sit. Just—help me get him in the back."

Janice nods, her hands shaking as she grabs his feet. Nate's at the ready, opening the hatch and laying down a ratty blanket. Alissa stares, face unreadable, until Janice yells, "Help us!" and she's there, bracing Marcus's shoulders while we lever him inside.

Once he's settled, Janice perches beside him, stroking his hair like he's her little brother and she's the only thing keeping him alive. Alissa shuts the hatch and turns on me, not with relief, but accusation.

"Start talking," she says.

I glance at Marcus, then at Janice, who is watching me through a screen of tears and suspicion. Nate just hugs himself, shivering.

"Marcus was in the tunnel," I say, keeping my voice low. "Somebody hit him and tied him up. I found him in a storage room with this—" I reach into my pack and pull out the Scholarship Committee folio, then the thumb drive.

"This is what they didn't want anyone to see."

Alissa doesn't reach for it. "How did you know where he was?"

I exhale, hands shaking now that the adrenaline's leaking away. "After Janice's emergency text, I went back inside. I heard the guards on the radio. They said there was a problem, and I followed them. Blueprints said the only way out was through the utility corridor. I guessed."

Janice narrows her eyes. "You guessed. Or you set him up?"

Explaining myself wouldn't help. It never does when someone's scared.

Nate shifts his weight, glancing between us, jaw tight.

I open my mouth, then close it again. "He wasn't supposed to go in at all. You were all supposed to—"

Janice cuts me off. "He went in because you asked him to." Her voice is shrill, the edge of it cutting deeper than the words. "If he never wakes up—"

It lands where my armor is thinnest.

I want to protest, to correct Janice, to remind them their job was only to gather information, not break into municipal property—but I don't.

"He will," I say instead. "He's tough."

Alissa steps forward, her tone more clinical than angry. "Let's get him warm and make sure he doesn't have a concussion. Then we'll talk about who did what."

Janice sniffs and nods, but her eyes linger on me a beat too long.

We pile into the Jeep, Nate driving, Janice and Marcus in the back, Alissa riding shotgun. I squeeze into the last seat. The Jeep rattles down side streets, every pothole jarring Marcus's head against the glass.

Janice cradles his neck, whispering, "Hang in there," over and over.

At the first red light, Alissa twists in her seat, fixing me with those midnight eyes. "Give me the drive," she says.

I hand it over, no argument. "There's a lot on there. Bank records, internal memos. It links my uncle to everything."

Nate, eyes locked on the road, mutters, "That's all we need, right?"

Alissa flips the drive in her hand, thinking. "It's not enough. Not if the cops are on your uncle's payroll. We need a backup plan."

"Blackmail?" Nate says, half-joking, half-terrified.

"Leverage," she corrects. "If we drop the entire file online, they'll bury us. If we use it right, we get Mel and Abby clear. Maybe the rest of us, too."

Janice drags her gaze from Marcus, jaw trembling. "You're not going to just hand it over, are you?"

I shake my head. "I'm not working for the cops, if that's what you're thinking. This is for Mel. And you."

A silence settles in, as cold as the night outside. These kids trust very few people, especially me. In their eyes, I'm just another Maddox—someone who gives orders, withholds reasons, and lets other people pay the price.

I don't defend myself. Instead, the side streets slide by—the old mills and shuttered storefronts, the city that built and broke my family a dozen times over.

Lila, pacing our apartment, wondering if I'm alive.

My dad, bent over his case files, not knowing how close I am to blowing the lid off his brother's entire operation.

Rafi, waiting in his car—maybe worried, maybe just rooting for me.

We stop long enough to buy aspirin and an ice pack. Back in the car, no one says anything. We stare out our separate windows.

"Don't screw us," Janice says. "You want to be the hero? Start acting like it."

Before I can answer, Marcus stirs. He groans, squints, then fixes his gaze on Janice

"Hey," he mumbles. "We win?"

Janice laughs, then presses her forehead to his.

Alissa comes back with an ice pack and presses it to Marcus's head. He winces, but his eyes clear. "Nice hit," he says, and I almost smile.

"Can you talk?" I ask. "Do you remember what happened?"

He answers slowly. "Some guy in a jacket. Grabbed me from behind. Said something about 'leaving it alone.' Then, lights out." He touches the lump on his temple. "Guess I didn't leave it alone."

Janice reaches over and squeezes his hand once. Doesn't say anything.

We drive without a destination. The evidence is in my bag. The weight of it settles anyway.

When the others doze, I lean forward and say to Alissa, "We're going to need help. Someone who can take this public without getting us killed."

She keeps her eyes on the road. "I know a guy."

After a beat, she glances over. "Are you really a Maddox, or are you just pretending?"

I don't answer right away. The city slides past the window—brick and shadow and old promises.

"I'm whoever you need me to be," I say.

9

Partnership Under Pressure

I t's almost 1 AM by the time I limp into the apartment. The lobby stinks of boiled cabbage, and my hands are still trembling from the tunnel sprint and the weight of Marcus against my shoulder. Up here, the only light in the kitchen is a thin neon stripe under the microwave clock. The rest of the apartment's a tangle of overlapping shadows, laundry piles, and the scattered fragments of whatever life I have outside this job.

Rafi's already inside, pacing the kitchen in tight circles, hands shoved into his jacket pockets. The door slams, and his head snaps toward me, his face shifting through half a dozen expressions before settling on furious but relieved. The kitchen counter is a war zone of case files, sticky notes, and empty mugs. The smell of burnt coffee lingers above everything, mixing with the chemical stink from my gloves.

I drop my bag onto a chair and fish out the drive, then toss it onto the counter like a spent bullet. "It's done," I say. My voice is so hoarse I don't recognize it.

Rafi just stares at me. "You could've been killed."

I shrug, then regret it—my shoulder twinges, fresh and deep. "No one saw me," I say, even though it's a lie. "Security was chasing its own tail."

He steps forward, voice low and strained. "We dragged a bunch of kids into a black-ops run on the Genesee. Cassie, what the fuck were we thinking?"

I open my mouth, then close it. The anger on his face is new, and I hate how much it stings. "We didn't drag them anywhere," I say. "You were there. They were already in, going against my directions, a half a step from doing something even dumber. If I hadn't intervened…"

He shakes his head, lips pressed so tight they're white. "We should have gone to the cops. You should have looped your dad in."

The mention of my father is a lit match. "Oh, right? Because that's always gone so well for me."

He's not backing down. "It would have gone better than this. Marcus could have died, Cass. You barely made it out yourself."

I push past him and go to the sink, running water over my wrists. The sting is sharper than I expected. "I'm not helpless, Raf."

He leans in, hands braced on the counter, eyes locked to mine. "I know you're not. But you're not invincible, either." He gestures to the drive on the counter. "We could have gotten this without turning it into a movie heist. Without risking those kids."

I bite the inside of my cheek. "The kids went in on their own."

"But they admire you," he says, his voice sharp and bitter. "They followed your lead. I never should've agreed to this reckless plan."

I slam the faucet off. "Then why did you?"

"If I hadn't, it would have gone much worse," Rafi says. "Do you think being reckless is proof you're not your dad's shadow?"

"You think I want to be him?" I hiss. "You have no clue what it was like growing up in his orbit. Every mistake, every fuck-up—he made me wear it like a badge."

Rafi's voice drops, almost pleading. "You're not him, Cass. But tonight? Tonight, you sounded just like him. Only worse, because you dragged people with you."

The words hit harder than anything in the tunnel. I wrap my hands around the edge of the sink, knuckles white.

Rafi circles around, unable to stand still. "This can't happen again," he says, louder now. "You want me on your team? Then you keep it above water. No more rogue operations. No more using people who didn't sign up for the risk."

I turn, jaw clenched. "You could have said no. You were the one who cloned the security badges and ran point from the car."

He bristles, voice going tight. "You asked for my help because you knew I'd say yes. Because you knew I'd never let you walk into that alone."

"And you're mad because you care?" I snap.

"No, I'm mad because you don't." He yanks his hand through his hair, hard enough I hear the strands snap. "If you go down, Cass, it's not just you. It's me, Lila, everyone who ever stuck their neck out for you."

I take a step back. The anger drains out, leaving a raw pit in my stomach.

He keeps going. "You want to be a PI? Be a PI. But stop acting like you're the only one who gets to decide what's right. You can't keep treating people like chess pieces. You're not your dad, and you're not your uncle."

I want to fire back, to tell him he's wrong, but nothing comes out. I just stare at the drive on the counter, at the mound of evidence I bled for.

It's not a victory.

Not yet.

Rafi's pacing again, voice low and shaking. "If this is how you're going to run things, I'm out. I mean it, Cass. I'm done."

The words are so final I almost laugh, but I choke on it. "You don't mean that."

He steps closer, close enough I smell his aftershave and sweat and adrenaline. "Try me."

It should scare me, but exhaustion settles over me. I shake my head and reach for the mug. It's empty, and put it down hard. "You know what, Raf? If you had wanted to play it safe, you should have stayed in IT. Not joined up with me. Because this is what I do."

"And what, exactly, is that?" he says, sharp enough to draw blood.

I meet his gaze, matching him inch for inch. "Whatever it takes."

He stares at me for a long, tense moment, jaw flexing. Then his voice goes quiet. "If you wanted to be a cop, you should have stuck with the police academy instead of letting your hangups about your father dictate your decisions."

I flinch, the words cutting straight through every defense I've built. My cheeks go hot, and my eyes sting, and I'm twelve years old again, standing in the hallway outside the precinct, listening to my father and his partner argue about what a disappointment I'd turned out to be.

I grip the counter so hard the laminate creaks. The world blurs at the edges.

Rafi softens, but it's too late. I don't want his pity, or his apology, or the hand he reaches out to place on mine.

"I'm sorry," he says, voice hushed. "That was—"

But I pull away, the shame and anger boiling into something I can't even name.

The kitchen is silent except for the low hum of the fridge. My hands tremble, and my throat locks up.

In the dark, I spot the faint glimmer of the thumb drive, sitting right where I left it. For a brief instant, I want to grab it and hurl it, perhaps toward Rafi's head, to shatter the spell.

Instead, I shove both hands into my pockets and storm past him, into the bathroom, and lock the door. I slide down to the cold tile, back pressed against the wall, and try to catch my breath.

What kind of person would let it all go? Who would just say, 'You're right, and I'm sorry,' and mean it?"

Outside, I hear Rafi pacing, then the soft clink of mugs being gathered from the counter. He doesn't leave, but he says nothing. Somehow, that's worse than arguing.

I count to a hundred, then two hundred, until the burn in my cheeks cools to a dull ache and the pressure behind my eyes subsides. When I unlock the door and step out, the kitchen is empty. Beyond the kitchen, Rafi has turned on one of Lila's dumb crystal lamps, washing everything in a pinkish haze, and it makes him appear younger and smaller than usual. He's slouched on a couch, elbows planted, head in his hands.

After a moment, he stands, moving toward me with careful steps. "Cassie, I—" He reaches for my shoulder, but I flinch away, more reflex than decision. He pulls his hand back and lets it hang at his side.

"That was too much," he says. "I shouldn't have—" He stops, frowning at the floor.

I want to say something cutting, something meant to land hard—but I don't. Not now. I breathe instead, slow and shaky.

That's when the door swings open, and Lila barrels in, carrying a paper bag of groceries and wearing the world's ugliest sleep mask on her forehead. The sudden brightness of the hallway light hits me like a slap. Lila's gaze jumps from my face to Rafi's, to the mess on the counter, and back to me. Her eyes go wide. I catch my reflection in the microwave door—mascara smeared, hair half-collapsed, adrenaline still clinging to my skin. I grab a napkin and wipe my face.

She drops the bag on the table, apples and celery rolling everywhere, and peels off the mask. "What happened?" she asks with a shriek. It's the same voice she uses when a spider the size of a mouse is in the shower.

Rafi and I answer, voices tangling:

"Nothing—"

"I fucked up—"

Lila holds up a hand, traffic-cop style. "Pause. Sit." She gestures to the kitchen chairs, and I obey without thinking. Rafi sinks down across from me, arms folded, face blank.

Lila moves around the kitchen, gathering apples from the floor and kicking the fridge shut with her heel. She plucks the evidence drive from where I left it and examines it, eyebrows high. "So. Is this what I think it is?" She sets it in front of me, like she's placing a bandage on a wound.

My voice drops. "It's everything. The blackmail, the payoffs, the admissions fraud. All of it."

Lila's gaze flickers to Rafi, then back to me. "And you risked your ass to get it."

I don't answer. My eyes burn anyway.

Lila's voice drops, softer now. "Why do you keep doing this, Cass? Haven't you proven your point? You're the best damn investigator in the city. You don't have to kill yourself to make anyone believe it."

The words tumble out before I can catch them. "If I don't, nobody else will. If I quit, all of this—" I gesture at the drive, the files, the exhaustion coating every surface in the room—"would be for nothing."

Rafi jumps in, voice tight. "It's not for nothing. But it's not worth your getting killed. Or losing everyone who gives a damn about you." He says it like a confession, each word heavier than the last.

Lila makes a little sound, not quite a laugh. "You two are a mess."

I almost smile. "Tell me something I don't know."

Lila pours herself a glass of water and leans back against the counter. She's still in her work attire—a blazer wrinkled with stress and her hair sticks out at wild angles. "Listen, I'm not your therapist, but maybe—just maybe—you should listen to the people who care about you. Because if you keep pulling this solo hero shit, you're going to end up alone. Or worse."

I wipe my eyes on my sleeve and stare at the spot on the table where she set the drive.

Lila moves closer, her tone gentle but unyielding. "Do you remember when I almost got fired for giving leftover food from the coffee shop to a homeless person?" She doesn't wait for me to answer. "You once told me if you're going to break the rules, you need a damn good reason and a backup plan for when it all goes sideways. Sound familiar?"

I remember holding her hand in the HR office while she tried not to cry.

Lila glances at Rafi. "And you—stop acting like you don't love the drama. If Cassie played it safe, you'd be bored to death in two weeks." She points the empty glass at him, mock stern. "So maybe stop pretending you're just along for the ride."

He tries to protest, but Lila cuts him off. "Don't bullshit a bullshitter, Raf. I've seen the way you soften around her. You're not fooling anyone."

Rafi glances upward, then at me, then back to the ceiling. "Fine," he mutters. "Can we agree to include the police next time?"

I don't argue. It's easier than explaining that I already plan to—and that it still won't make him safe.

Lila grins, and the tension in the room softens, just a little.

She grabs a mug from the shelf and sets the kettle to boil. "You both need to eat. And sleep. And then tomorrow, you'll decide what to do with the evidence." She gives me a pointed look. "No more midnight heists. I mean it."

Rafi stands, like he's going to leave, but he hesitates by my chair, then crouches down so we're eye level. "I really am sorry, Cassie. I shouldn't have said any of that."

I want to tell him it's okay, but it's not, and I don't trust myself not to cry again if I open my mouth. So I just nod.

He gets it. He always does.

My phone buzzes on the counter, and Lila picks it up, reading a string of texts with her eyebrows arched. "Marcus and Janice got home okay," she reports. "Alissa too. They all want to know what's next."

I reach for the drive, turning it over in my hands. "First, we sleep. Then we blow the whistle so hard the whole city hears it."

Lila grins, wolfish. "That's my girl."

Rafi heads for the door, pausing with his hand on the knob. He turns, meets my eyes, and for the first time tonight, he releases a gentle exhale and smiles.

"I'll see you tomorrow?" he says.

"Yeah," I say, and my voice almost cracks, but not quite. "See you."

He goes, easing the door shut behind him.

The apartment is quiet except for the whistle of the kettle and the soft click of Lila typing on her phone. She moves around me with the easy grace of a best friend who's seen me through every bad decision I've ever made.

She pours two mugs of tea and sets one in front of me. "Drink," she says. "You'll feel better."

I do, and for a moment, I almost believe her.

We sit in silence, side by side at the kitchen table, watching the steam curl up and vanish.

Maybe tomorrow I'll fix things. Or maybe I'll just keep making it up as I go.

10

The Gala Plan

Dad is already sitting behind my desk, arms folded, his trench coat draped like a flag over the back of the chair. The sight of him in my office—my office—does something strange to my heart rate. I set a fresh coffee in front of him, not because I want to, but because of how he gets when the caffeine runs out.

Rafi is all business today. He's parked at the edge of the conference table, tapping away on his laptop, three different signal repeaters blinking next to the battered Asus. Every few seconds he glances at the whiteboard, where I've sketched out the Genesee floor plan in blue and highlighted security positions in angry red. Over on the windowsill, Alissa, Janice, and Mel are trying to look anywhere but at my dad. If any of them are nervous, only Janice is showing it—her leg vibrating under the table.

I take a seat, marker in hand. "Alright. From the top."

Dad's eyes flick from me to the whiteboard. "Security's doubled since the last time you worked there. Alfred's not taking chances." He stabs a finger at the map. "Patrol at every entrance, cameras here, here, and here—plus two plainclothes minimum."

"Good," I say. "That's exactly what we want."

He cocks an eyebrow. "You want to get caught?"

"Not caught. Just noticed enough that Alfred acts like Alfred." I point to the main event space. "He gets cocky in crowds. He'll want to put on a show."

Janice raises a hand. "What if the show is us getting perp-walked?"

"Then you play dumb," says Rafi, eyes fixed on the laptop. "Or faint. Whichever gets you out of cuffs faster."

Alissa snorts. "I'll take fainting. Janice could win an Oscar for melodrama."

Janice flicks her wrist. "You're welcome."

Mel's voice is quiet but clear. "What if they recognize us? Last time, the manager practically had us memorized."

"That's why you're all going in as staff. Temporary hires for the fundraiser—no one thinks twice about a coat check girl, a server, or a bored patio attendant."

I give Dad a sideways glance, daring him to contradict me. He sips the coffee, like he's already decided how this is going to go.

"Assignments," I say, writing them out as I speak. "Mel, you're on coat check. That means you'll have access to everyone's pockets—phones, wallets, keys. If anyone shows up with a burner, you let us know."

Mel nods, her face a careful mask.

"Janice, you're on patio and service entrance. They run most of their deliveries through here," I tap the schematic, "and Alfred always leaves himself an escape route. You spot anyone coming or going who's not staff, you log it, and if it's the big man himself, you hit the panic."

Janice beams, likely picturing herself in a movie. "Roger that, boss."

"Alissa, you're serving food. That gets you everywhere—main hall, VIP lounge, even the kitchens if you play it right. You'll be closest to Alfred during the speeches."

Alissa glances at the other girls and shrugs. "Got it."

Rafi unplugs one repeater, turns it over in his hands. "You'll all have comms. One tap for check-in, two for alert, three for abort. Keep the mics out of your mouths unless it's urgent."

Dad watches all of this, silent. His jaw works as if he's chewing on a counterargument, but he says nothing yet.

I let the silence stretch, then fix the cap on the marker. "Questions?"

Mel raises a hand. "If something goes wrong?"

Rafi jumps in. "You bail. No heroics. There'll be a go-bag under the coat check desk with a change of clothes and cab fare home. You leave everything behind and don't stop to explain."

Janice says, "And what about you?" She means me, but her eyes flick to Dad.

"I'll be inside. Blending in with the donors," I say, ignoring the way my father's jaw tightens.

He speaks. "I still don't like the idea of putting kids in the middle."

I cross my arms. "They're not kids. They're the only ones who can get close without tipping our hand."

He frowns. "You saw what happened to Marcus. That could happen again."

The girls gaze at the floor, except for Janice, who's attempts to appear unfazed and partially managing.

"We're being careful," I say, keeping my voice even. "That's why Nate's on the outside, running extraction. Marcus is on ice until further notice."

Rafi adds, "He's got a concussion. Can't risk his screwing up a stakeout."

"Hey!" Janice protests. "With Nate out, he's the only driver."

"We're not using the Jeep for this. Too conspicuous," I say. "You're all taking Ubers to the club. Paid for in cash. It's clean."

Dad leans back, tapping the desk. "You're going to need real police support."

I sigh, hating that he's right. "That's where you come in, Dad. Rafi will feed you every move, but you wait until we have proof. If you go in too early, Alfred walks."

He considers. "Ten minutes head start. Then we move."

"Five," I counter, "or they'll know it's a setup."

"Deal."

The girls fidget.

I clear my throat. "One last thing. No improvising. Stick to your roles. If you see anything you can't handle, you bail."

Mel, voice thin: "Even if it means losing the evidence?"

"Especially," I say. "I'd rather lose a thumb drive than a person."

This time, Dad doesn't argue.

Rafi kills the laptop screen and turns at me. "You want to run it again?"

I shake my head. "They've got it."

Janice says, "I have a question." She leans in, voice a stage whisper. "Is it true you once broke into the school gym and rearranged the trophy cases?"

I raise an eyebrow. "Not the time, Janice."

She grins, unrepentant. "Wanted to make sure you're as badass as you say."

Dad tries to hide a smile and fails. "She's worse."

I roll my eyes.

Rafi stands, stretching his back. "Okay, comms check. Alissa, say something."

Alissa puts on the earpiece and tests: "Testing. One two."

Janice: "I can hear you."

Mel, softer: "Me too."

Rafi gives a thumbs-up, then glances at me. "We're good. I'll monitor from the car."

Dad's eyes settle on me. "You sure about this?"

I glance at the girls, at the whiteboard, at the network of red and blue lines. "No," I say, "but that's never stopped me before."

He nods once. "See you on the inside."

When they all clear out—Rafi trailing last with the laptop and the box of comm gear—my office too big and too empty. I take a long sip of cold coffee and stare at the whiteboard. Every line on the board is a piece of what it took to get here. As usual, the plan isn't perfect, but it's enough.

I pull out my phone, hesitating. I dial.

He picks up on the first ring. "Cassie?"

"Hey, Marcus. You resting?"

A pause. "I'm going crazy," he says, voice dull with painkillers.

I laugh—soft, but real. "I wanted to say... I couldn't have gotten the evidence without your help."

"Did you get him?"

"Not yet. But tomorrow, he's done."

He laughs. "Kick his ass, Maddox."

"Copy that, Kahale."

I hang up, put the phone on the desk, and take in the room. The only sound—the faint hum of the comm repeater down the hall.

Tomorrow, we take down Alfred Maddox.

* * *

By seven the next morning, Rafi's at the office, sorting the gear on the conference table like he's prepping for a spacewalk. The girls show up together, each carrying a duffel bag and an air of panic.

Dad arrives right on time, fresh from the gym and already in his Lenape PD civvies. He brings fresh donuts. Janice makes off with two donuts, eyes never stopping.

"I don't like the parking situation," Dad says. "If it's too obvious for me, it's too obvious for Alfred."

"Noted," I say, and try not to sound like a brat about it.

He scopes the gear on the table—Rafi's comms, the burner phones, even the coat check tags. He picks up a comm and studies it, then gives me a slow nod. "Nice setup."

"Wait until you see the trackers," Rafi says, grinning. He grabs a powdered donut and stuffs half of it in his mouth.

The others chatter among themselves, filling the room with the eagerness of one last run before graduation. I'm ready. They all are. I herd everyone toward the table and start the briefing.

"First off," I say, holding up the little server pins, "these are mics. Tap them once, and they record. Hold for three seconds, they go live and patch through to us. Nobody's going to notice unless you rap on your chest."

Janice tries hers out. "Testing, one-two-three, is this thing on?"

Her voice comes through the repeater, annoyingly crisp.

"Yep," Rafi says, "and if you say anything you don't want everyone to hear, hit mute first."

Janice pantomimes zipping her lips.

"Mel," I say, "you're the relay if anything goes wrong."

"Cool," Alissa says and pockets a phone. She's all business, but there's a glint in her eyes that reminds me she's still a teenager. Maybe a better liar than I am.

Dad brings out the badges. Each one is heavy, laminated, and—if you squint—they pass as legit enough to get us through the first cordon. He hands them to me and Rafi last. "You'll go in and observe, and keep an eye on the kids. But you have to hang back until we're inside. We get one shot at this, Cass."

"Got it!" I state, his gaze meeting mine, the years of lessons and letdowns conveyed in one glance.

He addresses the girls next. "Listen—if you get caught, you say the offer of scholarship money lured you in. That's it. You don't mention Cassie, you don't mention me. Play dumb and let the process work."

Janice raises her hand. "And if they offer us pizza in the holding room?"

He almost smiles. "Eat it. But say nothing else."

Rafi takes me aside while the girls practice "casual" greetings and Mel tries not to hyperventilate.

"You alright?" he asks, voice low.

"I'm fine," I say, maybe too fast.

He leans in, checking the fit of my mic. "You don't have to go in with the raid team. You could hang back, let the kids do the heavy lifting for once."

"Not how I'm wired," I say, but I appreciate the effort.

He hesitates. "If it gets hairy, I want you to call it off. No heroics, okay?"

I don't argue. We both know how this could end.

Back at the table, Janice runs through small-talk scenarios—"Hi, can I take your coat? Is that cashmere? Did you know cashmere comes from goats?"—and Mel is memorizing the coat check manifest. Alissa practices walking with a full tray, eyes laser-focused.

"Okay, team," I say, drawing everyone together. "We have two objectives: confirm Alfred's dirty money operation is running through the Genesee and get proof of the handoff to the Ivy League scouts. If we're lucky, we also catch the other board members in the act."

Mel asks, "What if we don't get the handoff?"

"Then we fall back on the drive," I say, patting my bag. "It's got enough to scorch Alfred and everyone he's ever bribed, but the goal is to get him on something he can't talk his way out of."

Between mouthfuls of her second donut, Janice says, "So we just spy and report back?"

Alissa's eyes sharpen. "And if there's a double-cross?"

I like the way her mind works. "If you see anyone you don't recognize, anyone from out of town, or anyone who carries the kind of trouble that will break up a high school party for fun, you flag them. We keep our heads down, we watch each other's backs, and we let the cops handle the rest."

Dad, who's been listening, adds, "You let us know if you see anything suspicious. Even if it's just a feeling."

Mel swallows, then nods.

It's almost time. The girls collect their gear, and Rafi hands out cab envelopes, each with a time and pickup location. The plan is to converge at the club entrance at 5:45, staggered at fifteen-minute intervals. No cluster, no pattern. If anyone's watching, they'll see a bunch of bored teens clocking in for menial labor.

As they shuffle out, Mel lingers, pulling her ponytail tight. "Cassie?"

"Yeah?"

"Thank you. For trusting us."

I can't say "You earned it," because I don't want to pile on the pressure. I smile, and she smiles back, then disappears down the stairs.

Janice is last out. "Wish us luck, Detective," she says to my dad, and he gives her a grave nod.

Alissa, halfway to the street, calls over her shoulder: "See you in the action."

When the three of us are alone, Dad gets quiet. "You think this will work?"

"Not a clue," I admit, "but I've learned to trust the long shot."

He gives a single nod. "Ten minutes. After that, I come in."

"Don't wait for the sirens," I say, "because I won't."

Rafi snorts, then checks his watch. "Let's go, Cass. It's showtime."

I grab my bag, the drive, and a spare badge. For a second, an eerie calm settles over the office. The whiteboard wiped down and the evidence boxes lined up at the ready—evidence of what I've worked for. My heart is a live wire, but I don't let it show.

Outside, the world is bright and freezing. Rafi's car waits at the curb, exhaust curling into the morning. The girls are already in their separate cabs, each one a tiny moving piece in a plan that must work.

Dad lingers in the lobby, watching me. "Be careful, Cassie."

"I will," I say with a wave, grateful for Dad's support.

We split. Rafi and I drive, the city rolling by in a blur of salt-stained pavement and faded banners. Neither of us speaks as we rehearse our plan. Rafi parks a block away, sets up the repeater, and gets to work.

As I step out, I catch my reflection in the window—hair tied back, blazer too sharp, eyes wide and ready. I don't recognize myself.

The last thing I do before heading in is check the drive one more time. The folders blink up at me—evidence, confession, proof. Everything I need to bring down Alfred. Everything I need to finish the job.

I breathe once, slow. Then I go.

There's time yet before five. Time to make the stops that keep the world steady.

And time to see the one person who makes me want it that way.

11

Friendship on the Rocks

I shoulder my way into the apartment, fingers barely managing the deadbolt, wrist already checking my phone before I even put down my bag. It's not even five, and the hallway outside smells like detergent and burnt toast. I dump my keys onto the counter—they clatter, bounce, land next to the notepad where Lila leaves reminders I never read.

Before I can even shed my coat, Lila is there, emerging from the kitchen with a bottle of wine in one hand, two glasses in the other, wearing an actual party dress. Her hair's done up in a way I've only seen on job interview days or wedding guest selfies. She beams when she sees me, like I've returned from a six-month trek instead of a Tuesday at work.

"Hey!" she says, holding the glasses aloft as if to catch my attention through sheer force of will. "You're home! Early!"

"Hey," I echo, already halfway to the bedroom, dragging my messenger bag behind me, scanning for the portfolio with the fake ID I need for the gala. "Big night. You're all dressed up?"

She sets the glasses on the counter and follows, wine bottle dangling from her fingers like a prop. "I was hoping you'd be back before seven. I have news."

My hands are already in the closet, digging past my own clothes and some old sweaters of hers that migrated over last winter.

"Is it the thing at work?" I ask, muffled, still scanning.

She stops, halfway between the kitchen and the hallway, and says it with more pride than I've heard in months: "They promoted me, Cass. Team leader. Permanent."

I freeze, at least long enough to meet her eyes, and manage a smile. "That's amazing, Li." It's not a lie, but it sounds like one in my voice. "Congratulations." I move past her, duck into the bathroom, and fish through drawers for the micro-recorder I left in a makeup bag last week. Lila's still in the doorway, waiting for me to join her.

She pops the cork herself, and there's a hopeful little bounce in her step as she fills both glasses. "Come on," she says, "let's toast! Just one—I even got the good stuff, not that grocery store swill you always buy."

I come out, find her already holding out my glass, and take it. My hands won't stop fidgeting; I'm already trying to one-hand my phone while I take the first sip. I half-expect her to call me on it, but she waits, lips pressed together, eyes watching my face.

"To the Peterson Group's new team leader," she says, raising her glass. I clink and try to match her smile. The wine is cold and sweet, leaving a little burn at the end.

"So when do you start?" I say, swiping at my phone, searching for the last text from Rafi. Security passes confirmed for 5:45. Need to grab comms. Don't forget the burner. I scroll, thumb hovering, mind already back at the office.

Lila sips her wine, then sets it down. "I'm already training the other girls. They want me to design the onboarding. I even get to pick my schedule, Cass. I'll have time." She cuts herself off. "Are you... Are you here right now?"

"I'm here," I say, meaning it, but only in the physical sense. I slide around the counter, snag the manila envelope tucked under the microwave, and shuffle the contents until I find the stack of donor profiles. "It's just I have to prep—there's a lot tonight. I might not be back until late."

Her face folds in at the corners. "Right." She tries for a light laugh, but it lands flat. "It's always about a case."

I know this is supposed to sting, but I can't let it. "It's the last one, Li. If it works, I'll have enough to put Alfred away for good."

She pushes the wine glass aside; the sound sharp on the counter. "That's what you said last time."

I open, then shut my mouth. Words refuse to come to mind as I rub the bridge of my nose. I try again. "I'm sorry. I just—this is important. Everything else can wait."

She shakes her head. "But it never waits, Cassie. It's always urgent. It's always more important than—" she stops. She picks up her glass again, but doesn't drink.

A silence settles, the kind that fills up every inch of space, closing in the walls in the tiny apartment. Lila stands there in her best dress, her hair perfect, holding a glass meant for celebration, but now, with no one to share in the celebration. Guilt twists in my gut, like leftover pizza and a cheap hangover. I don't even know how to fix things between Lila and me.

"Do you want me to cancel?" I ask, even though I know she'd never say yes.

She doesn't answer for a long time. When she does, her voice is quiet: "You could stay, just for a minute. Just... sit."

I let out a sigh and sit on the stool at the counter, set the envelope down, and face her. I even put my phone on the laminate and turn it screen down, as if that will help.

We sit like that for a few seconds, the clock on the wall ticking and a distant neighbor's dog barking at nothing.

"I'm proud of you," I say, and this time it comes out right. Lila searches for the lie, and when she doesn't find it, she smiles—small, but real.

"You're an idiot," she says, and I almost laugh.

"Yeah," I admit. "But I have good taste in best friends."

She sips her wine, reaches across the counter and takes my hand. Her skin is warm and soft. I've missed this, the simple closeness of it.

"I want you to be careful tonight," she says. "And not just for the case."

"I will," I say, though we both know I can't promise that.

She lets go, and stands, her shoulders a little straighter. "Go save the city," she says. "But maybe call if you're going to be late."

"I will," I say again, meaning it.

As I gather my things and double-check my pocket for the drive, I glance toward the kitchen. Lila stands there, swirling the wine in her glass. My unfinished glass sits on the counter, lonely and accusing. Her shoulders sag. The wine turns slow circles.

"Break a leg, Cass," she says.

"Always do," I say, and close the door behind me, the latch catching on the first try for once.

The hallway is colder than when I came in. I walk to the elevator, envelope clutched in my hand, and try not to think about the way I left things. But it follows me, a phantom weight, all the way to the parking lot, and I know it'll still be there when I get back.

I step out into the parking lot illuminated by an indigo sky over the street lamps. The cold bites my cheeks while I scroll through my phone, check the time, and see a text from Rafi: "All set. See you at the drop." I text back a thumbs-up, but my fingers are slow.

As I climb into my car, Lila's silhouette in the upstairs window moves through the kitchen as if she's trying to keep busy. She pauses once, glances out at the lot, and draws the curtain. The glow behind the glass fades, and I'm left staring at the reflection of my face in the windshield: dark eyes, hair coming loose, lips set hard.

I grip the wheel, trying to steady my hands, and wonder how many times I'll have to choose between the work and the life I keep promising to build around it. I start the engine. The heater rattles, struggling to keep up.

I pull away, watching the apartment shrink in the mirror, and promise myself—again—that this will be the last time.

But I don't even believe it.

The night is a long corridor; the headlights slice out enough of the road to get me to the next disaster. And behind me, the wine and the party dress and the best friend I keep letting down, all waiting for something that I may never be able to give.

I put the car in gear and drive, the operation ahead of me and the weight of home lingering like a bruise, impossible to ignore and impossible to heal.

12

Gala Night

If you walk into the Genesee Ballroom tonight, your corneas will sear from the glare of wealth. Everything is oversized: the vases of imported lilies, the glimmer of a full orchestra wedged between two tiers of marble, and the guests—each one built from the blueprint of a different Mid-Atlantic dynasty. Chandeliers hang like planets, scattering gold light over enough formalwear to bankrupt the city's two best tailors. Some nights, you see a ballroom like this on a TV show and think, "Nobody actually lives this way." Tonight, it's real, and it's a perfect camouflage.

I don't pretend to blend. Not with the stiletto that already bit a blister into my heel, or the chip in my molar from gnawing ice chips on the drive over. But it's easier to be invisible when you know nobody wants to see you, and the rich see waitstaff the way they see a sink—useful, then instantly forgotten. So I loiter near the edge, behind a decorative urn taller than I am and painted with scenes of Lenape City's invented history. My vantage point is prime: one angle on the grand staircase and two on the arched doorways. I can see Mel posted at the coat check, Janice patrolling the doors, and Alissa already in motion, head down and tray up.

Mel is in her element, but just barely. She's gone for "unflappable efficiency," which means she's logging every guest like she's counting ballots in a swing state. She's got her hair twisted into a bun, and every time she smiles at a patron, the smile is a little too bright, a little too rehearsed. She tags a fur coat, slips a ticket into an outstretched hand, and then subtly scans the guest's face, probably committing every wrinkle and brow arch to memory. If someone is going to crack, it won't be Mel. It'll be the rich idiot who forgets he left a phone or, more likely, a loaded Glock in his overcoat.

Janice is more obvious, but that's the play. She's stationed by the patio exit, with a heavy black flashlight on her belt, a lanyard with an official "Event Safety" badge, and an attitude that screams, "I dare you to cross this line." She's making a show of inspecting the e-cig vapes and the glass flasks smuggled in by the prep school rebels and the washed-out debutantes. Now and then, she fidgets with her earpiece, then pretends it's nothing. If security is watching anyone, they're watching her.

Alissa is the most dangerous. She's got a tray of amuse-bouches in one hand. Her other hand is white-knuckled and glued to her side. She moves through the room like a shark through a kelp forest—just enough side-eye to track the VIPs, just enough momentum to seem like she belongs. The service staff is mostly local college kids and a few Genesee legacies earning "character" points. None of them suspect Alissa is here for anything but the tip. She circles the outer edge of the main hall, ducking expertly around a cackling hedge fund trio, then drifting closer to the high table.

At the center of all this is Alfred Maddox, silver in the hair and gold in the cufflinks, smile so wide you can see the pink of his gums. His court is a mixture of donors, university provosts, and, tonight, the city's DA—who, if you listen closely, is already half in the bag and dropping hints about "mutual benefit." Alfred works the room with the precision of a surgeon, touching wrists, sharing a backslap, murmuring something confidential every time he leans in. There's nothing he likes more than an audience, except maybe a well-oiled machine. Tonight he has both.

I press a finger to my earpiece, careful to not reveal I'm wearing one. The device is buried under my hair, which Rafi insisted I wear down tonight "for cover." He's on the comms, posted in a beater sedan three blocks down, monitoring everything through a cobbled-together web of baby monitor frequencies and a police scanner. So far, he's mostly reported the traffic on Broad Street and an unscheduled police presence in the lower parking lot, which he suspects is a tipoff from someone inside.

"Status?" I whisper, barely moving my lips.

The reply comes back fast. "Janice is a twitch away from making the security director. Mel's fine, and Alissa is closing in on the VIP lounge. You've got three cameras on your six, but none are moving. Over."

I resist the urge to check the cameras myself. "Any word from my father?"

A pause. "He's parked. Says to hold, he'll text if he's going in early. Be careful, Cass. They've got at least two private security with earpieces."

"Copy," I say, and kill the transmission.

I check the ballroom clock—eight on the dot, still an hour before the first round of speeches.

The floor settles into its rhythm. Musicians tuning up. Waiters topping off glasses. Guests feeding on one another like wolves in formal wear. The energy is thick, but the room is too bright for panic.

Mel is near the coat check, juggling two incoming jackets and a string of pearls that won't unclasp. She glances up and catches my eye for half a second. Her lips move: *In position.*

Janice talks to a young security guard, who blushes when she draws closer to him. She points to the patio, then at her badge, then gives a little exaggerated roll of her eyes. He's buying it. She palms something off the end of the bar—a napkin? a keycard?—and tucks it into her waistband. She hams it up for the crowd, but her jawline is taut, the corners of her eyes pinched tight. Nobody with a face like that is having fun. A guest directs a comment at Janice. She puts her hand to her chest and laughs. She's nervous, but she's good at hiding it.

Alissa has made it to the perimeter of the VIP section. She slows down, distributing the canapés to the donors, but never breaks pace. She locks her eyes onto Alfred who is now laughing with the DA, hand on the man's shoulder. At one point, the DA reaches for a crab puff and drops it on the carpet; Alfred bends to pick it up himself—too quick, too practiced—then says something that makes the entire table burst into laughter. He keeps the bag close. It's a performance, but of the kind only a few can appreciate.

I roll my shoulders, stretching out the tension. The evidence drive in my jacket pocket is a constant ache. I recheck my pocket, just to be sure—still there, taped to the inside lining, ready to burn every bridge if things go sideways. Two more copies exist, but this is the real deal; the final backup plan. I can't stop thinking of Lila, back in the apartment, finishing the bottle of wine and waiting for a text that I'll send hours too late, if at all. I hate the thought that slows me down, makes me human when I need to be a machine.

There's movement by the stage. A man in a dark suit—one of the private security—leans in to speak to Alfred. He whispers, Alfred nods, and then both scan the room. I duck slightly behind the urn, angle my body like I'm tracking a drink order, and listen.

Alfred doesn't go for the microphone. He doesn't call anyone over.

Instead, he drifts—casual, unhurried—toward the coat room, passing the high table like he's just stretching his legs. One of the private security shadows him, close and incidental.

At the edge of the crowd, a second man peels off from the orchestra side, carrying a garment bag that hangs too heavy for fabric. Eyes forward and never slowing.

Mel stiffens behind the counter. She doesn't reach for the bag. She lets Alfred do that himself.

That's the handoff.

Quiet. Clean. Personal.

The music swells. There's the clatter of forks and glassware, and over that, the growing hum of the crowd. The program says the next speaker is from the mayor's office, but that's not until ten. Whatever is happening, it's off script.

I check on Mel again. She's taking a break from coat check, standing near the stairwell, and holding a tray of champagne. She's watching a knot of teens from St. Augustine's Prep—they're here on scholarship, which means they're the photo op, not the beneficiaries. One of them, a girl with a buzz-cut, gives Mel a weird, lingering gaze. But Mel smiles—a real one, not her customer service face—and the girl smiles back. Mel is steady, but I can see the shake in her fingers when she sets a glass down.

The guard talking to Janice steps away from his post and into the staff hallway. Janice waits three beats, then follows. I want to radio in, but I trust her. She's the only one who can improvise on short notice and still land upright. I turn my attention to the VIP lounge, where Alissa is now pouring drinks. She edges closer to Alfred, and for a split second, he glances up and makes eye contact. Shock, then the calculation passes over his face. Does he know her? Maybe, but he hides it fast. Alissa doesn't flinch; she pivots, moving to another table, but her steps get tighter, her eyes wider as she's running the math on how many ways this could go wrong.

I circle the perimeter, keeping to the outer lanes, then duck into the catering anteroom. The kitchen is a madhouse, but I glimpse Janice and the security guard through a slatted door. She's got him pinned against the utility sink, talking low and fast. He's nodding, eyes glazed. She's flirting. Then she palms his keycard, pats his chest, and slides back out. She catches me watching and gives a quick double-blink: Mission accomplished.

I double back to the ballroom, scanning for Alfred. He's still at the table, but now he's standing, a hand raised to gather attention. His voice booms even before the PA kicks in.

"Ladies and gentlemen—if I can beg your indulgence?"

The crowd quiets, and for a second, every eye is on him. It's theater, but it's also a smokescreen. While everyone's watching my uncle, the real business is happening somewhere else.

"Tonight," he says, "we celebrate not just the future of Genesee, but the promise of every student, every athlete, every dreamer who calls this city home. That is what legacy means. That is what the Genesee family stands for."

He pauses, lets it settle. However, behind the words is the careful inventory of every face, every position, every leak. Alfred's running the same op as I am, just with a bigger budget.

I tap my earpiece. "He's about to make the handoff. Janice, are you in position?"

A whisper: "Patio door. There's a second guard in the alcove. I can stall him if you need."

"Wait for my mark," I say, then catch Mel back at the desk, logging something on her phone.

"Mel, status?"

She replies instantly: "Got the master coatroom key. Security is running a check on the east exit. They're onto something."

"Stay put," I say, and move toward the VIP section.

The next five minutes are a blur of logistics: glasses clinking, plates swapping out, guests rising and falling in small tides. Alissa keeps circling, but she's moving toward the bar now, positioning herself for a better angle. I follow, but keep my distance. If I get too close, I'll tip someone off; if I lag, I'll miss my window.

Alfred fields congratulations, holding court near the grand fireplace. I spot a woman with a notepad, probably a reporter, and two men in university livery. A waiter brings over a decanter, and Alfred pours for everyone at the table. Alissa steps forward, offers a canape, and just as he's about to refuse, she leans in.

"Mr. Maddox," she says, soft but clear.

He freezes. For a moment, the world shrinks to the space between them.

"I remember you," he says, voice low.

She smiles—cool, professional. "You said to come back if I ever needed a reference."

There's a beat. He studies her face, then gives a small, private nod. "Of course. You were a standout." He motions for her to wait, then turns back to his table. The conversation moves on.

I exhale, relief and dread in equal measure. If he recognized her, he'll be watching. But he also didn't blow her cover. Maybe he respects the hustle. Or maybe he's saving it for later.

I scan the room for Janice. She's in place, leaning against the patio door, chatting with the second guard. I can't hear the words, but her posture is all ease. She's good.

Mel texts: "Guest at the coat check is asking about you."

I frown. I haven't interacted with anyone yet.

"Description?" I text back, thumb shaking.

She replies: "Male, late 40s, suit. Private security. The stance gives it away."

I check the perimeter. Sure enough, a man in a blue suit is scanning the room, eyes lingering on every staff member. When he spots me, he tilts his head and starts walking my way.

I move fast, ducking into the staff corridor and double-back toward the kitchens. I wait, heart pounding, then peek out. He's gone.

I'm halfway to the staff hallway when a dainty teenage waitress catches my attention. She's at the edge of the kitchen, angled like a chess piece, dressed down in a server's tunic, but the eyes give her away. She's scanning for someone—then spots Alissa and bee-lines over, moving so smoothly she barely leaves a wake.

Alissa doesn't see her coming, not until her counterpart is practically in her lap. They collide, and the waitress's hand clamps onto Alissa's wrist, steadying the tray.

"Don't react," the girl whispers, lips not even moving. "Maddox is watching you. Don't look now."

Alissa's grip spasms; one glass wobbles, but she recovers. For a beat, neither moves. I can see the struggle in Alissa's jaw, the impulse to run. Instead, she does the bravest thing I've ever seen: she breathes in, holds the tray perfectly level, and keeps walking.

I scan the ballroom. Alfred is at his donor's table, but his face has changed— champagne frozen mid-air, smile brittle. He recognizes what Alissa is doing here. Two security goons in rented tuxes peel off the wall and move, slow but direct, toward her. Their stride too deliberate as they casually mingle with the guests. I know this tactic. Pinch the target between two lines, leaving no escape except the one you want them to take.

My earpiece clicks, and Rafi's voice has a sharp edge: "Cass, you have two incoming on Alissa. South stairwell and main floor. You have thirty seconds, tops."

"Copy," I whisper. "Janice, can you get to Alissa?"

Janice is at the edge of the service corridor, pulling her best "bored security" face, but her eyes flicker in quick Morse code. She angles left, skimming the buffet, and closes in on the intercept.

The guards tighten their triangle around Alissa. One is tall and bald, with a scar that slices through his eyebrow. The other is nondescript, but his smile is too smooth. Alissa tries to pivot toward the nearest guest cluster, but the guards close the space.

My pulse is a tuning fork. I move along the wall, keeping the urn between me and Alfred's gaze, and edge toward the commotion.

The ballroom door's slam against the wall with a crash of metal-on-metal. Half the room freezes; the other half explodes into motion, everyone scrambling for phones, purses, and exits. Some idiot shouts about "rights," and another about "donations"—like money buys immunity. For a moment, the only other sound is the hiss of champagne splashing onto tile as a pyramid of glasses tips and falls, cascading down the steps in a sparkling landslide.

"Police! Everyone stay where you are!" Adrenaline and acoustics amplify the voice, one like an avenging god. Uniformed officers in black-and-blue bristle in with radios, shields, and zip cuffs. The first three advance in a wedge, fanning out to cover every escape. It's surgical, brutal, and I can't help but admire it.

From my hiding spot behind the urn, I track the movement of Alfred Maddox. He's not in the line of fire—he's not even in the room. All I catch is a glimpse of the back of his head as he glides through a side door behind the bar, a silver blur cutting away from the chaos. Of course. While everyone else panics or postures, the real operator slips the net.

Powered by twitchy adrenaline, I leap through the gap and dart along the wall. I'm through the side door in three steps, then in a narrow corridor lined with crates of liquor and stacks of catering trays.

The hallway is empty except for the echoes of Alfred's shoes. I can hear the commotion in the ballroom receding behind me—voices rising, guests cursing, the faint buzz of someone's phone left on a counter. Ahead is a flash of movement: a door slamming, then the wheeze of a mechanical latch.

I run. The carpet turns to tile, then to bare concrete, each footfall sending up a cold jolt through my heel. The smell shifts from old money and perfume to something harsher—bleach, ammonia, the tang of spilled cheap vodka. There's a sharp ninety-degree turn, then a set of stairs leading down, and I nearly pitch myself headfirst trying to keep pace.

The stairwell is pitch black. I flick on my phone's flashlight, holding it low and close to the wall. Every step is slick with condensation. I count them out—twelve, thirteen, fourteen—and then there's a landing, and a battered steel door, painted gray but flecked with rust. Someone left it open just a crack, and it swings gently like it's breathing.

I edge closer and listen. Nothing but the faint echo of steps, farther off now, almost lost in the bowels of the building.

"Rafi, do you copy?" I whisper, half expecting the comm to be dead in the concrete.

It isn't. His reply is thin and frantic. "Cassie, where the hell are you?"

"Sub-basement. Alfred went to ground."

There's a beat of static, then: "He's not showing on any security feed. That area's blind. Be careful."

"I'll call you when I can," I say, then silence the earpiece.

I push open the heavy door. On the other side is a tunnel: old brick, rounded at the ceiling, running in both directions as far as the light will show. The air is cold and stale, but at least it's not the choking bleach of above. I follow the only sound there is—the click, click, click of expensive shoes somewhere ahead.

It's hard not to think about the times I've walked tunnels like this. Here, there's something else, too: the knowledge that the person I'm chasing is the last loose thread. If he gets away, nothing changes. If I catch him—maybe everything changes for Mel and the donors who've thrown their lot in with the Genesee.

The tunnel narrows, then widens again, opening into a long-forgotten wine cellar. There's a scattering of crates, a half-collapsed rack of bottles, and a weird hush makes even my breath sound like an air horn.

Alfred stands halfway down the room, fiddling with the lock on an iron grate, hands steady even as they work the code. There's a duffel bag at his feet, something bulky—a go bag packed with a few days' supply, and maybe enough evidence to put this case to rest.

He gets the grate open. Before he can step through, I move. My heels scrape on the stone, and he hears it, whirling around. For the first time tonight, his composure cracks. There's fear, but mostly irritation.

"Cassie," he says. "I thought you'd be celebrating your little victory upstairs."

"Dad always taught me to finish the job," I say, closing the distance.

He lifts his chin, tries a smile. "You think you have me cornered?"

"No. You've run out of ways to lie," I say, and point to the bag. "Is it all there?"

"More than you can imagine," he says, but there's no triumph in it—just resignation.

I keep the phone up, camera on, recording every second. "Hand it over. Walk away with whatever dignity you have left."

He laughs. "Dignity? That's for people who can afford to lose."

He makes a move for the bag, but I'm faster. I kick it out of reach, then plant my foot on the handle.

"Don't," I say, and I mean it.

He studies me, eyes flicking from my face to the phone, to the iron gate, to the far, dark corner of the room. He's calculating, as always.

"What's next, Cassie? You drag me upstairs? Let them take their pound of flesh?" He says it as if he's asking for the script, as if he's still running the show.

"Not my call," I say. "But if you're lucky, the cops are too busy with the donors to notice you tried to run."

He holds my gaze. His fists clench, then relax. He sits, slow and controlled, right on the floor. For the first time, how tired he is becomes impossible to miss—maybe how tired he's always been.

"Your father would have done the same," he says.

"Yeah," I answer, voice flat. "But he'd never let me do it myself."

We wait in silence. The air is thick with everything that's ever gone unsaid in this family.

Above us, I hear the heavy tread of boots. The police are coming, and even my uncle can't talk his way through three feet of brick.

"You want me to do it?" I ask. "Call them down?"

He shakes his head. "Let's not make it a show, Cassie. Not for them."

I sit down opposite him, the bag between us. I recorded it all just in case.

For a while, we say nothing. The echo of our breath is the only proof we're still alive.

After a few minutes, the boots arrive, and the door opens. The light is blinding, and the voice is the one I've dreaded and longed for in equal measure.

"Cassie?" My father's voice rough as gravel.

"In here," I say.

He steps in, gun holstered, badge out. He takes in the scene, nods, and then says, "Alfred Maddox, you're under arrest."

Alfred shrugs. "I was always going to lose to a Maddox, one way or another."

My father cuffs him. His expression lands on me: pride, threaded with regret.

"Nice work, kid."

I want to say a million things. None of them will land right.

"I know," I finally say.

He ushers Alfred out. I stand, dust myself off, and grab the duffel. I check the contents—hard drives, binders, envelopes—everything we need.

At the top of the stairs, the light is pure and hard. I blink against it, step into the noise and heat of the police operation. My father is waiting, hand on my shoulder.

"Want to see it through?" he asks.

I match his pace, and we walk out together.

The last thing I take in of the Genesee is the ballroom—lights blazing, every guest penned up and howling for their lawyer.

Mel and Janice hang over the balcony railing, waving like maniacs. I wave back. Alissa is there too, arms folded, grinning. Even Rafi is outside, camera rolling, capturing it all for posterity.

The bag rests heavy in my hand — the evidence, the proof.

Lila's home waiting, probably worried sick.

Tomorrow. The day after.

For once, I let myself believe that maybe—just maybe—we changed something tonight.

And I'm not sorry.

Not even a little.

13

Breathing Space, Breaking Points

A wall of noise and hormones already claimed Slice's back booth, even on a Tuesday. The red vinyl is glossy with sanitizer, and the windows are fogged over, each pane etched with the fingerprints of a thousand restless teenagers. In the far corner, a cluster of varsity jackets, thrift-store flannel, and drama club hoodies signals my target: Marcus, Alissa, Janice, and Nate, plus Mel, Rafi, and—at the end—Lila, all arranged like a jury with extra pizza.

I get three steps into the dining room before I hear Janice's voice ricochet off the tile: "—And then I told him, I don't care if you're the vice principal, if you want the closet key you have to go through me." There's a general eruption of laughter, led by Marcus, who's wearing his concussion like a badge of honor, a bruised knot high on his forehead. Alissa sits beside him, socking his arm every few sentences. Mel sits next to the coat rack, picking at a slice, and smiles like she won something. Rafi's at the edge, orchestrating the chaos with a few well-placed quips.

Lila's there, but not there, like she has yet to find her place among the group. She sits in the first seat on the end, half-turned toward the window, a glass of wine hovering in her hand. She smiles at the right moments, but it's too practiced, the way someone smiles at a story they've heard three times before.

Rafi's the first to see me, and he signals with two fingers. I navigate around a table of junior lacrosse kids, and slide into the open spot next to Lila, letting my coat drop on the floor.

"Cassie!" Janice raises her arms like a prizefighter, and points at the enormous bruise on Marcus's head. "Have you seen what you did to our fearless leader?"

I laugh. "Last I checked, you were the brains of this operation, Janice."

She puts her hand to her heart. "You honor me."

Marcus rolls his eyes. "Don't feed her ego. It's already a health hazard."

Alissa chimes in: "It's not her ego I'm worried about. It's yours. You wanted to back into the tunnel with a head injury, dumbass."

Janice launches into a retelling of the night's events, this time with twice the drama and three new plot twists. She pantomimes the "epic takedown" of a security guard (who was, in reality, an underpaid temp with a limp), and exaggerates the gravity of Mel's coat check espionage ("She intercepted a burner phone with nerves of steel!"). Mel's face goes cherry red, but she shrugs it off, muttering, "It was nothing. Just a lucky grab."

Rafi leans in, dropping his voice over the hum of the soda fountain. "You missed the pre-show. Marcus tried to sign his discharge papers with the wrong hand and almost fainted in the ER parking lot."

Marcus snorts, then regrets it, wincing as he touches the bruise. "I'm fine. See? I can still eat." He inhales half a slice of pepperoni, almost choking before Alissa smacks his back.

Nate, who's been content to observe from a safe distance, pipes up. "Did you hear about the press conference?"

Alissa nods. "The DA's already spinning it. 'Thanks to the brave efforts of law enforcement and community volunteers, justice was served.' No mention of our undercover work, of course."

Janice wags a finger. "They're saving that for the Netflix documentary."

The table breaks up into smaller conversations. Mel and Janice debate whether it's better to go public with their story or keep it secret as a "legend." Marcus and Alissa swap war stories, each one trying to outdo the other with minor acts of recklessness. Rafi checks his phone, probably monitoring the latest news on the case.

Lila is silent, her thumb tracing the rim of her glass. I wait until the others immerse themselves in another round of story-swapping. I lean over, keeping my voice low just for her. "You okay?"

She hesitates. Her voice so quiet I almost miss it: "Did you mean what you said? About it being the last time?"

I take a second to process. "Yeah," I say, because it's the only answer I have. "I want it to be."

She turns away, blinking hard. "You always say that, Cass."

"I know." I take her free hand under the table. It's cold, and she doesn't squeeze back, but she doesn't pull away either.

From the main table, Janice's voice surges back into focus: "We need to celebrate! I mean, we toppled a criminal empire and nobody even got expelled. That's historic." She raises her water glass. "To the weirdest, best team ever assembled at Lenape High!"

There's a chorus of "hear hears" and pizza slices held aloft. Even Lila manages a small lift of her glass.

When the attention swings back to their next adventure—something about "liberating" the principal's private snack fridge—I turn toward Lila, blocking out the booth and the noise.

"Talk to me," I say.

She laughs, short and bitter. "There's nothing to say. You did the thing. I knew you would."

"Li—"

"I know your work is important, but..." Her words catch, and she steadies herself with a sip of wine. "It felt like you disappeared on me. Like I was the only one not in on the secret."

"I'm sorry." I mean it. The words come out hoarsely, and for a moment, the rest of the pizza joint drops away. "I should have made space. For you."

She shrugs, but her chin quivers. "It's not your job to make space, Cass. Just... remember you don't have to do everything alone. You can lean on me sometimes."

The table behind us erupts as Marcus demonstrates the "proper technique" for getting knocked out, which involves more pizza than physics. I smile, but my chest aches.

Lila puts her hand on my knee, light as a feather. "Are you okay?"

An answer forms on my lips, but my thoughts return to a call from my father this morning. Alfred's lawyers were already filing countersuits and spinning the narrative on every morning news show.

"I'm okay," I lie, "but it's not over yet. He's already on the offensive. His lawyers filed three new motions, and he's publicly denying everything. Said the whole thing was a conspiracy to destroy his 'legacy'."

Lila huffs. "Figures. The only thing that man cares about is winning. Sounds like a Maddox."

I cringe at the jab, but direct my attention to tracing the wood grain in the tabletop. "We can fight it. But it'll be slow, and messy, and I'm probably going to get subpoenaed by Christmas."

She leans in, bumping her shoulder to mine. "I'll bring snacks to the deposition."

I laugh, really laugh, for the first time in days.

The others stack their plates; the celebration winds down. Mel checks her phone and says, "My mom's outside."

Janice and Nate gather their stuff, already plotting out a midnight run to the donut shop on Broad Street. What I wouldn't give to have the metabolism of a teenager again. Marcus and Alissa linger. Marcus tries to explain the physics of concussion recovery with lots of hand gestures and zero science.

Lila places her hand on my shoulder. "You sure you're good?"

"Never better," I say, and this time I almost believe it. "But what about you?"

"I've been better," Lila says, and there is more truth to those words than I can even express.

Lila and I sit together, each of us nursing a glass of wine as the teens gain their second wind. Janice commandeers the jukebox, which now blares a rotation of pop punk and Broadway hits, alternating between off-key singalongs and shrieks of laughter.

After about an hour, the bench gets too cramped. I slip out on the pretense of getting more napkins, but it's just to get a moment to breathe. Rafi intercepts me by the register, holding up a plate with two fresh slices.

"Hungry?" he asks. When I roll my eyes, he adds, "Well, you looked like you were about to chew a hole through the table."

I grin. "Chivalry's not dead. It's just undercooked and covered in red pepper flakes."

He laughs, and for a minute, we're two people standing under the fluorescent lights, away from the noise. He nods toward a corner booth, away from the crowd.

"Let's sit," he says, "before Marcus tries to eat the vinyl."

I slide into the booth, and he follows, setting the pizza between us. For a while we eat in silence, accompanied by the low hum of the soda machine and the far-off chaos of the others. It's almost peaceful. I can see the street through the window, the wet pavement reflecting neon and headlights, the world going on as if there wasn't a minor revolution in the heart of Lenape City.

After a few bites, Rafi wipes his mouth with the back of his hand. "So, real talk."

I brace. "Hit me."

He taps a finger on the Formica. "Do you ever tire of being right all the time?"

I make a face. "Are you implying I have a god complex?"

He pretends to consider it. "Not a god complex. More like a benevolent dictator. You run the show, but you actually care about your minions."

I laugh, but then he gets serious. "You took on a lot, Cass. More than anyone should've had to."

I shrug, but he doesn't let me deflect.

"No, I mean it. You're relentless. And you're gonna burn out if you keep putting the entire city on your back."

I lean back, picking at the edge of my plate. "Someone has to."

He studies me for a second, the way he does when he's about to say something risky. "You know, you could just... let people in. Let them help. That's what the rest of us are here for."

I want to argue, but I remember Lila's words. "I'm trying. Really."

He nods, like he can see all the gears grinding inside me. "I know. It's why we follow you. Even when you're being a giant pain in the ass."

A comfortable silence settles, broken only by the clatter of a dropped pizza pan in the kitchen. Rafi finishes his slice. He leans across the table, elbows braced, eyes locked on mine.

"So, what now?" he says, voice soft.

I don't have an answer.

He laughs. "You know, this is the first time I've ever seen you stumped."

"Don't get used to it," I shoot back, but there's no heat in it.

He glances at the others—still singing, still debating whether pineapple belongs on pizza (it does)—and back to me. He hesitates, then says, "I'm glad you're okay, Cass."

My chest loosens a little. "I'm glad we're okay."

The moment hangs between us, neither of us sure what comes next. Rafi reaches out, brushing a loose strand of hair behind my ear. My heart does a weird, jittery thing, like I just pulled off a ten-thousand-dollar bluff at a poker table. I lean in and so does he.

Before anything can happen, there's a yell from the main booth: "CASSIE! GET OVER HERE!"

Janice, naturally. I pull back, cheeks burning, and Rafi smiles, a little crooked. "Rain check?"

I can't keep the stupid smile off my face. "Rain check."

We rejoin the group, where Nate has already started stacking empty glasses and Alissa is valiantly trying to explain the concept of a "victory lap" to Nate. Lila is back at the end of the bench, this time with a refill on her wine, watching the chaos with quiet amusement. When she sees me, she waves me over, patting the seat beside her.

As I slide in, she pours some of her wine into a second glass, offering it to me. "Long overdue."

I take it, raising it in a mock salute. "To best friends and pizza?"

She rolls her eyes, but clinks my glass anyway. "To making it out alive."

We both drink, and for a moment, everything is as it should be: the warmth of the wine, the roar of the booth, the knowledge that—at least for tonight—

I'm surrounded by people who get me.

There's a TV mounted on the wall above the counter, the kind that's always stuck on local news or weather. Nobody's paying attention, but the anchor's voice carries over the room noise:

"—in other city news, the Scott-Calder redevelopment project is expected to bring hundreds of new jobs—"

I freeze, glass halfway to my lips. The name Calder hangs in the air like a bullet. I stare at the scrolling headline on the screen: "MAYOR SCOTT ANNOUNCES NEW CALDER-LED INITIATIVE."

Rafi notices and follows my gaze. "What is it?"

I put the glass down, mind racing. "Calder," I say, almost to myself. "That's the name from the foundation records—the one Alfred was funneling through. It's not just his show. There's someone else. Someone bigger."

The others catch on to my tone. The booth quiets as they lock onto me, then onto the TV, then at each other.

"Are you saying this isn't over?" Alissa says.

I don't trust myself to answer.

Janice grins. "I knew there'd be a sequel."

Marcus shakes his head, but he's smiling, too. "You won't to let it go, will you?"

I gaze at Rafi. He's watching me with the same steady, unflinching confidence. "What's our next move, detective?"

For a second, I let myself imagine the future—a future full of pizza nights and Lila's hugs and Rafi's quiet support, but also of more mysteries, more walls to knock down, more of the world to fix.

I pick up my glass, raising it to the TV, to the booth, to the whole stubborn city outside.

"Tomorrow," I say, "we get to work."

And the story, like the best nights at Slice's, is far from over.

We step into the freezing night. For a moment, the entire city is small and soft, and manageable. Lila's arm snakes through mine as we walk. She shivers, so I squeeze a little tighter.

At the curb, Rafi waits, leaning against his beater sedan, hands in his pockets. He sees us, and for a second his face breaks open with real, pure relief.

"You're alive," he says, mock-serious. "Didn't think you'd survive that pizza."

I grin. "I'm no teenager, but it takes more than sodium and cheese to put me down."

He opens the passenger door for me, and as I duck in, I glance back at Lila. Her eyes are bright, maybe from the cold, maybe not.

"I'll see you at home," she says.

"Yeah," I say, "you will."

She heads down the block, and turns the corner.

Rafi gets in, starts the car, and lets the heater blast. We sit in silence for a bit, the city lights flickering past as we drive.

He glances over. "You're not okay, are you?"

I shake my head. "Not really."

He nods, understanding more than he lets on. "Want to talk about it?"

I study my hands, the faint smudge of ink still staining my knuckles from the police station. "Maybe later."

He lets it be, and we drive on.

The night outside is empty and alive all at once.

This peace feels borrowed.

Not a finish line, but another mile marker, another night survived, another round of pizza and war stories and promises made in the dark.

I lean my head against the cold glass, close my eyes, and let myself imagine, just for a second, what it would be like if the world really was safe. If I stopped fighting.

But I know better.

There's always another case, another mystery, another piece of the puzzle waiting to be pried loose.

And that's okay.

I have Lila, and Rafi, and even Marcus and the Musketeers.

I'm not alone.

Not anymore.

14

On the Stand

The walls of the Lenape County Courthouse are off white, the color of expired milk. Under the flicker of fluorescent lights, the chamber of justice is more like the waiting room for a colonoscopy. I sit at the witness stand, massaging my temple, a cardboard cup of coffee clamped in my hand. It's already gone cold, but the taste is so bitter I'm not sure it started hot.

The judge calls the room to order. There's a cough from the gallery, and the bailiff straightens like he's about to personally tase anyone who so much as whispers. The prosecutor—James Branham, bespectacled, mid-thirties, every inch a man who played trombone in high school—leans over the lectern and asks me to state my name for the record.

"Cassandra Marie Maddox," I say, and my voice is steadier than I expect. The defense attorney scribbles something on a yellow legal pad, head never lifting. At the table in front of him, Alfred Maddox sits in a suit so expensive it's probably immune to sweat. His lips are pursed, his expression betraying his annoyance.

"Ms. Maddox, what is your current occupation?" Branham asks.

"Paralegal with Sampson & Sampson. Also licensed as a private investigator in the Commonwealth of Pennsylvania."

He nods, as if my résumé is the only thing standing between us and chaos. "And what was your relationship to the events under review here today?"

I glance at the jury. Three of them wear identical shirts—subtle blue stripes, like they're in a cult. One is already blinking hard, fighting the urge to nap.

"I was retained to investigate irregularities at the Peterson Group. Later, I was retained to investigate the Genesee Country Club's scholarship fund," I say. "That investigation led to the discovery of financial records linking the Genesee Foundation to multiple instances of admissions fraud."

A few heads nod in the box. Maybe they care. Or maybe they're just relieved to hear someone talk like a spreadsheet.

Branham clicks a remote, and a projector throws my evidence spreadsheet onto a yellowed screen beside the jury. The text is jagged, hard to read. "For the record, Exhibit A is the analysis of scholarship grant distributions from Genesee Foundation, Inc., cross-referenced against acceptance data for the Ivy League Three and—" he checks his notes, "—Pennamore College. Can you walk us through your findings, Ms. Maddox?"

I nod. "Sure. Over a three-year period, the Genesee Foundation disbursed approximately $1.7 million in scholarships. Of that, nearly sixty percent was awarded to students from five specific families—all of whom had prior business dealings with the foundation's leadership."

"Specifically?"

"Alfred Maddox, acting as Chair," I say, not looking at the man himself. "But also through a nonprofit conduit called Ignite Global. I traced the funds through 501(c)(3) returns, campaign donation databases, and private correspondence."

I pause, letting the numbers settle like ash. In the gallery, Rafi sits three rows back, head low, hands fidgeting with a pen that I know he keeps as a nervous tic. He doesn't lift his head, but he's listening.

Branham cues up the next slide. "Tell us about Ignite Global."

"A shell foundation claiming to fund STEM programs for underprivileged youth, but it's basically a black hole for donor money. From 2021 to 2023, it received over $900,000 from Genesee and passed along less than ten percent to actual programming. The rest cycled between consulting fees, 'research' expenses, and direct transfers to the personal accounts of its board members—including the defendant."

There's a whisper from the jury box. The judge, who has the patience of a stone, lets it slide.

Branham pushes on. "Did you find any direct evidence of misconduct?"

"Two sets of emails. The first is from a fundraiser in March 2022—subject line, 'Urgent: VIP Placement'—which details a coordinated effort to secure spots for specific students at Penamore College. The second is a set of wire instructions, signed by Alfred Maddox, moving $80,000 to Ignite Global the same week as the scholarship decisions."

"Was this unusual?"

I resist a laugh. "It's unique. Most scholarships have an open application process, reviewed by a committee. These were closed-door, invite-only, and the recipients were hand-picked. In a few cases, the acceptance letters were drafted before the scholarship applications were even filed."

Branham turns to the judge. "Your Honor, we'd like to submit the full document chain as evidence."

"Sustained," says the judge, and the bailiff stamps the evidence bag with a date and time.

Alfred doesn't move. There's a shimmer at the tip of his nose, a tiny bead of sweat, but otherwise he's all marble and angles.

Branham pivots. "Ms. Maddox, can you tell us about your relationship to the defendant?"

I expected the question, but it lands like a sucker punch. I take a breath, counting to three.

"He's my uncle," I say, and for a moment the entire courtroom leans in, like they've all been waiting for this single, soapy detail. "I grew up in Lenape City. Our families were close until... until my father ranked up in the force."

Branham lets the words sit. "Did your familial relationship impact your investigation?"

"Only to make it more thorough," I say. "If I'd missed anything, the defendant would have found a way to use it."

There's an almost imperceptible smile from Alfred, the kind a chess player gives after losing a pawn while setting up the next three moves.

"No further questions," Branham says, and steps back.

The defense lawyer stands. He is shorter than expected, with a machine-made tan and a suit at least ten years out of style. He approaches with hands folded, like he's about to apologize for bumping my cart at ShopRite.

"Ms. Maddox," he begins, "you stated you're a licensed private investigator?"

"That's correct."

"And your employer is Sampson & Sampson, who—if I recall—are currently representing several parties seeking damages against my client's business interests?"

I keep my voice steady. "Correction, sir. I'm employed by Sampson & Sampson as a paralegal. The law firm sponsored my initial P.I. license and assigned me to the case with Shenandoah Partners. I acted independently, under Maddox Investigative Services during my investigation into The Genesee Country Club. To your point, my job is to find facts, not take sides."

He gives a thin-lipped smile, then rifles through his notes. "You testified that you traced scholarship funds to recipients with 'prior business dealings' with Mr. Maddox. Can you specify what those were?"

"Donations to the Genesee Foundation, but also co-investments in real estate, country club memberships, and, in one case, a directorship at Ignite Global."

"So, just to clarify," he says, voice syrupy, "these recipients were successful, well-connected, and—by all accounts—outstanding students?"

I know where he's going. "That's accurate," I say, "but the scholarships were never publicly advertised. Other qualified students never had a chance."

He pounces. "Isn't it possible, Ms. Maddox, that these were simply 'merit-based' scholarships and that the connections you mention are coincidental?"

I almost snort, but stop myself. "Possible, but unlikely. Especially when the award letters were drafted before the applications were received."

He flips to a new page. "You mentioned your uncle's role as Chair. You are aware, I'm sure, that the Genesee Foundation's board includes half a dozen other individuals. Are they also on trial here?"

I shake my head. "Not today."

"And yet you choose to focus on Mr. Maddox."

I glance at the jury. "Because every major transaction required his signature. He was the controlling voice."

He lets that hang, then goes in for the kill. "Isn't it true, Ms. Maddox, that you have a personal vendetta against your uncle? That your father's estrangement from your uncle left you with... feelings?"

It's an amateur play, but it hits. My leg starts bouncing under the bench, and for a second, I taste blood in my mouth. I keep my voice as level as I can manage.

"I do have feelings," I say, looking him dead in the eye. "Mainly disappointment."

A ripple of laughter from the gallery. Even the judge allows herself a micro-smirk.

The defense attorney sighs, realizing he's lost the point. "No further questions, Your Honor."

The judge nods. "Ms. Maddox, you're excused. Please don't discuss your testimony with anyone until the trial concludes."

I rise, knees creaking, and exit the witness stand. The bailiff herds me to a holding row just inside the gallery. The prosecutor gives a tight smile, and Rafi, sitting in the third row, catches my eye. One corner of his mouth lifts, then settles.

* * *

The rest of the day is a parade of expert witnesses, each more boring than the last. I tune out most of it, just watching Alfred's hands. He never fidgets. Never scratches his nose, never checks his phone. The only movement is when he scribbles a note to his lawyer, or glares at the DA.

At 5:04, the judge gavels out for the day. I gather my things, which are mostly loose papers and a lip balm I haven't used since fall. I'm halfway to the doors when Rafi intercepts me.

"That was clinical," he says, offering a high-five I don't take.

"Don't gloat," I mutter. "It's not over."

He shrugs, but follows me out anyway, sticking close as we navigate the courthouse lobby. "You didn't acknowledge him once. That rattled him."

"It rattled me," I admit. "You ever seen a ghost, Raf?"

He snorts. "Only when you text me after midnight."

We step outside, into the flat gray of another Lenape winter. The sky is the same color as the courthouse walls.

Rafi kicks a pebble off the steps. "Tomorrow it's Mel's turn, right?"

"Mel, then Janice. Alissa, if she doesn't get cold feet. They're all lined up."

He studies me. "You think they'll hold?"

"Kids these days?" I say with a cracked smile. "They're tougher than they seem."

He nudges me with his elbow. "So are you."

We walk to the curb, silent for a minute. The streetlights flicker on, casting everything in sodium gold.

"You want a ride?" he asks.

I shake my head. "I need the air. Gonna walk."

He shrugs, but doesn't push it. "See you tomorrow, Cass."

"Yeah," I say, and watch him disappear into the dusk.

I cross the street, every ache in my knees and ankles registering as I head home. The sidewalks are empty. The world is muffled, soft with the threat of snow. I replay every question, every answer, every glance from my uncle. It's the first domino in a line about to come crashing down.

In the morning, I'll do it again. I'll put on my cleanest blazer, pour burnt coffee down my throat, and try to pretend that I'm not terrified of what happens when the truth finally gets its turn on the stand.

But for now, I take a minute.

Then I let it go, and keep walking.

15

Under Oath

If I were writing the script, I'd give Mel Albright a better entrance: some triumphant walk up the courthouse steps, a slow pan to her jaw set with determination. Instead, she's just a seventeen-year-old kid in her best thrift-store cardigan, fingers twisting a silver lacrosse bracelet until it leaves an imprint on her wrist.

On the second day of testimony, hostility courses through the courtroom. The bailiff is cranky from lack of sleep, the judge already on her second mug of coffee. A new crowd fills the benches—reporters, teachers, half the faculty from St. Augustine's—plus the usual army of lawyers in starched collars, all waiting for the next whiff of drama.

When the bailiff calls Mel's name, she jumps a little, like a freshman about to get cold-called in Chemistry. She walks to the stand, sits, and immediately starts scanning for a friendly face. I raise a hand in a half-wave from the gallery. She finds me, exhales.

The prosecutor today is Heller—a woman in a charcoal pinstripe suit whose block heels click across the courtroom floor like a metronome keeping time. She approaches the stand with an encouraging smile, but the warmth doesn't quite reach her eyes. Heller is here to win.

"State your name, please."

"Melanie Albright." A faint clear of the throat. Then louder, steadier: "Melanie Ruth Albright."

"Ms. Albright, how do you know the defendant?"

Mel's gaze flicks toward the defense table. "He's a family friend. I used to caddy for him at Genesee Country Club. Sometimes he'd show up at my uncle's Fourth of July parties. I know him from around."

Heller nods slightly, then changes lanes. "And did you receive a scholarship from the Genesee Foundation?"

Mel shakes her head immediately. "No, ma'am. I wasn't on their list."

A soft ripple of laughter from the jury. Mel blushes, then pushes on.

"But I know who was. They announced the scholarship recipients at the Spring Gala last year. I was working coat check. It was a big deal."

Heller circles, her tone light—velvet covering a blade. "Can you describe anything unusual about the scholarship program?"

Mel nods. "Usually the scholarships go to kids in the city. People who actually need them. But last year... three awards went to students from St. Augustine's. None of them applied. They just got them. One was a board member's daughter. The other two... I don't know their families, but they're all club regulars."

"And what about your own scholarship—the one you received? Where did it come from?"

Mel swallows, hands tightening in her lap. "I was told it came from Penamore College. But the paperwork listed Ignite Global as the sponsor, with funds routed through the Genesee Country Club Charitable Trust."

Heller steps closer. "Was that accurate?"

"No." Mel's voice sharpens. "It wasn't even supposed to be mine. The email congratulated the wrong student. When I pointed out the mistake, I was told to sign anyway. That 'opportunities like this don't come twice.' They said if I didn't accept, it would 'cause problems for my uncle'."

A murmur through the gallery.

"Your uncle is Charles Albright, correct?"

"Yes, ma'am."

"And what happened to him?"

Mel closes her eyes for one beat. "He... he took the fall for the kickback schemes at Shenandoah Partners. The ones tied to the property development bids." Her voice cracks, then steadies. "He didn't act alone. He just signed what they told him to sign."

The jury shifts uneasily.

Heller lets the silence stretch, then: "Is that when you contacted Ms. Maddox?"

"Yes. I needed a way out. I knew the scholarship wasn't legitimate, and I didn't want to get trapped in something criminal. I asked Cassie—Ms. Maddox—to help me figure out what I could do."

Heller gives a small nod. "Let's go back. You mentioned overhearing a conversation. Can you tell the court what you heard?"

Mel glances at the bracelet on her wrist, grounding herself. "It was after the Spring Gala. I was cleaning up the coatroom. The door was cracked. I heard Mr. Maddox talking to a woman—I'm pretty sure it was Mrs. Sloane from Penamore Admissions. He said, 'We can guarantee spots for our preferred applicants if you expedite their review. Make it appear legitimate, but get it done before the next board meeting'."

She lifts a shoulder. "They weren't whispering."

Heller retrieves a sheet of paper—Mel's scrawled timeline. The same one I'd stared at for hours two months earlier.

"Is this your writing?"

"Yes, ma'am."

It's handed to the defense. The attorney glances at it as one would gloss over a grocery receipt.

Heller steps back. "No further questions."

The defense lawyer rises slowly, performing with an air of calm superiority. He walks toward the stand with his hands clasped behind him, as if ready to lecture on "how the world really works."

"Ms. Albright, how old are you?"

"Seventeen."

"And how long have you worked at the Country Club?"

"Two years. Off and on."

"So you were a junior when these events occurred?"

"Technically a senior. I graduated early."

He jots a note meant to imply significance. "And this conversation you overheard—through a cracked door. Is that a habit of yours? Eavesdropping?"

Mel tenses, but her voice remains steady. "I don't make a habit of it, sir. But people talk loud when they think nobody's listening."

A few jurors nod.

"Is it possible you misheard? Or misunderstood? That Mr. Maddox was advocating for qualified students, not... manipulating the process?"

Mel's jaw tightens. "He said, 'Make it appear legitimate.' Those were his exact words."

The lawyer frowns, changing strategies. "Do you dislike Mr. Maddox?"

She blinks. "No. He's always been nice to me. Tipped well."

The lawyer's rhythm falters. "Then why report him?"

Mel's voice becomes a whisper, but every word lands. "Because it was wrong."

He waits for more. After a beat, he says, "No further questions."

Mel steps down, head high, though her hands tremble as she passes me. I reach out and squeeze her shoulder. She gives me a small, grateful smile before slipping through the double doors—lighter for having told the truth, but not free of its weight.

Next up is Rafi. He's more at home in a courtroom than most lawyers, but tension shows in the way he tugs at the collar of his dress shirt. When the bailiff calls his name, he steps up, squares his shoulders, and sits without fuss.

Heller is in command. "Please state your name and occupation."

"Rafi Alvi. I'm an IT consultant with the Lenape City Police Department. On the side, I also work alongside Ms. Maddox with her firm. I specialize in digital security and forensic data recovery."

She flips to her notes. "Did you participate in the investigation into the Genesee Foundation?"

"Yes. I conducted the digital forensics—collecting and analyzing emails, bank records, and server logs."

"And were you able to authenticate the evidence submitted by Ms. Maddox?"

He nods. "Every byte. The email chains were intact; the bank records unaltered. The hard drive image from Ignite Global's office matched the data set from the foundation's servers. No evidence of tampering."

Heller walks him through the boring technical stuff, but Rafi makes it sound simple. When she hands him a printout of an email chain, he glances at it and recites the hash values by memory, like he's reading from a song sheet.

Heller: "Did you find any evidence of deleted or hidden communications?"

Rafi: "Several. I used open-source tools to recover deleted emails. They contained language about 'expediting applicants' and 'taking care of our own,' which, in context, clearly refers to the scholarship placements."

The defense doesn't bother to challenge the data. Instead, they try to poke holes in Rafi himself.

"Mr. Alvi," the lawyer says, "you're close to Ms. Maddox, aren't you?"

Rafi doesn't blink. "Yes. I've known Ms. Maddox and her family all my life. In my role with the LCPD, I also work with her father. We're close friends."

The lawyer leans in. "Would you say you're biased?"

Rafi shrugs. "I'm biased toward facts."

The court reporter, who hasn't smiled in two days, actually cracks up. The judge tells her to strike the last sentence from the record, but the point is made.

Rafi is excused. He passes me, and this time I squeeze his hand. It's warm, solid—a steady reassurance that we have a shot.

Then come the Musketeers, one by one, each with their own flavor of disaster.

First is Marcus. He walks stiffly, head still bruised, but unbandaged from the tunnel incident, eyes dark with sleep deprivation. He answers questions with the blunt honesty of someone who's spent too much time around cops: "Yes, ma'am. No, sir. I saw the envelope. I didn't touch anything else." He describes the hidden room in the Genesee's sub-basement, the folio marked "Scholarship Committee," the thumb drive I'd later present as evidence. When the defense asks why he broke in, Marcus shrugs: "Because the grown-ups wouldn't listen."

The jury loves him. The judge less so, but Marcus is too deadpan for anyone to call it bravado.

Alissa is next. She's a different animal—cool, poised, voice clear as a bell. She recounts overhearing conversations in the club, including one where Alfred Maddox joked about "locking in legacies" over crab puffs and gin. She remembers everything, even the brand of pen the man used to sign a check. When the defense tries to rattle her, Alissa just leans forward and says, "You know, if you're trying to gaslight me, you should have picked someone less competitive." A ripple moves through the courtroom. Not loud. Just enough.

Janice, of course, is pure theater. She's a one-woman show, narrating the discovery of the "secret tunnel" with so much suspense that half the jury leans in, mouths open. She describes the gold placard in the hidden room, even imitates the voice of the guard who nearly caught them. When pressed about her motivations, she says, "Listen, I watch a ton of Law & Order. One witness never gets the facts right, and I refuse to be that person." Even the judge snorts at that.

Nate goes last, as always, and is the only one who seems genuinely bored by the process. He gives a matter-of-fact summary of their surveillance operation—who followed whom, what equipment was used, how they managed to outsmart the club's security. When the defense tries to paint him as a "juvenile troublemaker," Nate shrugs and says, "Better than being a juvenile delinquent."

From the gallery, it all comes down at once—every story, every detail, every flicker of doubt in their voices, each one hitting like a punch to the ribs.

They're young. Too young for this. And I'm the one who put them here.

Whatever they carry, the weight of it still comes back to me.

* * *

At recess, Rafi finds me in the corridor. He hands me a juice box—tangerine, my favorite. "You okay?"

"I'm the worst mentor ever," I say.

He laughs, "You're the only one they'd follow into a sewer."

I take the juice, sipping slowly. "You think it's enough?"

Rafi leans against the wall, folding his arms. "You saw the jury. You saw Alfred's face. They're rattled, Cass."

We watch the court staff scurry past, arms loaded with files. In the distance, Mel and Janice sit together, heads bent close, as if plotting the next caper. Marcus is alone, staring out the window, with his hands in his pockets.

I want to go to him. I want to tell him I'm sorry. I want to take back every risk I ever let them run.

But I know better. There's no do-over for this.

Back in the courtroom, the judge glances at the clock and announces they'll reconvene in the morning for the final witnesses.

Alfred straightens in his chair.

Tomorrow, he takes the stand.

As the day ends, I linger by the courthouse steps, watching the Musketeers pile into the Jeep and vanish down Broad Street. Age settles over me along with a quiet I don't rush to fill.

Rafi stands beside me. "Tomorrow, it's done," he says.

I know that's never true. The story just changes shape. The villains get smarter and the heroes get tired.

But for tonight, I let myself believe it.

"See you tomorrow, Raf."

He smiles. "Count on it."

I go home. I sleep. And I dream of gold placards, and secret tunnels, and the impossible lightness of being a kid who believes the world can change if you're just brave enough.

* * *

On the third morning, the courthouse buzzes with the kind of anticipation reserved for coronations and executions. I know the game is rigged before I even see the lineup—reporters loitering near the metal detectors, half of City Hall's blue-blazered administrative staff filtering in to catch the show.

Today's headliner is Alfred Maddox.

He enters the courtroom with the stride of a man who's just won a golf tournament: hair perfectly in place, suit sharp enough to serve hors d'oeuvres on, shoes that reflect the overhead lights like surgical steel. He smiles at the bailiff, bows slightly to the judge, and takes the oath with the breezy confidence of someone who's donated enough to have his name on a wing of the building.

Rafi leans over from the next bench and mutters, "He even color-coordinated with the stenographer." I roll my eyes, but he's right. Alfred's tie is the exact navy of the court's upholstery.

The prosecutor begins with gentle questions, the kind that could double as a lifestyle segment on morning news. "Mr. Maddox, can you explain the mission of the Genesee Foundation?"

Alfred turns to the jury, voice syrupy. "Absolutely. The Foundation exists to support youth development, especially in underserved communities. We offer mentorship, scholarships, and after-school programs—all with the goal of building tomorrow's leaders."

He makes eye contact with the foreman, who beams back as if he's being inducted into a secret society.

"And your role?"

"I was proud to serve as Chairman of the Board. I oversaw grant distributions, coordinated fundraising events, and ensured that all our programs aligned with our mission statement."

If the court had a bottle of wine to pop open, they'd do it right now. It's masterful.

The prosecutor dials up the pressure. "Can you explain the decision to award three consecutive scholarships to students with personal or business ties to the Foundation's directors?"

Alfred shrugs, projecting fatherly concern. "Our pool of applicants is naturally smaller than, say, a state university. Many of Lenape's best and brightest happen to be connected—this is a small city, after all. If a candidate is deserving, why penalize them for their network?"

He pivots to a story about a struggling student who made good. He never says her name, but I know who he means—she was in my class, and she left after her "merit" scholarship fell through. The way he tells it, she's a paragon of hard work. There's not a hint of malice, not a whiff of guilt.

The prosecutor moves on. "Mr. Maddox, were you aware of funds being routed through Ignite Global?"

"Ignite Global was a partner, yes. We used their infrastructure to coordinate events and manage donor relations."

"Were you aware that less than ten percent of their budget was spent on student programming?"

"I was surprised to learn that, yes," he says, face unreadable. "I have since initiated a full review of their finances, and I'm deeply disappointed in their leadership."

He's positioning himself as the victim—of fraud, of misplaced trust, of a system too complex to be micromanaged. The jury eats it up. I start to sweat, wishing the bench had armrests to dig my nails into.

After half an hour, the prosecutor pivots to the email evidence. He reads aloud a message from Alfred to the Ignite board: "We can guarantee the outcome if you expedite the next round of applicants." He puts up the hard copy, which bears Alfred's digital signature.

Alfred doesn't blink. "That email has been taken out of context," he says, every syllable shaped for maximum plausible deniability. "I was referring to a funding deadline, not admissions."

It's so slick. For a moment, the whole case is one loose motion away from unraveling on live television.

The prosecutor keeps at it, but Alfred's patience is inexhaustible. He weathers each question with a slight nod and an occasional "I can see how you'd interpret it that way." He never loses his smile, never raises his voice.

When they reach the part about the legacy placements at Penamore College, Alfred leans back and steeples his fingers, as if he's about to offer career counseling to the DA.

"We have always prioritized local students and the local college," he says. "If some of those students happen to be the children of board members. That's a reflection of our community's strength, not a conspiracy."

The prosecutor closes his folder, defeated. "No further questions."

The defense lawyer stands, strutting to the stand with the swagger of a man whose case just got easier. "Mr. Maddox, have you ever been convicted of a crime?"

"No, sir."

"Ever even cited for a civil infraction?"

He shakes his head. "Not to my knowledge."

The lawyer paces, pausing to let that hang in the air. "You're aware that the charges today stem largely from the testimony of a single witness—your niece?"

Alfred's eyes flick to me for the first time. He offers the faintest of shrugs.

"I have great affection for Cassie," he says. "She's brilliant, resourceful, and, frankly, I wish I'd had her on the Foundation's audit team. But I do believe she's misinterpreted my actions, perhaps due to our complicated family history."

The lawyer feigns surprise. "Complicated how?"

Alfred smiles, gentle as a knife. "Let's just say the Maddoxes are a passionate bunch. Sometimes passion leads to... misunderstanding."

The lawyer thanks him, then sits, as if the job is done.

I plant my feet flat on the floor and don't move. Not yet.

The prosecution has one last move. They call Warren Keller—a name I barely remember and a man I only met once one summer while working as a server at The Genesee. His presence triggers something primal in the base of my skull.

He walks with a limp, a man in his late sixties with thick hands and a shock of white hair. He takes the stand, is sworn in, and answers the first few questions in a deep, raspy voice. He was a contractor for the city, worked on three redevelopment projects, and had regular contact with Alfred regarding funding and logistics.

"Mr. Keller," says Heller, "can you describe the payment process for the Old Town Plaza project?"

Keller nods, scans the room. "Sure. Most of the money came through the city's development budget. But there was a chunk—about three-quarters of a million—that passed through a consulting group called Eschelon Nexus

LLC."

The prosecutor's head snaps up. "Was this documented?"

Keller shrugs. "Not really. The invoices were generic—'consulting services,' 'project management,' that sort of thing. But when I asked, I was told to 'run it through Eschelon, then deliver as instructed.'"

"And who instructed you?"

"Usually a go-between from Shenandoah Partners. Sometimes Mr. Maddox directly."

The room goes still. The judge, for the first time, sits forward in her seat.

The prosecutor presses. "Did you see any overlap between Eschelon Nexus and Ignite Global?"

Keller nods. "Sure. Same addresses, same staff on the emails, same damn P.O. Box."

"And was the scholarship program used as a cover for these payments?"

"Absolutely. They'd hold a 'scholarship luncheon,' pay the caterer, then two days later a check would hit the books for twice the amount."

The defense is up in arms, shouting for the judge to strike the testimony. She sustains, but the words are already in the air, polluting every corner of the courtroom.

On cross, the defense tries to paint Keller as a disgruntled subcontractor who lost out on a better deal. Keller just laughs. "I got paid, son. I'm just tired of the city getting grifted."

The judge orders the jury to disregard the details about Eschelon Nexus, but the court reporter's hands don't stop moving. Every word is a nail in the coffin.

* * *

When the day adjourns, the defense team practically sprints from the room, trailing interns and paralegals like a panicked flock. The Musketeers—Mel, Janice, Nate, Marcus, and Alissa—congregate near the vending machines, talking in low, excited voices.

I linger in the courtroom, staring at the empty chair where Alfred sat, replaying his testimony over and over in my head. All the pieces are there: the nonprofit, the shell companies, the city contracts. The college scam was just a side hustle. The real money was in city development, and we had only pieced together enough to land Thomas Pence, Shenandoah's CEO, and Chuck Albright, his assistant, in jail.

Rafi finds me at the back, hands jammed in his jacket pockets. "You okay?"

I shake my head. "We missed the whole picture, Raf. The scholarships were just a front."

He shrugs. "That's how it works. They start with one scam, then build the next one on top. You ever see a grifter who only has one trick?"

I laugh, but there's no joy in it. "What if we're just playing catch-up forever?"

He nudges me, gentle. "That's how you know you're in the right job."

We walk out together. The hallway is empty except for the janitor, whose mop leaves streaks of pale water on the tile.

At the exit, Rafi stops, turns to me. "You know what happens next, right?"

"Alfred walks," I say, bitterness sharp in my throat.

He shrugs. "Maybe. Maybe not. But you've got ammo now. You know what to look for."

I stare out at the city skyline, the old stone facades and the half-built towers of Old Town Plaza. Somewhere in one of those offices, someone is already laying the groundwork.

"You ready to go back to work?" he asks.

I meet his eyes, then gaze at the city, at the scaffolding and the neon and the millions of stories that will never see daylight.

"Yeah," I say, and this time I mean it.

We walk into the night, two more ghosts in a city that never forgets.

But I have a file folder under my arm, a head full of names, and the certainty that this isn't finished. Not even close.

The courthouse doors shut behind us with a thud.

Tomorrow is waiting, and I am wide awake.

16

A Trail to the Mayor's Office

My office smells like toner, cheap takeout, and the faint burn of electrical components somewhere past their warranty. Three layers of Genesee Country Club records—printed emails, notary seals, and cross-referenced ledger sheets—cover the desk. On the monitor, I'm halfway through an Excel macro that might as well be a suicide note for my remaining faith in human honesty. My eyes swim with numbers. It's almost midnight, and the only light is the screen and the alley sodium glare leaking through the blinds.

I have the trial testimony up on one half of the monitor, evidence folders open on the other, and a Post-It pyramid of shell company names blooming up the left side of the bezel. For the last two hours I've been toggling between Alfred's own words ("our partners at Ignite Global," "the stewardship subcommittee," "routine expenditure, nothing unusual") and the actual wire transfer logs, all of which as routine as a Vegas slot machine with the brakes cut.

The more I dig, the less sense it makes. Which, I guess, is the point.

My coffee is cold, but I drink it anyway, scraping the bottom for grounds and bitterness. The building is dead quiet except for the distant elevator hum. Every once in a while, the radiator pipes groan, like they're arguing about how much longer they want to keep working. I take out my phone, scroll through last week's voicemails, and delete two reminders from my dad and an automated survey about the DA's "community engagement." Nobody calls with good news after ten.

I turn back to the spreadsheet. There's something off about the last set of invoices. The numbers round to even hundreds, which is usually a red flag. Nobody pays a consultant $12,000 on the nose unless it's hush money or some kind of laundering fee. But every time I try to pull the vendor's actual name, it traces back to another LLC, then to an address in Delaware, then—poof—nothing. I'm missing a link.

I start to re-read Alfred's deposition transcript, skimming for anything that doesn't fit the pattern. He's careful, but not perfect. In one response he refers to "necessary logistical overhead" for the Old Town Plaza project, but the next time he's asked, he says the funds were "strictly for youth program development." I make a note: see if any Plaza consultants match Ignite Global's board members.

The clock on my monitor blips over to 1:07 AM. I rub my eyes and refocus.

Rafi lets himself in without knocking, juggling a carrier tray with two coffees and a pharmacy's worth of caffeine pills. He's dressed for the night shift: hoodie, athletic pants, sneakers with holes at the heels. His hair is still perfect, because Rafi's hair does not know the meaning of stress.

He sets the drinks down with a thunk and glances at my screen. "You're through the looking glass, Alice. I thought we were going to ease up for a night."

I bite my lower lip. "I'm close, Raf. There's a pattern here, but I can't get to the endpoint. Alfred was lying about the Plaza disbursements."

Rafi slides into the chair beside me. He pulls up the sleeves of his hoodie and starts sifting through the spreadsheet. "Alright. Give me the rundown, starting from the last confirmed transaction."

I give him the basics: Ignite Global receives a donation from Genesee's foundation. Three days later, "Drexel & Pittman Consultants, LLC" receives a payout in that exact amount. After that, a matching amount lands in the campaign account for Lenape Forward, which is supposed to be an unaffiliated city improvement PAC, but the names on the signature card are the same as the ones on the scholarship committee. Every time I try to trace Drexel & Pittman, the paper trail vanishes.

Rafi taps at his laptop, syncing his screen to mine. "Try running the EIN on that consultant. Sometimes the state records lag behind the IRS ones." He pulls up a database I've never even seen before, keys in the number, and grins when the server chugs back a result.

"Registered to a co-working space in Philadelphia," he says. "But here's the officer list. One of the names is Elaine Winters. Didn't she testify as Chief of Staff for the Mayor's Office?"

I freeze. "She did. And she's on three of the Genesee committee meeting minutes."

Rafi whistles. "Mayor's fingerprints all over. So what are you thinking? Kickbacks for city contracts? Quid pro quo with scholarships as a smoke-screen?"

I pinch the bridge of my nose, eyes squeezed shut. "It's worse. If this is the same Elaine, she's funneling city money through shell companies and back into the PAC. That's money laundering. On top of everything else."

Rafi slides a fresh coffee in front of me. "You're not alone in this. We'll patch it together, step by step. Maybe take ten and let the dopamine settle."

I want to punch something, but I'm too tired to muster the energy. "I just—it's never-ending, Raf. Every time I cut off a head, three more grow back."

He shrugs, but it's the gentlest, most understanding shrug I've ever seen. "Hydra was Greek. We're in Pennsylvania. The odds are in your favor."

I almost laugh. Instead, I drink more coffee.

We sit in silence for a few minutes, screens casting us in zombie blue. Outside the window, the street is empty except for the soft stutter of a motion sensor light two buildings down. Rafi types, pulling up campaign donation records, cross-referencing city project approvals. I circle through the emails again, and this time I notice a cc'd address on one of the old Genesee memos: mayor.scott@lenapecity.gov.

I jab at the screen. "That's direct contact. No way Alfred's operating solo."

Rafi leans in, eyes bright. "You think the mayor's the actual puppet master?"

"Alfred was just the middleman. The real money's coming from city development. Genesee was always just the cover."

We're interrupted by a rattling knock on the office door. I flinch, because anyone knocking at this hour is a cop or a psycho, and I'm not sure which is worse.

But it's Lila, holding a plastic bag heavy enough to break a wrist. She has on sweatpants, sneakers, and a messy pixie-cut. The moment she steps in, she brings a warmth to the office.

"Hell, are you two hatching a coup?" she says, setting the bag on the desk and pulling out cartons of dumplings, noodles, and boba tea. "It's a Wednesday, Cassie. You know people usually sleep on Wednesdays?"

Rafi grins and holds up his hands. "Not me. I'm strictly nocturnal."

Lila eyes the mess, then me. "How bad is it?"

I protest, but she cuts me off. "You only pull all-nighters when someone's about to get indicted. Or you're about to get indicted. Which is it?"

I gesture at the folders and my screen. "We're following a money trail. Ignite Global was a dead end until Rafi found the city development overlap. Now it's pointing straight at Mayor Scott's reelection PAC. Elaine Winters is the link, but I don't know how she fits in yet."

Lila pulls up a chair, cracking open a carton of dumplings and using the lid as a makeshift plate. "I know nothing about PACs, but I know it's sketchy if someone reroutes donations through more than two shells. That's money laundering, right?"

Rafi shovels noodles into his mouth. "Textbook."

Lila glances at the screen. "Show me what you've got."

She's not just humoring me. She scans each page, reading every line. I slide the monitor over. We spend the next hour cycling through every spreadsheet, every flagged transaction, every cryptic invoice.

At one point, Lila laughs. "Sorry, but 'Drexel & Pittman'? That's not even a real law firm. My uncle used to run the legit Drexel, and it closed down in 2008."

I scroll down. Sure enough, the company's registered in 2021—two months before the first Plaza payment went through.

Lila nudges me. "You have them. If you can prove the city's funneling through fake consultants, you have leverage. You can take it to the press, or the Feds, or both."

Tension hits my shoulders like an avalanche. "I need to see it for myself. The original project files, the city's vendor list, anything that connects Drexel & Pittman to Mayor Scott's office. It's probably all public, but what we need will be buried. That means City Hall."

Rafi stretches, arching his back. "Want me to run a honeypot on the city's procurement server? It'll ping whenever someone logs in from an admin account."

"Do it," I say, barely hearing myself over the pounding in my chest. "And check any emails from Ignite Global in the city's correspondence archives."

He nods, typing at warp speed.

Lila pops a dumpling in her mouth. "If you need backup tomorrow, I can play the dumb assistant. Or the angry girlfriend. Dealer's choice."

I reach over and squeeze her hand, the only solid thing left as everything else shifts. "Thanks, Li. For all of it."

She shrugs, cheeks flushed. "I'd just rather you not get murdered by a corrupt city manager before I get to see the new Fast & Furious."

We all laugh, the kind of laugh you only get when you're three seconds from a nervous breakdown.

At some point, the city's procurement portal pings. Rafi's face goes serious. "You have to see this."

He flips the laptop so I can read. There's a login from "ewinters@lenapec ity.gov," time-stamped two minutes ago. They're not just monitoring the contracts—they're actively cleaning up.

I stand so fast I almost tip my chair. For a second, I just pace in a tight figure eight, the realization slamming into me like a wave. "He's not the top of the pyramid," I say, voice shaky but getting stronger. "Alfred was just another node in the network. Just like Pence, just like Albright. The Mayor is the keystone."

I stop dead in the center of the office and face the notes, the screens, the evidence.

Lila and Rafi wait for my cue.

I take a deep breath and say the only thing that matters.

"Tomorrow," I say, "we go to City Hall."

* * *

City Hall is built to make you feel small—thirty-foot ceilings, more marble than a Roman mausoleum. The echo of your own footsteps follows you from the security desk all the way to the elevator bank. There's a rotating display of local student art by the bathrooms. Today it's watercolor bridges and one particularly haunted interpretation of the city skyline. All details ignored by everyone except the janitorial staff. The place is a museum for bureaucrats.

I'm here early, but not so early that the staff hasn't put out the first coffee urns. The air is sharp with lemon disinfectant and the waxy, not-quite-organic whiff of "industrial bakery" muffins. I keep my head down as I sign the visitor log, using a throwaway variant of my real name: "Cassandra M. Maddox—Records Research, per Chief of Staff appointment". The guy at the desk doesn't even glance up. I'm just another functionary, which is exactly what I want.

Inside my messenger bag: a color-coded folder with highlights and sticky tabs, and a single-page printout of the Drexel & Pittman shell-company registration. In my pocket: a burner phone with Rafi on speed dial, and a USB with an image of last night's honeypot intercepts. I'm not here to play hero. I just want to see the people behind the paper—smell them, hear their voices, maybe catch a tremor in their hands when I ask the wrong question.

The elevator dings, and I step out onto the third floor, where the offices go from "public access" to "authorized personnel only." I know the route by heart. My dad spent half my childhood dragging me up here to sign paperwork, collect parking permits, or explain why he still hadn't responded to HR's "mandatory training modules." The same ancient brass nameplates line the hallway. Behind a frosted-glass double door is the mayor's office with a waiting area decked out in a funereal blue. The receptionist is new—fresh-faced, braces glinting in the artificial sunlamp—but her eyes have the glazed ten thousand-yard stare of anyone who screens calls for a politician.

"Hi, I'm here to see Elaine Winters?" I say, giving her my most harmless, slightly apologetic smile.

She checks the calendar, then points me to a seat. "She'll be with you in a moment. Would you like coffee or water?"

"Water, thanks," I say, and wonder how many interns they burn through in a month.

The waiting area is all fake warmth: motivational posters, a fish tank with a single, listless tetra, a plastic plant drooping from too many dustings. I sit, open my folder, and pretend to read through the printouts while actually watching the movement behind the frosted glass. I count four separate silhouettes, two of which I recognize from LinkedIn stalking. One of them—tall, square-shouldered, likes to keep his tie at half-mast—is definitely on the mayor's strategy team. I flag that for later.

After exactly six minutes, the inner door opens, and out steps Elaine Winters.

She is impeccable—power suit so sharply tailored it could have been 3D printed. Hair set in a helmet of calculated volume. Makeup that says, "I could do this interview on national TV and not sweat a drop." She smiles at me, but the teeth don't show, and the eyes are unreadable.

"Ms. Maddox?" Her voice is a perfect neutral alto.

"Thanks for taking the time on such short notice," I say, matching her smile with my version: relaxed, just slightly deferential, but not cowed. "I appreciate the flexibility."

She leads me past a bank of cubicles—each one lined with photos of spouses, dogs, and marathon finish lines—then into a small, glass-walled meeting room. There's a carafe of water, two glasses, and a phone on speaker mode in the center. The table has a few nicks and scratches, but otherwise it's surgically clean.

Elaine sits, gestures for me to do the same, and folds her hands on the tabletop. Her nails are flawless: pink, just shy of the line between "tasteful" and "wealthy." When she talks, she never blinks for more than half a second.

"So, what brings you to us today?" she says.

I slide my folder onto the table, open to the spreadsheet page. "Just a background audit for the Genesee Foundation matter," I say, using the phrase that appears on every public-facing document in the last six months. "Some inconsistencies in the financials popped up, especially in the city's redevelopment contracts. I was hoping to clarify the relationship between the mayor's office and some of the consulting firms involved in Old Town Plaza."

Elaine glances at the document, then back at me. "We've provided all our disclosures to the DA's office, as I'm sure you're aware." Her tone is pleasant, but there's an edge to it, like she's letting me know I'm two steps behind already. "Which specific firm are you referring to?"

I pretend to flip through the tabs, knowing exactly which one I want. "Drexel & Pittman. Their payments match Ignite Global's intake, but they didn't itemize the consulting work. There's just a notation about 'community partnership initiatives' and a set of matching wire transfers."

Elaine nods, doesn't even blink. "That was a sub-grant arrangement. Completely above board. The city's procurement team recommended Drexel & Pittman after a vetting process. We were careful to avoid any appearance of impropriety, especially after the trouble with Shenandoah Partners."

She says the name as if it's just a footnote, not a black mark on half the city council. I let that pass. "It's strange, though. Drexel & Pittman incorporated just three months before the first Plaza payout. And their officers list includes a former campaign staffer, Sally Riggs."

Elaine's smile widens. "It's not unusual for small consultancies to staff up with campaign veterans. They know the city, and they know how to get things done. Sally is a hard worker—she's done projects for several nonprofits in the region."

I keep my tone light. "Of course. I'm just trying to get a sense of the workflow. Sometimes funds get double-counted, or earmarked for overlapping purposes. Here, it appears the Genesee routed money through Ignite, then Drexel, and then into the city's own project accounts. Is that typical?"

She leans forward, tapping the table with one manicured finger. "Transparency is our highest priority. I can provide the full chain of custody for every dollar if you'd like. But I should tell you—our compliance team is already preparing a supplemental disclosure for the auditor general. You'll have the report within the week."

I don't miss the subtext: *You're not the only one digging into this, and you will find nothing we haven't already sanitized.*

I flip to the next sheet, this one showing email headers. "Mayor Scott was cc'd on several communications between Alfred Maddox and the Ignite Global board. In one, there's a reference to a 'guaranteed placement' for applicants if the board expedites their review. Do you know what that was about?"

Elaine doesn't even hesitate. "That's boilerplate. Our office always advocates for local students, but we don't have influence over admissions. The phrase 'guaranteed placement' is aspirational, not literal."

"Sure," I say, "but then why was the conversation routed through Ignite's legal counsel instead of the city's education outreach team?"

A pause—just long enough to register. "That must have been an error in communication. Ignite Global is an independent entity—we have no jurisdiction over their operations. Sometimes our partners mis-attribute roles or titles. I can assure you, Ms. Maddox, that everything is completely legal."

The smile is back, but the eyes are flat now. She's done playing. I could push, but she'd just stonewall, and she'd enjoy it. I'm not getting anything useful until I break something they care about.

I close the folder and push it to the middle of the table. "Thank you for your time. I might follow up if the audit team has more questions."

She stands crisp and unhurried. "I'm always available. If you need access to our compliance files, just email my assistant. She can set up a secure portal for you."

We shake hands. Her grip is cool and perfectly calibrated: not too hard, not too soft, but just long enough to make it clear who's in control.

I leave the meeting room and walk back down the hallway, pretending to check messages on my phone. In the reflection of a side window, Elaine steps back into her office, picks up the landline, and starts dialing before the door is even closed. She's reporting in, probably to the mayor, possibly to someone even higher up the food chain.

I don't linger. I get out, down the elevator, and out the front doors as fast as I can without running.

The air outside is ten degrees colder than when I came in, but the adrenaline is keeping me warm. I duck behind a planter and call Rafi.

He picks up on the first ring. "You good?"

"I'm good," I say, scanning the windows above for any movement. "She had answers ready for everything. Either I'm way behind, or they've had someone prepping for this all week."

Rafi snorts. "Honeypot's been pinging nonstop. Either the city's cleaning house, or they want you to know they're watching."

I shiver, but not from the cold. "Elaine mentioned a supplemental audit report. They're going to flood the system with paperwork, making it impossible to trace the real money."

"So what's your move?"

"I'll think on it. But we're running out of time."

A pause, then: "I trust you, Cass."

"Yeah," I say, "I trust you, too. And if I end up face-down in the Schuylkill, avenge my death with maximum flair."

Rafi laughs, and it helps a little.

I hang up, then walk to the curb, clutching the messenger bag like it's the only armor I have left.

In the third-floor windows, behind the glare, a silhouette—could be Elaine, could be the mayor, could be nobody at all—watches me as I cross the street.

Let them watch.

They don't know how stubborn I can be.

17

Torn Between Two Worlds

The office is down to its skeleton crew: me, Rafi, and the wheeze of the server in the closet. At 2:30 a.m., Lenape City is a layer cake of dead office windows, but Maddox Investigative Services is lit up like a submarine at crush depth. Every surface in here glows blue—Excel spreadsheets on the UltraWide, browser tabs in dark mode, the blinking green LED of the office router flicking Morse code for "You Should Go Home."

I am not going home.

Rafi hunches over the little folding table between us, setting up another nest of browser tabs. He's got his shoes off, knees drawn up like a six-foot-tall kid, typing with the tip of one finger while cradling a Red Bull like a baby bird. I'm at my desk with a legal pad and a ballpoint, circling numbers until the ink bleeds through the paper.

Every five minutes, he checks to see if I'm still awake. Every time I meet his eyes, a delay lands between us, unspoken.

The latest evidence haul is a two-inch stack of printouts, all stamped with Lenape City's official watermark and, more importantly, a set of suspiciously generic payment memos. I've been at it for hours; my contact lenses have turned into dollar-store plastic wrap. I rub my eyes, and the headache comes roaring back.

"Want another coffee?" Rafi asks, half-standing.

I wave him off. "Last one hit my nervous system like a semi. I'll ride this

135

out, thanks."

He grins. "That's the spirit."

The clock says 2:34. I can't remember the last time I checked my phone. Maybe that's a good thing.

The numbers on the page swim and double up; for a second, I'm not sure if I'm reading or hallucinating. I blink hard, and the words "DREXEL & PITTMAN CONSULTANTS" snap into focus. Next to it, three payments, all for exactly $50,000. No client details, no contract number, just "Consulting: Q3/Q4."

I circle them, underline the date: January 3rd, 2023. The other two are spaced perfectly 30 days apart.

"Hey, Raf, check this," I say, holding up the page. "Who the hell pays an even fifty K every month without a retainer or an invoice to show for it?"

He rolls his chair over, toes shoving off the tile. "Shell company," he says, voice confident. "Watch this."

He's already logged into the Secretary of State's business database. He types "Drexel & Pittman," hits enter, and the listing pops up. No website, no phone number, just an address in a downtown WeWork and a "Principal Agent: S. Riggs." He's so damn fast it makes me mad.

"Who's Riggs?" I ask, even though I already know the answer.

He pulls up LinkedIn. "Sally Riggs. Used to work for the mayor's campaign. Now listed as 'Operations Consultant' at D&P. Six months, no endorsements, no post history."

I scrawl a note in the margin. "You think it's city money laundering?"

Rafi shrugs. "Could be, but it's too clean for that. Usually they go with odd numbers—forty-nine-seven-fifty, or something that won't ping the compliance bots."

I press the page flat on the desk. "So it's a pass-through. A holding pen for dirty funds before they get funneled somewhere else."

"Or," he says, pointing at the next column, "it's black budget. If you can't track the deliverables, you can claim whatever you want in the 'consulting' category."

I take a breath, letting that settle. My pulse is weirdly loud in my ears.

Rafi pushes off the desk and disappears into the kitchenette. I listen to the sound of the electric kettle filling, the click of the switch, the rattle of instant coffee packets in the drawer. It's all white noise, but somehow comforting.

While he's gone, I pick up my phone and check for messages. None from my father—likely asleep or trying not to think about his daughter blowing the lid off half his department's budget with a single Google Sheet. I text Mel, just a "You good?" because I haven't heard from her in days. It sits unsent because I can't think of a way to sign it that isn't desperate.

Rafi returns with two mugs. He sets one down next to me, close enough that our hands touch for a second. There's a small jolt, like static.

He doesn't pull away.

"You ever think we're just in over our heads?" he asks. His voice is softer now, the kind of voice you use at a sleepover right before someone admits they're scared of the dark.

"All the time," I say. "But I don't know how to stop."

He laughs, but it's not a full laugh. "That's what I like about you."

I pick up the mug. The coffee is cheap and burnt, but it's hot, and that's all I want.

For a long minute, neither of us talks. There's just the hum of the server and the blue glow of the monitors.

Then, quietly, he says: "Can I ask you something?"

I brace for a question about the case, but he surprises me. "Why do you keep pushing everyone away?"

I grip the mug and swirl the coffee, trying to buy time. The real answer is simple—a lack of trust. But saying it out loud makes it too real, and me too vulnerable.

"You ever see someone get used up by this job?" I ask, voice low.

He nods, understanding instantly. "Your dad."

"And Alfred," I say. The name tastes sour. "Everyone who tries to do the right thing gets chewed up. I'm not trying to be next."

He leans forward, elbows on his knees. "You're not them, Cass."

"Maybe not," I say, "but I'm stubborn enough to repeat their mistakes."

He gives a small smile, the kind that makes his eyes go warm. "You know you're not doing this alone, right?"

The words hang in the air, heavier than anything I've found in the spreadsheets. I know what he's implying.

My throat is suddenly tight. I want to say something brave. Instead, I just stare at the surface of my coffee. My hand shakes. I set the mug down before it spills.

Rafi reaches over, and this time his hand closes on mine. It's warm and solid, with calluses from all the years of typing, soldering, and pulling cables through ceiling panels.

My first instinct is to pull away.

I don't.

"I'm not good at this," I say, barely a whisper.

He squeezes my hand. "Me neither."

I force myself to meet his eyes. They're dark and open, containing everything he's trying to tell me. That he's scared, too; that maybe this is the only safe place either of us has.

"I want to trust you," I say, and it comes out brittle.

He smiles, softer now. "You already do. Otherwise, you wouldn't let me anywhere near these files."

I laugh—real this time—and tension uncoils inside me.

We sit like that, hand in hand, until my phone buzzes on the desk.

It's a text, no caller ID, just a string of numbers and letters in the subject line.

I read it once, then again.

Rafi leans in. "What is it?"

I show him the screen.

It says: "You missed something. D&P isn't the end of the line. Check the transfer logs 3/14/23—recipient is a ghost. Meet at the waterfront, 4:15 a.m. If you want to live."

Rafi stands, eyes wide. "That's less than two hours from now."

I set the phone down, my hand suddenly cold.

The moment between us is gone—evaporated, replaced with the familiar surge of fear.

I reach for my coat, and Rafi does the same.

"Want backup?" he asks, voice trembling just a little.

I don't answer right away.

Because I do.

But I also know that if something goes wrong, I can't risk anyone else getting burned.

I say, "I'll think about it," but I already know the answer.

I'll go alone.

Because that's who I am.

Because that's who I've always been.

I seek an anchor in Rafi, and let myself hope that maybe, one day, I won't have to be.

"Read it again?" Rafi asks, and I pass him my phone.

He reads it, lips moving silently, then sits. "You think it's a setup?"

"Someone's scared enough to use burner texts," I say. "Either that, or they want us dead."

He sifts through the new emails, eyes darting line to line. "If it's legit, we need to move fast. These logins—the access time." He taps the screen. "Someone else is in the Drexel & Pittman account. And if it's not you or me..."

"It's whoever's at the top of the food chain," I finish.

I open the transfer logs from March 14, 2023. There's an outbound payment, the same amount as before, but instead of a shell company, it's routed through a nondescript savings account at First Commonwealth Bank. The account number ends in four zeroes—a trick for laundering.

"No registered name," I say, scrolling further. "But the memo field just says, 'Honorarium—per agreement.'"

Rafi is already on it, cross-referencing the routing number against every other transaction in the city's history. "Shit," he says, flipping his screen toward me, hands shaking.

There are ten more payments, all routed through Drexel & Pittman, and then out to the same account, sometimes the same day. The pattern is too regular. He overlays it on a chart of known organized crime payouts from a few years back.

"They're copying the old Scarpo money-laundering pattern," he says, breathless. "It's not just city contracts. It's everything—kickbacks, bribes, even election money."

My stomach is a fist. "So the mayor's office isn't just complicit—they're running the show."

Color drains from his face. "Cass, you can't go down there alone."

I lean back, watching the ceiling rotate slowly above me. "You know I have to," I say, but I'm not sure if it's resolve or just the inertia of being me.

He stands, paces the length of the office, then wheels on me. "At least tell your father. Let him run surveillance, get a squad car in the area—something."

"No," I snap, louder than I mean to. "We can't trust anyone, not with this. If even one cop's in on it, we're burned."

He slams a fist on the edge of the desk. "You're going to get killed."

I laugh, sharp and ugly. "Not before I get the proof."

Rafi sits, shoulders folded up to his ears. The rain starts up again, rapping on the window, drowning out the low hum of the router. It makes the silence between us even bigger.

"I don't want you to go," he says, voice barely audible.

"I know," I say, but I'm already thinking ahead—what to bring, what to hide, what to say if someone tries to make me disappear.

He pulls his chair close enough that our knees touch. The blue light from the monitors softens his profile, and shadows pool beneath his eyes. "You think I'm just scared for you," he says, "but I'm also scared of what happens if you don't come back. I'm not good at being left."

I try to hold his gaze, but it hurts too much. "You won't be."

"Promise?" he asks, and the word hangs, heavy and impossible.

The only promise I can make is to show up, to keep fighting, to keep being the last stubborn Maddox standing.

He leans his forehead against mine, just for a second, and in that second the world is quiet.

Then the phone buzzes again. Another message, same anonymous number. You're being watched. Don't bring backup. East slip, warehouse 7. 4:15.

I pull away, grab my jacket, and double-check the gun in the desk drawer.

Rafi stands, blocking the door for a second. "Text me every five minutes. And if you see anyone, anyone you don't recognize—"

"I know," I say.

He takes my hand, squeezes it, and then lets go.

"Let me at least keep watch from a distance," he says, adjusting his seat.

Though we have less than an hour before the meeting, I agree. The office becomes a war room in the final phase of prepping for an assault: no jokes, no music, just the frantic shuffle of digital files, the whir of a USB stick, the tight, staccato rhythm of Rafi typing passwords.

Rafi sets up a burner tracker on my phone—something custom, "untraceable by normal means," he says. Hardly a comfort. He hands it back to me, and when our fingers touch, I'm still shaking from the last text.

"There's a panic protocol," he says. "One tap and it pings me every ten seconds. Three taps, and I call the cavalry. Not just your dad—I've got half the LCPD on a deadman's switch if I don't hear from you by 5 a.m."

"Overkill," I say, but I'm grateful.

He opens a velvet pouch—one I recognize as a holiday gift from my father, meant for expensive pens or jewelry. Inside is a lipstick tube, matte gold, with real weight to it.

"Wear this," Rafi says. "Mic's in the base, SD card in the cap. Press once to record. If you unscrew it, it triggers a live feed to my laptop."

I take it, studying the color. "Nice. Not my shade, but I'll manage."

"Matches your eyes," he says, and he almost blushes. I pocket it, not sure if I should laugh or say thank you.

We run through the plan twice more. I'm to park three blocks from the meeting point, approach on foot, stay in open sight as much as possible. We set check-in intervals: first when I park, then at the warehouse, then at the end. Rafi writes the code phrase for emergency extraction on a sticky note, sticks it to my phone: "BLUEBERRY DANISH."

"Why that?" I ask.

He shrugs. "Nobody says it in real life. Least of all, you."

He tries smiling, but his fists clench.

I get up, slide my gun from the drawer, and check the magazine. I pull on my old army-surplus jacket, the one with the ink stains and the torn lining, then glance at the mirror above the filing cabinet. The skin beneath my eyes has darkened. A crease cuts deeper along my mouth.

At the door, I hesitate. Rafi stands a few feet back, like he wants to say something but can't find the shape of it.

I turn, and for the first time since I was a kid, I let myself lean on someone. I close the distance, wrap my arms around him, and rest my forehead against his chest. His heartbeat is fast, nervous, but steady.

He puts his arms around me, careful at first, then tighter. I don't want to let go.

I pull back just enough to see his face. He's biting his lip, trying to keep it together.

"You know, this is the part in the movie where the hero promises to come back," I say, voice barely above a whisper.

He shakes his head. "Just make it to sunrise."

I stand on tiptoe and kiss him. It's clumsy—my nose bumps his cheek, I taste coffee on his mouth—but it's real, and I mean it.

When I pull away, I whisper, "Just in case."

He nods, and there's nothing left to say.

I step into the hallway, the carpet cold and rough beneath my shoes. At the bottom of the stairs, I stop. Rafi's at the window, outlined in blue by the office lights. He raises a hand, and I do the same.

Outside, the rain is heavier. I pop my collar and walk fast, every step a countdown.

I reach the car, settle behind the wheel, and check the time. 3:45.

I take out the lipstick, roll it between my fingers, and think about Rafi's lips on mine—about what it means to let someone care for you, even when you're terrified it will all go wrong.

I drive toward the river. Warehouse 7 looms against the waterfront, a bruise-black block behind the chain-link. The sky lightens, and for a second a shape moves behind the gate.

I take out my phone, type the check-in, and wait for the reply.

I get one word: "Tracking."

I smile, even though I'm alone.

The next move is mine.

I get out, pull my coat close, and walk toward the water.

The city behind me, the rain on my face, and—maybe for the first time—someone who gives a damn if I come back.

18

The Man in the Middle

I f you want to know what the city smells like at four in the morning, go stand by the river in March. Rain soaks everything, even the air, until it's more liquid than gas—diesel, rust, cigarette butts, the ghost of a thousand dead fish. There's no sunrise coming, just the flat gray of night smudged out by storm clouds and one sodium bulb stuttering above the east slip. I kill the engine two blocks from the rendezvous, rain hammering the windshield so hard it's like driving inside a cement mixer.

Warehouse 7 squats on the waterfront like something the city forgot to demolish. The windows are blacked out or bricked over, graffiti half-buried under newer tags, the paint blistered down to rust. It's the only building on this stretch without a For Lease sign or foreclosure tape—too far gone even for false hope. Instead, it's ringed with eight-foot chain link, topped in razor wire someone's decorated with busted sneakers and one genuinely terrifying baby doll's head. The riverside gate is closed, padlock dangling, but I already know that means nothing. If you're a city employee or a dealer with the right friends, you can get in anywhere.

I text Rafi my location. He'll log it, cross-check it, and start counting heartbeats like he always does.

I pop the lipstick mic out of my coat pocket, click it twice, and wedge it deep in my collar. The earpiece is disguised as a cheap wireless bud; I fit it in place, then pull up my hood. The rain is coming sideways now, and I taste ozone on

144

the wind.

"Mic check," I whisper.

His voice is in my head instantly: "Got you. Audio's clean."

I can picture him grinning, but then he adds, "Keep low. I'm on the city's traffic cam feed. Someone looped a drone over the slip an hour ago—thermal scan. It's likely you're being watched."

I keep walking. Shoes squelch through puddles. The rain adds weight to my shoulders, like it's trying to slow me down.

There's nothing alive out here except rats and whatever needs a fix more than it needs dry feet. The warehouses on either side are blacked out, the windows painted or just caked in the kind of dirt that never washes off. If anything moves, it'll be easy to spot, but that's not a comfort. I edge along the fence, eyes straining to see through the blur.

I make the gate in 30 seconds. Keep going. The padlock is a prop; the chain's loose, and the whole fence panel rattles when I lean on it—two hundred yards to the river, then a hard left and the loading dock. The east slip is supposed to be abandoned, but a fresh set of tire tracks cuts through the mud, disappearing behind a stack of shipping pallets. Someone's here already.

My phone buzzes. I check the screen: "two heat sigs, 30 meters apart."

I slow my breathing, scan the dock. At first, there's nothing, just more rain and the distant clatter of a freight train on the bridge overhead. Then, a flicker of movement behind the first stack of pallets—just enough to confirm I'm not alone. My heart is a goddamn jackhammer. Every instinct says run, but the math says walk. The only way out is through.

I step onto the loading ramp, boots slipping on the green-black moss. A single floodlight flickers overhead, painting everything in bruised yellow. My hands stay in my pockets, the pistol tucked inside my waistband where it belongs.

The rain's worse under the overhang, the wind channeling it into a fine mist that soaks my jeans to the skin. I scan left and right—still nothing.

"Raf, status?"

Rafi comes through without raising his voice. "You've got company. Ten meters. Dockside, east."

I keep my posture casual, but every muscle coiled.

A guy in a business parka stands ahead of me, office clothes visible under the soaked gray shell. Mid-40s, thinning hair, clutching a manila folder to his chest like it's a life preserver. He moves with the loose, frantic energy of someone who's never done anything this illegal before.

He stops five yards from me, hood dripping, glasses fogged. For a second, we stand in the rain, sizing each other up. Then he gives a little nervous wave.

"Are you—?"

"I am," I say.

He exhales so hard his glasses fog again. "Call me Mark," he says, which is definitely not his name. "You alone?"

I glance around, making a show of it. "I'm never alone. You have something for me?"

He nods, thrusting the folder out like it's radioactive. "Take this and go. They're already erasing logs—procurement, project funding, the whole trail. If you don't get ahead of it now—"

"I know," I interrupt. "What's inside?"

"Ledger pages. Original drafts, not the sanitized PDFs. And a flash drive—encrypted, but the password's taped to the back. Start with 'Special Initiatives—Office of the Mayor.'" His voice shakes. "They're watching both of us."

I take the folder and slide it under my coat. "Who's 'they'?"

He turns sharply, scanning the rain-slick street, water streaming down his neck. "You know who. The mayor's office and the people who pull its strings. I just work with spreadsheets. That's how this landed on me—every time something got flagged. Duplicate vendors. Payments out of cycle. Weird invoices that didn't belong to any department."

He swallows hard, forcing the words out now, like he's running out of oxygen. "You know how much money the city burns every quarter? Millions. Most of it's invisible. You move a hundred grand here, two-fifty there, and nobody ever asks."

He taps the folder. "That's the paper chain. The log before the digital edit—the one nobody ever audits. They think if it's not in the system, it doesn't exist." A sharp, humorless laugh. "But Drexel & Pittman isn't even a shell company. It's a pass-through. 'Special Initiatives.' Zero employees. Unlimited draw. Campaign money. Hush money. Whatever they need."

My grip tightens inside my coat.

"The flash drive has admin credentials," he continues. "Two, maybe three tries before it wipes itself. City IT's running 'maintenance' at five-thirty a.m. They're not backing anything up. They're burning it."

He hesitates, then digs into his coat and presses something hard and plastic into my palm. A city-issued badge—Facilities, temporary access, the laminate scuffed like it's been used more than once.

"It still opens doors," he says. "They never bothered to revoke it."

He pulls a scrap of paper from his pocket and presses it into my hand. An address written in shaky block letters. "That's the node. Off the mainframe. Closet server in the old Scott-Calder Building. You get in, you rip the source. Otherwise, it's gone."

"Why risk this?"

His jaw locks. "Because I have a family. Because I want to disappear—not get murdered by an ex-cop on the city's payroll. And because you're the only one who can do something with it, Maddox."

Rain beads on his lashes. "They were at my apartment last night. Black SUV. No plates. Someone from Calder's office called this morning, said they wanted to 'clarify' some misfiled records." His voice drops. "If I vanish, it won't even make the news."

A sound echoes down the dock—metal on concrete. Mark stiffens.

"You need to move," he says. "Now."

I glance at my phone.

Rafi's alert pulses once: Move. Now.

I pocket the address. "How do I reach you?"

He shakes his head, already backing away. "You don't. If I'm alive next week, you'll know."

Then he turns and disappears into the rain.

I break into a run, following Mark's path back to the street. At the gate, I hear a car engine turn over—maybe Mark, maybe not. Somewhere downriver, a siren lifts and dies. My own footsteps slap too loud against the wet pavement, every one of them daring someone to follow.

"Cass?" Rafi's voice is back, softer now. "Talk to me."

"I've got it. Source is legit. They're burning the records in real time—if we don't move, we lose everything."

"Then Scott-Calder's your target," Rafi says without hesitation. "Sublevel node, west records wing. Old building, bad cameras. You use that badge, you'll get one clean pass before alarms catch up."

I hear typing, then Rafi's voice again, all steel and caffeine: "Then let's light them up before they get the matches out."

I smile, wet and shaky.

"I'm heading straight to Scott-Calder."

My phone vibrates.

Rafi: "Either you're sprinting, or you're about to do something reckless."

"Both," I say.

I duck under a loading dock awning and pull the folder from under my coat. Ziploc. One ledger sheet. One blister-pack USB.

I peel it open and scan the sheet. It's an old-school ledger, handwritten lines of vendor numbers and six-digit codes, red ink for debits, blue for credits. At the bottom, in blocky, neurotic handwriting, is a note:

Special Projects—Office of the Mayor—internal only.

Beneath that, three lines of numbers, each followed by "D&P" in parentheses. I don't need Rafi to tell me that's Drexel & Pittman.

I snap a photo and send it, then pop the USB drive from its tape and slide it into my phone's OTG adapter.

The upload bar ticks forward, slow and stubborn.

Rafi's voice cuts in, sharp with disbelief. "Cass—this is real. This is everything."

The splash screen is bare bones: two folders, both stamped within the last week. I open the first—hundreds of Excel files with names like *Redev-Plan3_FINAL* and *ConsultantReviewQ1*, fat with macros and audit trails. I don't try to read them here. That's how mistakes get made. This needs Rafi.

The footsteps grow louder, then pause. Someone's out there, but I can't see who. I press the folder to my chest, and slip out the far side of the loading dock, moving low and fast through the maze of trash and standing water.

Once I'm two blocks clear, I slow down, catching my breath under the awning of an abandoned bodega. I check the folder one last time—ledger, flash drive, network address, everything tight and dry in the plastic sleeve.

"Cass? You okay?"

"Still breathing," I say. "You ready to crash a city server?"

He laughs, the sound tight and brittle. "I was born ready."

I push off the wall, rain pounding the street, adrenaline already burning the edges off my fear.

Somewhere out there, Mark is running for his life. I just have to run toward the finish line.

And pray I don't get erased along the way.

Then the gunshot. Not loud, but flat and final, somewhere between me and the river. Something splinters near my leg—a chunk of crate erupts into wet confetti. I hit the deck, knees grinding into gravel, folder tight under my chest.

Another shot, closer this time. I can't tell if they're aiming at Mark or me, and it doesn't matter. I army-crawl behind a dumpster, vision tunneling in and out with every breath.

"Cass, talk to me!" Rafi's voice, urgent and raw, fills my ear.

I whisper, "Still moving. Shooter by the old rail line. Mark's in the wind."

Rafi's already pulling up maps. "You have ten meters to the fence; six to the left is a pile of concrete bags—use it as cover. You can vault the fence by the cut in the razor wire. Go now."

I go, counting steps in the dark, shoes sliding on wet moss, the smell of ozone and cordite thick as soup. Another shot slaps the chain link behind me, but I'm already through the gap, snagging my coat but leaving no blood.

Once on the street, it's all cold air and open space. I run, lungs burning, folder jammed inside my shirt, flash drive clenched so tight it leaves an imprint on my palm. Every shadow in the street watching me, ready to leap.

The city badge knocks once against my ribs, a reminder that doors can open as easily as they close.

My car is three blocks away, but it might as well be on another planet.

Rafi is counting down in my ear, voice clipped and precise. "Keep going. Two blocks, right turn. You're clear for now. No heat signatures except yours."

I'm moving on instinct now, a string of adrenaline holding me upright. The rain is blinding, but I don't dare slow down. I duck behind a row of trash bins, wait for headlights to pass, then cut through an abandoned lot to the next block.

The car is where I left it, thank God above. I fumble with the keys, hands shaking, and dive inside, slamming the doors and locking them. I just sit, shaking, the world still spinning a thousand miles an hour.

I thumb the phone, text Rafi the agreed code: BLUEBERRY DANISH. He replies in a heartbeat: "You're a machine. Are you hit?"

I check. Nothing but bruises and a torn sleeve. "All good," I type, then add, "Mark's gone."

Rafi: "You did everything you could."

I lean back, eyes closed, breath coming in short, sharp gasps. The rain pounds the roof like a million tiny fists. For a minute, instinct takes over— the absolute, animal need to survive. I grip the evidence so hard my hands hurt.

Then I start the engine, throw the car in gear, and drive into the dark. I've been running my whole life.

I pull the badge from my coat and set it on the seat beside me. Facilities. Temporary access. The kind of thing that works exactly once.

"You've got less than an hour before the maintenance window closes."

I turn the car toward downtown, tires hissing on wet pavement.

If I miss that window, the truth disappears.

And so do I.

19

City Hall's Hidden Machinery

The Scott-Calder Building is one of those old civic monsters that got a glass atrium stapled to its chest in the eighties, a kind of Frankenstein handshake between marble and carbon fiber. The main entrance is just three squat columns and a hurricane vestibule, but the inside opens up into a vault of stone, light, and echo.

I stand outside the double-doors for a second, hood up, gloves on, face gone numb from the walk in. I scan the glass for security film, spot the pitted patch where they replaced a pane after the last protest, and angle myself to avoid the camera above the lintel. The blueprint said it had a blind spot at the corner. Dad always taught me: never trust a building, but always trust a lazy contractor.

I swipe in on the city-issued badge, and the LED blinks green. I step inside, click the door closed behind me. The building's empty except for the echoing tick of a cleaning lady's rubber shoes two stories up.

"Update?" Rafi's voice is in my ear, all brisk and clear, like he's reading off a submarine status board.

I whisper, "Foyer is clear. No security at the desk. Janitor on three."

"Good. Elevator cameras are on a fifteen-second loop. Take the service stairs to two, then cut left. The archive is sub-basement, but they route the badge access from the second-floor reception."

I move.

The stairs are wide, cold, every step a possible siren. On the landing, I keep my head down, jacket zipped, and scan for movement.

"Clear."

I move my fingers on the banister, leaving prints on top of the layer of dust.

The second-floor reception is a bank of glass cubicles and a sign-in sheet that's only half full. I duck behind the open door of a "Wellness Room" and pop the laptop. The signal is weak, but Rafi's VPN handshake lights up green after a beat.

"I'm in," he says. "The sysadmin's still using the default passwords. Bless their lazy hearts. Give me the badge number."

I read it off the back of my lanyard. He's silent for three seconds, then: "Okay, it's mapped. Use it on the basement elevator. The door will open, but the camera won't log. You have a three-minute window before the next ping."

Down in the sub-basement, it's all cinderblock and utility paint, the color of anxiety. The air is colder, sharper—like a warning to keep your business quick and your mouth shut. I pass two locked doors ("STORAGE A" and "IT CLOSETS") and stop at "PROCUREMENT ARCHIVE." The badge reader is an ancient box with the brand worn off, but it chirps when I wave the card, and the lock thunks open. I slip inside.

The archive is a row of gray metal filing cabinets and a desk cluttered with receipts, dried-out gel pens, and a dead succulent. A battered whiteboard in the corner reads "MONTHLY AUDIT—NO EXCEPTIONS."

Has anyone ever read these words?

I breathe. Then I get to work.

Mark said to start with "Special Initiatives—Office of the Mayor." There are a dozen cabinets, all labeled in a cheap label-maker font. I start at "S," fingers numb, and flip through hanging folders by touch. Each one is a relic— city contracts, bid letters, invoices stamped in blue ink. I also scan for Drexel & Pittman, but the first pass is nothing but copy paper and legalese.

"Raf, I'm seeing a wall of paper. Maybe I should try a year."

He clicks his tongue. "Target last year, Q1. The cover-up would be freshest there. Start in the drawer marked 'Supplemental Vendor.'"

I find it. Second from the bottom, so heavy it almost snaps my wrist when it rolls open. The folders are packed tight, and in the middle—wedged between "LENAPE CUSTODIAL" and "FRIENDS OF THE PARK"—is a fat file labeled "D&P CONSULTANTS – URGENT."

I pull it out and thumb through it. The first ten pages are nothing: meeting notes, conference call summaries, a list of city staff invited to a "breakfast roundtable." But then the real payload: a contract addendum with three signatures—Mayor Calder's, S. Riggs's, and a witness, Elaine Winters. The language is classic: "expedited deliverable," "confidential per Section 9," "direct oversight to be maintained by Executive Office." There's a post-it attached written in smooth, connected stroke—Alred's practice hand written during the last municipal election, "Make sure this clears legal before EOY."

I pull out my phone and start snapping pictures. Every page, both sides, then the tab, then the signature block. Each photo, damning evidence.

A fresh shiver runs through me. Halfway through the file, there's a weird break in the pagination. A gap, as if someone had plucked out half a folder and hoped nobody would notice. I slide my hand in. The cardboard is stiff—a thin folder stuck to the bottom of the drawer with double-sided tape.

I peel it free. It's unlabeled, but inside: a stack of printed emails, flagged "HIGH PRIORITY," and a sequence of deletion logs—internal memos about "record correction requests" for the Old Town Plaza, Ignite Global, and six other foundations that have Alfred's fingerprints all over them. The edits are all time-stamped between midnight and six a.m. Each one is signed off by an "Archive Tech" who uses initials only.

I take pictures of everything, then pull the lipstick mic from my pocket and start recording a spoken log, just in case the phone gets wiped later. My hands are shaking. I scan every page into the laptop with the USB drive, using Rafi's "Ghost Sync" program. The progress bar inches forward.

"Talk to me, Raf."

"Seventy percent done. You have two minutes before the janitorial team checks the lower level. They just clocked in. Motion sensor says the main corridor's clear for now."

I double my pace. The evidence is heavy, but the room is heavier. I'm starting to sweat, even in the cold. My breath fogs in the air, and my phone's battery ticks down faster than I'd like.

Then, from the hall, a voice: "I swear, if he leaves one more pot of coffee on, I'm putting a rat in his desk."

Another voice, higher-pitched. "That's so gross, but honestly I'd pay to see it."

Two women, both city staffers, maybe two rooms down. They're moving toward me, laughter echoing off the stone. I stuff the last file in my bag, snap the light off, and duck behind a row of vertical file shelves. The door opens. Footsteps cross the room—one heavy, one light.

"I told you it's in here," the first voice says. "The clean-up order said archives by seven."

The second snorts. "Did you see who signed it? Calder's new guy. He's such an asshole."

"I know. But it's already been cleared upstairs. Compliance wants all working files closed out—anything that didn't make final. And scrub vendor identifiers while we're at it. Clean archive. No loose ends."

The blood in my ears drowns out their words for a second, but I hear them opening the cabinet I just emptied. Papers shuffle. A soft thump as they toss folders onto the rolling cart.

"Doesn't matter," the first says. "You heard the directive—if this leaks, everyone burns. And you don't want to be the one they trace it back to."

The second voice drops, suddenly nervous. "Do you think it's true? That there's, like, a list?"

"Of course there's a list. There's always a list. Just do the job."

I snap a picture of their shoes as they pass, then hunch down, mic open, and record every word. I steady my shaking hands and remain invisible behind the shelf.

They finish, dump a handful of files into a blue recycling bag, and head out, the door clanking behind them. I wait a beat, then two, before creeping back to the desk. The USB drive flashes: SYNC COMPLETE. I yank it, check the laptop—mirrored, every file, even the ones they were about to delete. I try not to laugh, but the sound bubbles up anyway.

"Cassie, are you moving?" Rafi's voice is tight now.

"On it," I whisper. "They're gone. Got the files, got the deletion logs. Heading for the exit."

"Service corridor to your left. Camera's dead for the next sixty seconds."

I slip out, feet almost silent on the cold tile. The service hallway is lined with crates of old election flyers and broken traffic cones. I follow it to the stairwell, moving fast but not running. The stairs dump me out behind the building, into a concrete loading dock with a half-frozen puddle at the curb. My breath steams in the air.

At the edge of the lot, I pause, waiting for the nerves to quiet down. I'm about to call Rafi when I hear a heavy door slam open above me.

"Hey!" A deep voice—the night guard, probably—echoes down the stairwell. "You! Stop!"

I don't stop. I hit the alley at a run, vault a low fence, and cut through the parking lot toward Broad Street. The phone in my pocket buzzes, but I ignore it, lungs burning, feet soaked. I don't slow down, not until I'm three blocks away and the only sound is the distant bark of a garbage truck.

I pause, catch my breath, and fish the phone out. The screen shows a string of texts from Rafi, each more frantic than the last.

I tap the mic, and my voice comes out shaky but alive. "Got out. Evidence is clean. Headed home."

He sends back a single emoji: a raised fist.

I smile.

The sky is just starting to go from blue to gold. The city's waking up, none the wiser that the truth is loose in its veins.

I text James Branham, the prosecutor from my uncle's trial.

"New information. Urgent."

His reply, instant. "45 min. Molly's Mug & Muffin."

I walk the last mile in silence, every step lighter than the one before.

* * *

The Mug & Muffin is the kind of cafe that no one would ever Instagram—

linoleum tables, bad fluorescent lighting, and a bakery case with three kinds of stale Danish. Branham's seated in a corner of the room, back against the wall, tie loosened—casual, but professional. I sit at an adjacent table, giving myself a line of sight on the door.

Crow's feet, and a hint of blue below Branham's eyelids betray his weariness. On the table in front of him there's a yellow legal pad open, half a page of notes in his meticulous block printing. He stirs his coffee but never drinks it.

"Ms. Maddox," he says, not quite a greeting. "Is this the whole set?"

I drop the flash drive and a Manila folder on the Formica. "Everything relevant," I say. "The logs, the contracts, and a recording you'll want to play with headphones."

He doesn't touch the drive yet, just a measured gaze to weigh my face against whatever rumors the city has been feeding him. "You know this is a career suicide move, right?"

"I know," I say. "But it's not my career I'm worried about."

He almost smiles. "No, I suppose not." He flips open the folder, scans the first page, then the second, making marks with a fountain pen so heavy the tip must cut through the paper. He reads like a scanner: full-page sweeps, then doubling back when something doesn't fit.

"You traced this through Drexel & Pittman?" he says.

"And Ignite Global, and two other shells—Shenandoah was a big player until the contracts got rerouted," I say. "They're laundering city money through the consulting fees, then using the same pipeline for campaign funds and, maybe bribes. Some of the payment codes match up with the St. Augustine's scholarships, but there's no paperwork for most of those. That's why I had to break in."

He glances up, mildly alarmed. "You—what?"

"Metaphorically. I mean, I used admin credentials, not a crowbar. The records were about to be wiped."

He makes a note, then scrolls through the files on the drive. "This is solid," he says, "but it's not enough. Not unless you want to wind up on the wrong end of a defamation suit. Calder's got friends in every oversight office, not to mention a couple of judges who owe him their seats."

"I've got the staffers on tape," I say, tapping the lipstick mic. "They admit to scrubbing the records. If you bring them in under subpoena, maybe one flips."

He shakes his head. "I don't want 'maybe.' I want a direct link, or else all I get is my name in the next day's obits. The last guy who tried to bring Calder down ended up running parking meters in Erie."

I sit back, frustration burning through my ribs. "So what—you let it slide? Pretend the money just fell out of a hole in the city's pockets?"

He sets the pen down and folds his hands. "You think I haven't tried? Every time I get close, the target moves. The last three grand juries choked on the paperwork alone, and when we called in the State Ethics Board, their chief auditor was suddenly off to a six-figure job in the private sector."

His face hardens. "You're a good investigator, Maddox. One of the best. But if you poke at this hive any more, it's not just you who gets stung. Lila, Rafi, your friends at S&S—everyone."

He says the names like a litany. Too late, I understand the mayor isn't the only one keeping score.

"You're saying walk away," I say.

He sighs. "I'm saying don't do it alone. I can put you in touch with a US Attorney—off the books, for now. But you need to be very careful. Calder doesn't just ruin lives, he ends them. There are names on these contracts that go back twenty years. I'm not even sure who's running the show anymore."

I push the folder across the table, my hand shaking just a little. "If you had this, would you go to the Feds?"

"I'd go to my family first and tell them to leave town," he says, dead serious. "Then I'd go to the Feds. But you'll never get to a court date unless you get someone to flip on the record."

The overhead light buzzes, then dims for a second, as if even the wiring can't stand the tension.

I make my decision. "You've got a week," I say. "Then I leak it to the press. I'm not waiting for another audit to buy the Mayor a condo in Belize."

He laughs, and it's not a nice sound. "Stubborn. Just like your father."

He stands, tucks the folder under his arm, and tosses back the rest of his coffee. "Be careful, Cassie," he says. "I mean it. One mistake and you're not just out of a job—you're out of time."

He exists the cafe, and his silhouette merges with the morning crowd outside.

I sit for another minute until the adrenaline leaves my hands. The waitress brings me a Danish on the house, powdered sugar gone gray in the cafeteria light.

I don't eat it. I don't even touch it.

I just think about the next move and how many more are left before I run out.

When I step outside, the sun's bright enough to hurt, but I let it hit my face anyway. I walk east, away from the courthouse, past three news vans and two cops on patrol. I keep my head down and try not to think about who's watching.

Every step is a countdown.

One week. That's all the time I have left to finish this.

And maybe finish myself in the process.

* * *

The apartment is much like a police procedural had a nervous breakdown in my living room. Evidence folders are everywhere: stacked on the coffee table, spread in color-coded grids across the floor, clipped to the edges of my laptop screen, and pinned to every square inch of corkboard I could dig out of the basement storage. In the center, my dining table is command central, four chairs occupied by nothing but binders, flash drives, and at least two dozen highlighters in various states of disrepair.

I'm so tired my teeth hurt, but the adrenaline won't let me crash. My hands don't shake anymore—they just ache from the constant motion: click, print, copy, paste, annotate, repeat. Every time I start to lose focus, I pop a jelly bean from the stash Lila hides above the fridge. My blood sugar ping-pongs between "about to faint" and "could bench-press a Prius."

There are three laptops running, all on borrowed time. The primary is patched into Rafi's remote server, siphoning off a mirror of the city's procurement drive. The backup is old, slow, but reliable; used only for transferring the heavy PDFs and making redundant copies of the logs. The third is a burner—just in case—and it's already encrypted and stashed in a gym bag under the coat rack.

I label every drive with two sets of initials—one mine, one Rafi's—so if someone ever finds them, they'll know who to subpoena and who to blame. I make triple backups, then split them across a dead drop at the office, another in a safe deposit box, and one in the hollowed-out algebra textbook I keep on my nightstand for exactly this kind of emergency.

It's nearly four by the time I finish the final backup. I'm staring at a screen full of barely legal contract language when I hear the bedroom door open behind me.

Lila's there, wrapped in a hoodie and pajama shorts, her hair sticking out in three directions. She doesn't say anything at first—just stands in the kitchen doorway, watching me do my best impersonation of a broken Roomba.

I brace for the confrontation, but she just asks, "Want some tea?"

"Yeah," I say, voice ragged. "If you're making."

She puts the kettle on, then leans on the counter. Her eyes scan the spread of evidence. "You know they're going to come after you, right?"

"Already have. The city's got people scrubbing the archives every hour. It's only a matter of time before they realize what's missing."

She opens a cabinet, searching for the good mugs. "You trust Branham?"

I shrug. "As much as anyone in a suit. He's not dirty, but he's scared. The mayor's people have reach."

"Do you?"

That makes me pause. "Trust him? Or have reach?"

She smiles, the sad kind. "Both."

I let the question hang. The water boils, and she pours two cups, brings one over, then perches on the edge of the sofa. She tucks her knees up, cradling the mug, and waits.

"I know what you're going to say," I start.

"Then why are you still awake?" Her voice is gentle, not accusing.

I glance at my watch, then at the progress bar crawling across the screen. "Because by now they've figured out we were in their system. Their lawyers are already drafting cease-and-desists, and some IT guy is probably tracing our digital fingerprints back to this apartment. If I don't finish this now, they'll bury everything we found under so much legal concrete we'll never dig it out."

She considers that. "And if you do finish?"

My attention drops to the table—to the stacks of evidence, the glowing rows of copy progress bars. "Then I have something nobody else does. The full chain—from city money to shell corp to payoff. If we go public, they can't just wave it away."

Lila takes in the apartment, then turns back to me. "You want to be a hero?"

I snort. "I just want to not be a footnote."

She sips her tea, then steps close and rests a hand on my shoulder. "You're more than a footnote, Cassie."

My eyes settle on her hand, on the faint scar across her knuckle from when she punched a locker door in high school. "If anything happens—"

She cuts me off. "Don't. Just... don't."

We stand there, the air thick with everything we can't say. Eventually, she releases me, refills her mug, and heads back to bed. At the doorway, she pauses a beat before closing the door.

* * *

At five, I start assembling the master binder. I take every photo, every screenshot, every hand-labeled contract, and slot it into the color-coded dividers. The blue is for city contracts; the red is for the scholarship fraud; the green is for every email or memo that ties it all together. At the end, I print a hard copy index and staple it to the inside cover. The binder is so full that the rings barely close.

I stare at it, exhausted and a little proud. Then I step back. I need to get it to Branham before I lose my nerve. I snap it shut, wrap it in a plastic grocery bag, and stick it in my backpack.

Before I go, I tack one more page to the corkboard. It's the "org chart" of the scam—every name, every shell company, every step from city money to campaign kickback. At the top, I put a printout of Mayor Calder, smirking for a ribbon-cutting. In red Sharpie, I write: "THE KINGPIN."

Underneath, I pin a photo of Alfred, then a blurry shot of myself from a college ID, back when I thought crime was just something that happened on TV. At the bottom, I tape a picture of Dad—one from a family picnic before everything went sideways, before Uncle Alfred made his first million.

I step back and take it in—the web of connections, the way they close around me. I'm in deeper than I ever planned. I'm not sorry. Not even close.

I grab the binder, the backup drive, and the burner phone, then slide out the door and into the still-dark hallway.

I make the drop at an all-night copy shop two blocks from the apartment. The guy at the counter barely glances at me, just hands me the prepaid envelope and points to the mailbox in the back. I slip the binder in, double-check the address, and shove it through the slot. It lands with a satisfying thunk.

When I leave, I keep to the shadows, eyes peeled for anyone watching. But the street is empty, except for the paper delivery van and a couple of drunks arguing over a slice.

I take the long way home, cutting through a park where the grass is slick with dew and the benches are all too cold to sit on. I find a dry patch, sit anyway, and watch the horizon for a sign of morning.

It's not much, but it's enough.

* * *

Back at the apartment, I collapse on the sofa, shoes still on, head buzzing with all the things I still have to do. The corkboard is there, waiting, a monument to my own obsession.

I'm about to drift off when the phone buzzes.

It's Rafi.

I answer, my voice half-asleep. "Yeah?"

He's in full crisis mode. "Check your email. Now."

I stumble to the laptop, log in, and see the first message in the queue:

SUBJECT: THEY KNOW

BODY: I just got a ping from the city's IT department. Someone accessed your home WiFi from a mobile unit—probably a van, probably law enforcement. You need to disappear. Now.

A chill runs through me. Then something steadier takes its place.

I text back: "Too late. The drop is done."

Rafi replies: "You're insane. You're brilliant. I'm on my way."

I let the phone slip from my hand and close my eyes for a second. Then I stand, tear the org chart off the wall, and stuff it in the backpack with the backup drive and a few cash bills.

When the knock comes—three sharp raps, then a pause—I know it's Rafi. I let him in, and he's wired, already talking strategy.

"We need to get you somewhere safe. We can route your signal through three proxies and set up a burner at the train station. If we time it right, nobody will know where you went."

He says it all so fast I barely keep up. I laugh, then begin to cry.

"Hey," he says, pulling me in. "It's over. You did it."

"Not yet," I say, voice muffled. "One more thing."

He pulls back. "What?"

I hold his gaze. "You want to help me bring down a mayor?"

He grins. "I thought you'd never ask."

We grab our gear and head for the door.

As we step into the hall, the sky is just starting to lighten, gold slicing through the blue. The city is waking up, and I'm ready for whatever it throws back.

We walk into the morning together.

The case isn't over.

And neither are we.

20

The Power Behind the Curtain

The City Hall lobby at 8:05 a.m. is just the way I remember it: high-gloss tile, banners with the new city branding, a gold-plated statue of Lenape's founder that looks extra ridiculous under the LED lights. My hair is pulled into a high ponytail. Neutral lipstick. Glasses to hide how little I slept.

On paper, I pass for professional.

My body hasn't gotten the memo.

The security guard at the desk—the same bored guy as last time, a big fan of morning podcasts—barely glances at my ID. He waves me through the metal detector, no questions asked. City Hall is a sieve for credentials, and it's even easier when you walk like you own the place. I catch a passing councilwoman's eye. She does a double-take, then ducks into her office like she's dodging a process server.

The elevators here move as if they're underwater, but I'm grateful for the extra seconds to steady my hands and let the sweat dry from my palms. The phone in my pocket buzzes once, then twice. Rafi's pre-meeting check-in: "Ping if you need me." I don't answer. If it's bad enough to need backup, he'll see it on the news.

The top floor is all hushed carpet and framed photos of the mayor shaking hands with every B-list celebrity who's ever passed through the city. Etched on the double glass doors to Calder's office, the city seal and the mayor's full

163

name appear in all uppercase and are unmissable. Behind them, a silhouette waits at the reception desk. There's a weird static in the air—like walking into a crime scene just before the tape goes up.

I take a breath, push the doors, and step inside.

The mayor's executive suite is a monument to the kind of power that never apologizes for itself. Heavy leather decks the waiting area, and plaques and photos of ribbon-cuttings line the walls. Through a second set of glass doors, I can see Calder at his desk, already deep in conversation with a man in a suit who radiates "chief of staff" energy. Calder spots me and lifts a hand, peeling himself away from his guest with a practiced curve of the mouth that disappears the moment he turns.

The receptionist—a woman whose job it is to make people grateful for being ignored—never lifts her eyes from the monitor.

I take a seat, cross my legs, and wait.

After exactly two minutes, the door to Calder's office swings open. The chief of staff strides past without acknowledging me, but I catch a sideways glance: not curiosity, but more like, "I hope you brought your own body bag."

Comforting.

"Ms. Maddox," the mayor calls, all warmth and nothing to show for it. "Come in."

The room is oversized, deliberately so—offices on either side swallowed and fused into a single power-flex arena. At the center sits a desk the size of a king bed, dark mahogany polished to a mirror. Behind it, a wall of windows frames the city and the river, catching the morning sun like it's auditioning for a postcard.

Calder himself stands as I enter, jacket off, shirt sleeves crisp and rolled. He's taller than he appears on TV—maybe because he always stoops a little, like he's trying to convince the world he's just a regular guy. His hair is the exact color of wet sand, and his eyes are blue enough to make you forget, for one second, that he's a career killer.

He gestures at the chair across from him. "Thanks for coming on such short notice."

"I didn't have a lot of notice," I say, and sit. "But I figured it was important."

He sits, then leans forward, elbows on the desk. "I always make time for bright minds. Especially ones who keep my city running after hours." My jaw tightens once, then unlocks.

I set the manila folder on the desk between us, then take out the list of bullet points I rehearsed all night. "I wanted to bring something to your attention, Mr. Mayor. It's about Drexel & Pittman, and the city's redevelopment contracts for Old Town Plaza."

He cocks his head, curious, as if he's never heard the names before. "Go on."

I flip open the folder. Three entries. Color-coded, flagged in the city's own system.

"Quarterly," I say. "Always just under the reporting threshold."

I slide the page closer. "Same vendor. D&P. No work logs. No backup."

I tap the margin. "The invoices are blank except for a memo and an initial."

I take a breath. "But the money still clears."

He nods, absorbing it all. "You're saying there's fraud?"

I keep my voice flat. "I'm saying there's no legitimate business. And when I compared the ledger to the list of city staff authorized to approve these payments, every single one is a political appointee. There's no signature from an actual department head."

He considers, then shrugs. "Consulting fees are sometimes mis-allocated. It's not always intentional. If you found a real error, I'm glad you brought it to me instead of going to the press." His smile is smooth, conciliatory, and already moving on. "Is that why you're here? To be the city's conscience?"

I keep my eyes on him. "I'm here because someone tried to erase the digital trail last night. Two city employees accessed the archive room after hours and began deleting records tied to D&P."

I let that sit. I don't mention the mirror or mention what survived.

"If they'd finished," I add, "there would be nothing left to ask questions about."

He studies me, weighing what I know against what I'm not saying. The corners of his mouth tighten a fraction.

"That's a serious accusation, Ms. Maddox."

I go for the throat. "Not as serious as what you'll find if you subpoena the internal communications of your own staff. The whistleblower said the orders came from the top. If that's true, you could be facing obstruction, maybe conspiracy."

He stands, walks to the windows, hands clasped behind his back. "You come from a law enforcement family, right?" The question hangs in the air, rhetorical and predatory.

"Yes," I say, careful.

He glances over his shoulder. "Your father was good. But certainly not perfect."

For a second, I say nothing. Calder does the same. He studies the river through the glass as if he's waiting for me to remember something.

He turns at last. "You know how these things start," he says. "A rumor. A discrepancy. Money that doesn't quite reconcile."

A beat.

"Years ago, it was a raid. Cash went missing. The city needed an answer."

I clench my jaw. I remember. I just want to hear how he tells it.

Calder leans forward, voice soft. "I was asked to conduct the inquiry. Painful business. But your father held up. Every dollar accounted for in the end. The real problem was a pair of supervisors running a theft ring out of the evidence locker. They got what they deserved. Dylan? He got a black mark. No promotion, not for years. Not until I insisted he get another shot."

He shrugs. "Your father is one of the last honest ones. What does he make of the excellent work you're doing?"

The way he says it makes me want to throw up. "He's supportive," I say, and it sounds like an apology.

He pivots, walks back to the desk, and sits on the corner, now looming over me. "But you have to understand: none of this is what seems. Drexel & Pittman isn't a shell. It's a legal firewall for sensitive work the city can't handle in-house. Sometimes we have to move fast—faster than procurement allows. Nobody gets hurt. If we want the best for Lenape, we need to bend a few rules."

He reaches for the folder, flips through my printouts, then holds up a sheet. "You see this name? Sally Riggs? She's not an operative; she's a contractor. The project was a rush; the documentation is messy, but nothing illegal happened. It's all above board, if a little... unorthodox."

He drops the folder, then fixes me with that politician's gaze—the one that makes you forget he could order a hit and call it urban renewal. "You want to blow the whistle, that's your call. But if you're wrong, you'll destroy lives. Including yours."

He lets the threat dangle, then changes the subject.

"You ever wonder why someone as talented as you ended up chasing paper trails for a living?"

I bristle, but keep my mouth shut.

He leans in, voice low. "I know what happened with your uncle. I know how hard you tried to save him. You think he was a player in this game. He was nothing—a pawn. The real players never leave fingerprints, Cassie. If you want to keep your friends safe, if you want to see those kids you've been working with graduate without a black mark next to their names, you'll walk away."

He lets that land. The air in the office goes heavy, and for a second, I'm twelve years old again, watching my father take a punch in a bar and refuse to hit back. The room narrows. I fold my hands under the table and wait it out.

He finally smiles, softer this time. "I like you, Maddox. You remind me of myself before I knew better." He stands, buttons his cuffs, and walks me to the door.

"You take care now. And if you ever want to work for someone who appreciates your tenacity, you know where to find me."

My lips press together until they go numb. "Thank you for your time, Mr. Mayor."

He holds the door open, and I step out, vision narrowing to a single point. The hallway is empty. I walk to the elevator, hands white-knuckled on the folder, and push the button with more force than it needs.

Inside the elevator, I let myself shake.

By the time I reach the ground floor, I've stopped caring what anyone thinks of me.

I step into the daylight, phone buzzing again in my pocket, and start walking.

It takes five straight blocks before my body remembers how to be alive again. The city air is January sharp, despite it being the end of February. The cold burns the inside of my nose and turns every shallow breath into a sob I refuse to let out. My legs take over, moving on memory, carrying me through the city's morning traffic and into the shadow of a church I've never entered.

I duck into the vestibule, hands buried in my coat, and pretend to study the bulletin board. My phone vibrates again—Rafi, still watching the live feeds, still keeping me anchored to something that isn't raw panic.

The tremor in my hands won't stop. I press my palms flat against the marble just inside the entrance, trying to force myself back into the moment, to think like the investigator I'm supposed to be. Instead, my brain replays the last ten minutes on a loop: Calder's smile, the way he pronounced my name, the casual references to my father as if he knew him better than I.

I step back outside, blend into a pack of parents dragging kids toward a daycare, and cross against the light. No one's following, but invisible lines tighten around my neck with every step. By the time I reach the trolley stop, I've already mapped three separate escape routes home and an emergency path to the nearest police precinct if things get stupid.

I ride the trolley past my stop, just in case, then double back on foot. I change my mind twice about which way to go and finally slip through the alley behind Rafi's family pharmacy, heart still pounding so loud I can hear it over the trash truck a block away.

Inside the pharmacy, it's business as usual. The bell chimes. Behind the counter, Rafi's dad is explaining a blood pressure cuff to a woman with forearms like braided rope and a stare that doesn't waver. I avoid eye contact and slide past the aisles, past the chip display, and straight through the door marked "EMPLOYEES ONLY."

The "safe room" is a storage closet that Rafi converted into an ad hoc bunker: signal jammer nailed to the ceiling, two old laptops on a folding table, blackout shades on the top window. The room smells like printer toner, burnt dust, and lemon-scented disinfectant wipes. I close the door behind me and lean against the wall until the shivers pass.

Rafi is already in the room, hunched over a rat's nest of hard drives and USB sticks. He's in civilian mode—gray hoodie, glasses, sweatpants, hair flattened by headphones. He takes me in and loses the jokey grin he uses to keep me from losing it.

"Cassie," he says, soft but not babying. "You okay?"

I shake my head, no words yet, just a tangle of throat and tears and anger I don't have time for.

He slides a chair my way, and I sit, hands balled so tight my knuckles crack. For a minute, we just listen to the hum of electronics and the muffled sound of Rafi's dad laughing at some customer's joke out front.

I finally say. "Calder knew everything, Raf. Like, not just the evidence, not just what we found—he knew about my dad, about an old investigation. Calder, get this, actually took the lead on the investigation into my dad. Did you know Calder was the one who eventually got my father promoted? What does that say about my father? He and Calder have a history together."

Rafi doesn't interrupt. He just lets me talk.

"He spun it all. Drexel & Pittman, the scholarships, the kickbacks—he had an answer for every point. But it's worse than that." I stare at the jammed signal light. "He said Alfred was just a pawn. He implied my uncle was being used the whole time, and that if we keep going, we're going to get other people hurt. That if I keep poking, those kids—" I can't even finish the sentence.

Rafi's hand closes over mine. His skin is cold but solid, and I let him squeeze as hard as he wants.

"He's not bluffing," Rafi says. "Not with your file, not with the way they've been cleaning house all week. The guy's dangerous because he's methodical. No panic, just process."

He gets up, paces once, then bends over the table, booting up one of the old laptops. "But that's why we do this the way we planned. No last-minute changes, no improvising. If you're ready, I'm ready."

I don't correct him.

He walks me through the playbook: "We've already completed phase one with the overnighted hard copies. Next, we send the encrypted email to the AG's office. Then, we trigger the press leak. I have three journalists lined up, all prepped with one-time access codes. The city's too big for Calder to shut down all the coverage at once, so we hit everywhere, all at the same time."

He flips the laptop toward me. "Everything's staged. All you have to do is hit send."

I hover my hand over the trackpad, but my finger shakes so badly that I have to steady it with the other hand. I meet his eyes, and for a second, we are kids again, crouched in the back of his dad's pharmacy, plotting how to prank the meanest teacher at our middle school. Only now, instead of vinegar and baking soda, we're packing enough legal dynamite to bring down City Hall.

I click send.

The world doesn't explode. But a lightness creeps up my spine, like the air pressure changed just a fraction of a degree. Rafi closes his eyes, then opens them, a weird mix of terror and relief on his face.

We sit in silence as the first responses ping in.

The state AG's office issues an auto-reply: "Your evidence has been received and will be reviewed by the appropriate party."

One journalist's inbox lights up, then another, then another—quiet pings spreading outward, too fast to stop.

Each time Rafi checks the tracker and confirms that the packages are live.

He takes a long breath, then grins, exhausted. "You did it. You really did it."

I laugh, but it comes out jagged. "Don't say that yet. Calder's going to retaliate. He'll go for the soft targets first."

Marcus. Alissa. Janice. Nate.

Mel.

All of them exposed.

Rafi knows what I'm thinking. "Those teens are resilient. I wouldn't worry about them. But as for you. You're not going home tonight."

He's already packed a go-bag for me: a change of clothes, a burner phone, protein bars, two hundred dollars in small bills. He's even remembered to include my favorite kind of pen, the one with the rubber grip and the micro-fine tip.

"Stay here," he says. "It's not Fort Knox, but it's off the radar. I'll check in every hour. You need to keep your phone off except for the burner."

I want to protest, to say it's overkill, but Calder's smile rises up instead—the way he bent my father's story into a blade. Then my uncle's face, slack with disbelief the day the door closed behind him. After that, it's not faces at all, just the knowledge of how easily a machine like his flattens anyone standing too close.

"Okay," I say. "I'll stay."

Rafi unpacks the rest of the war room: two burner laptops, a battery backup, an old-school tape recorder for analog redundancy. He shows me how to trigger the alarm on the signal jammer in case someone tries to get cute with wireless mics. He even gives me a rundown on the escape hatch—an old laundry chute that opens into the alley behind the pharmacy.

The whole time, he keeps one hand on my shoulder, or the small of my back, as if making sure I don't float away. He's scared, but he never lets it show for long.

By noon, we've staged every copy of the evidence, even one set for Lila in case something happens to both of us. The backup plan is so paranoid it makes me want to laugh, but after the morning I've had, I want all the paranoia I can get.

Rafi props open the window for a breath of fresh air. "You want to talk about it?" he asks, not pushing, just offering.

I shake my head. "Maybe later. Right now, I just need to not think."

He nods, then sits beside me, shoulder to shoulder. "I'm not going anywhere," he says, and I believe him.

For the first time in weeks, I let myself just sit. The dust motes dance in the shaft of winter sun, listen to the background noise of the city through double-thick glass, and count the slow, even beats of Rafi's breathing next to me.

I don't know what happens next. Maybe nothing. Calder could nuke the city government to save himself. I could never get to see those kids walk across their high school stage, or my mother's face—mapped out with stress lines as she hurriedly throws together a meal on a regular Sunday morning.

But for now, we're alive. For now, the truth is out there, ticking like a bomb in a dozen inboxes, a thousand times harder to erase than one girl with a grudge.

Rafi stands and stretches, then starts prepping for the next wave of contingency plans. I get up, too, and help him label the evidence drives, our hands bumping every few seconds as we work.

The last package is ready. He seals it with tape, then meets my eyes, brightness catching behind the smudged lenses of his glasses.

"That worked," he says—not a question.

I smile, and this time it isn't a lie. "Yeah. It did."

Our fingers brush as we clear the table, and for one perfect second, nothing else matters.

We don't say goodbye when he heads for the front of the store, because it isn't over. Not even close.

I lock the door, set the alarms, and sink into an office chair that rolls and creaks under my weight. The air still smells like burnt coffee—stale, familiar, my father's brand of vigilance.

I pick up my phone, thinking about calling him.

I don't.

By now, he already knows what Rafi and I pulled off. If there's fallout coming, he's already tracking it—same as I am—as I sit here and wait.

21

Fall of the Dynasty

The rain's been coming down hard for four straight hours and it doesn't let up for a single minute, not even as the police caravan idles at the mouth of Sycamore Lane. The city is still asleep, streetlights fizzing under the downpour, lawns shining like wet vinyl, but every cop in Lenape knows what's about to happen. SWAT vans line up bumper to bumper, headlights off, only the blue LEDs pulsing on the dash. Inside an unmarked sedan, my father drums a quarter against the steering wheel, waiting for the signal.

"Five minutes," he says, glancing at his watch instead of the road ahead. He's wearing his raid jacket over a Lenape PD hoodie, the fabric already soaked through at the shoulders. In this light, he could be any man—middle-aged, unremarkable, the lines at his eyes from years of poor sleep. But there's something sharp in him tonight, a current that runs under his voice—his eyes jump to the mirror mid-sentence, then back again.

"You sure you want to see this?" he asks.

My mouth is too dry for words. I know I shouldn't be here. There's no justification for bringing your daughter to an armed raid, especially not when the daughter is an adult and the raid is on the home of a sitting State Senator. But I asked, and he said yes, and we both understood it was less about what I'd see and more about what I'd need to remember.

He pulls a sheet of notebook paper from his jacket and hands it to me. It's

173

the target list—names, addresses, crimes scrawled in his slanted print. At the top, in red ink: "Wilkins, Senator. 135 Sycamore. PRIMARY."

I read the list twice, the words swimming in my head: County Commissioner, Zoning Board Chair, a construction CEO whose son once dropped out of my AP Chem class. My pulse ticks too fast to ignore, and there's a metallic tang on my tongue that refuses to go away. I want to say something—some clever line to break the tension—but there's nothing left to say.

* * *

At 5:02 on the dot, the radio cracks: "GO."

The first SWAT unit moves like a single creature, boots splashing across the manicured lawn, guns up, bodies hunched in the rain. They don't bother with subtlety—the battering ram hits the front door, and the sound is so loud it actually echoes, even through the weather and the white noise of my panic. Three dark figures inside scramble for cover, then the entire front hallway erupts in a tangle of arms and shouting and plastic handcuffs.

"Visual confirmation, Wilkins is present," the radio says.

My father doesn't smile, but his whole body lets out a breath. "Let's go."

He leaves me in the car, but the windows are down. The walk up the driveway is a slow-motion parade: SWAT guys in helmets, guns resting on chests, their faces blank and bored. They know this is the big one, the one that lands on TV, but they also know it's just another morning, another set of handcuffs. It's the third guy in who comes out with Wilkins, pajamas bunched at the ankles, face red with rage and sleep deprivation.

"You're under arrest for conspiracy and racketeering," my father says, voice calm, like he's reading from a training manual. "You have the right to remain silent—"

Wilkins spits at the sidewalk, the rain already washing it away. "You're dead, Maddox," he says, loud enough that every neighbor on the block can hear it. "You think you've won, but you don't know a goddamn thing."

Dad doesn't even blink. He finishes the Miranda and hands Wilkins off to the uniforms, then turns to watch the rest of the sweep. Two more come out behind—an aide in a bathrobe, a woman I recognize from the last fundraiser. Both in handcuffs, both shivering, but not a word out of either.

Over the next ten minutes, the radio fills the car with overlapping voices—status updates, clipped confirmations, the sound of doors closing.

"County Commissioner secured."

"Target acquired at two-one-five Pinecrest."

"Negative contact at Roosevelt."

It's a domino line of power falling, the city's entire shadow government scooped up and loaded into vans before sunrise.

Will anyone even notice?

Or is it like a forest fire—something that only makes sense months later, when the new growth comes in?

At 5:23, the rain lets up just enough to see the head of the Zoning Board dragged from his garage in a t-shirt and nothing else. He's yelling about a "setup," but few show interest. One neighbor in slippers films the whole thing on her phone, mouth open in disbelief. Two houses down, a little girl stands in the picture window with a bowl of cereal, watching it all unfold as if it's a cartoon.

This is supposed to be a triumph. It's cold instead. There's a disconnect between what I know—these people are criminals, the evidence is bulletproof—and what I see, which is just a line of men and women in rain-soaked pajamas, hands locked behind their backs, faces twisted in fear or shock or, in a few, nothing at all. Those who fight go down fast. The ones who don't fight barely make a sound, as if they've already rehearsed this moment a thousand times in their heads.

My father returns to the car, his hair dripping, jacket stained with mud. He doesn't speak right away. He sits, breathes, and wipes his hands on his jeans.

"You alright?" he asks.

"Yeah," I say, but the word is hollow.

He meets my eyes—and doesn't look away. For the first time in years, I'm not a problem to be fixed. "You did this, Cass," he says. "Don't let anyone take that from you."

For a moment, I believe him.

On the drive back to the precinct, the city is quiet, but the streets aren't empty. News vans are already rolling in, headlights cutting through the fog. Two reporters in parkas stand at the end of Sycamore, faces lit by their phone screens, ready to spin the story before the bodies are even cold.

"Never ends," Dad mutters, but he says it without bitterness. He's focused on the next step, the next arrest, the next page in the warrant book.

At the turn for the main drag, we pass the County Commission building. The lights on the top floor flicker on, then off, then on again, like someone inside can't decide whether to hide or surrender. By noon, the news will have everyone's names, and by dinner, half the city will talk about who's next.

Will any of them sleep tonight? Maybe they'll be like me—eyes open, heart pounding, waiting for the knock at the door that never comes until it does.

* * *

The after-action debrief happens in a windowless conference room with a fake oak table and enough donut boxes to give the whole department diabetes. My father stands at the head, running through the arrests with a dry efficiency that almost makes it funny. He points at a map, marks off the targets, and assigns the follow-up interviews like he's divvying up chores on a family road trip.

I sit at the back, clutching a mug of burnt coffee. The officers joke and jostle, boots leaving wet crescents on the floor, laughter a little louder than it needs to be. The relief is there—in the loosened shoulders, the easy swearing—but it never quite settles. Everyone knows tomorrow brings another list. New names. The quiet certainty that clearing one room never empties the building.

Later, my father finds me in the hallway. His shoulders are slumped in a way they usually aren't, the lines around his eyes deeper, as if sleep gave up on him hours ago. Still, there's something lighter there, a fraction of the weight gone. He hands me an envelope—plain, unmarked, already opened.

"For you," he says.

Inside, it's a copy of the warrant for Mayor Calder. At the bottom, in blue ink, is my name, circled three times.

"You ready for the main event?" he asks.

I stare at the paper, at the smudge of his thumbprint in the corner. I've never been more afraid in my life. There's nowhere else I'd rather be.

"Let's finish it," I say.

He puts a hand on my shoulder, just for a second, then heads for the car.

Outside, the rain has stopped. The city glistens, every streetlight reflected a thousand times over in the puddles on the blacktop.

People are waking up right now. Sirens cut through the distance. Stories will be told tomorrow.

Calder's face. The long chain of decisions that led us here.

My father—and what it means to do the job, even when nobody thanks you for it.

I follow him to the car.

The work isn't finished yet.

* * *

City Hall at dawn is already crowded and hostile. By seven, the lobby isn't full of city workers but media—tripods sprouting like scaffolding, power cables taped to the floor, little blue makeup cases dragged behind reporters who haven't slept and don't plan to. A sign is taped to the elevator: PRESS EVENT—8:00 AM, COUNCIL CHAMBER. Every reporter in the city is here.

So are two men in black jackets with no agency badges. You can tell what they are by the way they don't talk, by how their hands hover just above their belts as they scan the room.

Rafi and I take a position at the back of the chamber, third row, just behind a woman with a Channel 9 logo stitched onto her coat sleeve.

"Smile," Rafi mutters. "The world's about to change, and you'll want to say you were here."

I try to smile, but my face is stuck in neutral. The room smells like aftershave, panic, and too many bagels. I keep one eye on the dais and the other on the doors, counting down the minutes. When the Mayor enters, he's flanked by three staffers and a guy in an immaculate suit that probably costs more than my student loans.

Calder arrives immaculate—tie straight, cuffs aligned, smile fixed in place. He makes a show of shaking hands, nodding at every camera, and ignoring the fact that half the people in the room want his head on a plate. He takes his place at the podium, clears his throat, and launches into the script.

"Ladies and gentlemen of the press," he says, "I know there's been much speculation these past few weeks, and I want to assure you that the Lenape City remains committed to transparency, accountability, and—"

That's when the doors slam open.

For a split second, nobody moves. Then my father is in the room, federal agents right behind him, badges raised, expressions set to "no more games." The two black jackets fall in to block the exits. The cameras pivot as one, and every phone in the room points at Calder.

The mayor freezes, lips still curled around the start of his next word. For a heartbeat, he's just another guy with nothing left to say. Then his eyes flick from my father to the crowd, weighing the angles, searching for his best move. He opts for the full performance: hands raised, confusion painted in broad strokes, the "what is the meaning of this?" routine.

My father's voice booms out, no microphone needed. "Mayor William Scott-Calder, you are under arrest for conspiracy, racketeering, and obstruction of justice. You have the right to remain silent—"

A ripple of sound moves through the chamber: a few gasps, a laugh that dies before it can find a home. The mayor's chief of staff, Elaine Winters, goes pale as a paper napkin. Her gaze locks on mine, and if hate could kill, I'd be a stain on the wall.

Calder's performance slips. Sweat gathers at his hairline, his eyes flicking toward the exits, his voice losing its steady edge. He turns, tries to hand his phone off to an aide, but the suit guy intercepts it. Behind the podium, his knuckles are white. He makes one last play for the crowd:

"This is a political hit job," he shouts. "We all know it. I've done nothing wrong, and the truth will come out."

The press leans forward as one. Flashes stutter across the stage.

"Drexel & Pittman—care to explain?"

"Who's actually calling the shots at City Hall?"

The questions stack and overlap, urgency replacing order.

My father is unmoved. He reads the rest of the rights, then gestures to the feds. Two agents step forward and secure the mayor's wrists with a pair of black plastic flex cuffs. The sound—plastic on skin, the ratchet of the band—echoes in the hush that follows.

Calder leans close to my father and says, low but clear, "This isn't over."

I can see the way my father doesn't flinch. He just nods, as if to say, "It never is."

The feds take Calder by the arms and guide him down the center aisle. The press surges forward in a wall of raised cameras and white noise.

Calder keeps his head high.

His hands tremble anyway.

Elaine Winters doesn't move, not at first. When she finally stands, it's with a steadiness that borders on eerie. She gathers her files, turns once toward the room, then fixes her gaze on me. There's nothing left but venom. If she could, she'd snap her fingers and have the ceiling collapse on me right now.

Rafi leans over, voice just above a whisper: "I'm never going to stop being scared of that woman."

I grin, and this time it's real.

The mayor is gone, the room is chaos, but it's like the world has stopped holding its breath. The aides cluster in the corner, the press corps circles the agents for scraps of official statements, and my father stands at the edge of the dais, just out of the spotlight, watching to make sure it's really over.

The crowd thins, and Rafi and I slip out a side door into the blinding white of morning. Outside, City Hall is already ringed with news vans. There are more cops than usual, but no sirens, no alarms—just the low buzz of a city resetting itself.

We walk a block in silence, then another. Rafi nudges me with his elbow.

"You okay?"

"I will be."

"You're a legend," he says.

I shake my head. "I'm not. I just had the receipts."

He studies me for a second, like he wants to argue—then doesn't.

I don't know what to say, so I just stand there, watching the news tickers scroll across the big screen in the square: "MAYOR WILLIAM SCOTT-CALDER ARRESTED—MORE TO COME."

I stop beneath the courthouse, where my uncle once stood with the world at his feet, and wonder if any of this will ever really change.

For now, I take the moment of triumph.

The balance has shifted.

And I don't plan on blinking first.

22

The Long Shadow

The courthouse smells like mildew and anxiety, and it's packed tighter than a Black Friday electronics aisle. Every bench is full, and the overflow room downstairs is standing-room only. I take my usual spot in the gallery, second row, one seat over from an old woman with a cane and a bag of orange Tic Tacs. She smells like menthol. We share a nod, then fixate on the defense table, where Alfred Maddox sits, flanked by his legal team like a general surrounded by lieutenants who stopped believing in the war weeks ago.

The trial is a three-day blur of exhibits, witness lists, and procedural tantrums. The new charges—perjury, financial misconduct, conspiracy— stack on top of the old ones like so many cinder blocks. The prosecutor, a sharp-featured woman with a taste for red power suits, runs the room like a traffic cop with a personal vendetta against white-collar crime. She calls her first witness before the coffee in my cup has even cooled.

"State your name for the record," she says, and the witness—some ex- accountant for the city—launches into a monotone about vendor payments and misappropriated funds. On the monitors, scanned ledgers and bank state- ments flicker past. Each one is a hammer blow: $50,000 here, $75,000 there, all flowing through Drexel & Pittman into a netherworld of "consulting" and "outreach." The accountant testifies with a dead-eyed monotony, but you can see the relief in his face when he's dismissed. He's done. He's safe. He gets to go back to a world where the numbers always add up.

Day two, the prosecution brings out the emails. Hundreds of them. Alfred's name shows up in every chain, sometimes as an author, sometimes as a CC, always lurking in the metadata. The highlight reel is ugly: "Accelerate the disbursement"; "If questioned, refer to section 9." Each message is another thread in the web, until even the defense lawyers stop objecting and just start taking notes on which arguments they can still make with a straight face.

Alfred's confidence unravels as the evidence piles up. First, he sits tall, arms folded, chin at a defiant angle. But by the afternoon, the suit hangs loose, the tie is crooked, and his eyes have lost the glassy sheen of self-confidence. Instead, there's a kind of desperate patience, like he's waiting for when it all stops and the old world resumes. There are flashes of the old Alfred—a smirk at a terrible question, a roll of the eyes when the DA fumbles a document—but mostly it's just erosion, slow and visible.

On the morning of the last day, Warren Keller takes the stand. He's been waiting for this. He walks like a man who's had too many surgeries, but his voice is strong and clear. The DA asks about the scholarship fund, and he smiles—almost friendly, almost sad.

"They said it was for the kids," he says, "but every cent came with a string."

He tells the story of the Old Town Plaza project: the fake bids, the kickbacks, the way the city's own oversight committee was in on the deal. Every sentence lands on Alfred like a punch, and his hands grip the edge of the table harder and harder.

The cross-examination is a disaster. Keller's memory is sharp, and he's got nothing left to lose. He recalls names and dates, and never once meets Alfred's eyes until the very end.

"I wish it were just about the money," he says, and glances over. "But it never is."

The judge calls a recess, voice flat, already moving on. The gallery empties, everyone hungry for gossip and bad vending machine coffee. I stay put. I want to see Alfred alone, to catch whatever expression he wears when no one's watching.

He doesn't disappoint. The second the room is clear, he turns in his chair and finds me. The mask slips: his eyes are wet, the jaw slack, but there's a fire burning behind the misery. I brace for a glare, but he just stares—long enough that the bailiff steps forward, then backs away when he sees what's written across Alfred's face.

I want to wave, or mouth something comforting, or even just turn away. But I don't. I hold the stare until it's Alfred who blinks first. Then I stand and walk out, down the stairs, and into the lobby, where the press scrum is already gathering for the post-mortem.

I sit on the bottom step, out of their line of sight, and wait for the verdict.

It takes the jury three hours. I spend most of it in the bathroom, splashing water on my face and running the hand dryer until the roar drowns out my thoughts. When I return, the Tic Tac lady is back in her seat, waiting for the show. She nods at me, then whispers, "You his daughter?"

I shake my head. "Niece."

She smiles, toothless, and taps my hand with hers. "Family, then."

The jury files in; the judge calls the room to order, and the rest is a formality. The foreman stands and reads off the charges: "Guilty, guilty, guilty." With every word, the room gets smaller, the air thicker. The press doesn't cheer, but the hunger is there—the need for a fall guy with a good story. Alfred stands, and for a second he's poised, not with arrogance, but with relief. Then the judge reads the sentence, and the sheriff cuffs him, and the legacy of the Maddox name changes forever.

He walks out, eyes fixed ahead.

When the room is empty, I let myself cry—just a little.

* * *

Outside, the sun is too bright and the wind tastes like old cigarettes. Rafi is waiting by the steps, hands in his pockets, a smile somewhere between "are you okay?" and "I told you so."

"You want to grab a burger?" he asks.

I wipe my face with my sleeve. "You think there's a restaurant in this city that isn't running a Maddox special tonight?"

He laughs, and for the first time in days, so do I.

We walk down the street, away from the courthouse, away from the history we both just helped write. The weight of the day presses on me, but also something else—freedom from a future unmoored from the past.

"You did the right thing," Rafi says after a few blocks.

"I know," I say, but I don't know if it's true. I'm not sure I ever will.

At the corner, we stop. The traffic light cycles through red and green, but no cars come. The city is in limbo; the world suspended for just a second.

I take him in—the scar on his chin, the way his hair never stays down. I want to tell him something important, something that matters. Instead, I just say, "Thanks for being here."

He shrugs, but his face says everything. "You want to keep walking?"

I do.

Rafi's hand brushes against mine as we walk, and I reach for his fingers, letting them intertwine with my own. The warmth spreads up my arm and settles somewhere beneath my ribs—a small, steady flame of hope. For a moment, I forget about Alfred, about the trial, about everything except the slight callus on his thumb and right against my skin.

* * *

The second hearing is in the new Federal Courthouse downtown, a box of glass and steel with security lines like an airport and the world's least forgiving fluorescent lights. They call me in as a witness for the prosecution, but the place is packed like I'm headlining a stadium show. Although cameras are banned, every lawyer, reporter, and city official stares as I thread my way through the marble corridor to the witness room.

"Showtime," Rafi whispers, straightening my collar and giving my hand a squeeze. He sits in the front row, just behind the prosecution bench, notebook balanced on his knee. Every eye in the gallery tracks me as I take the stand.

The assistant U.S. attorney is a young guy with a nice tie and a nervous habit of clearing his throat before every question. He starts slow: my name, my credentials, my job at the firm, my work as a private investigator. Then he builds. He leads me through the audit trail, the emails, the bank records. On a big monitor, he cues up the evidence: a string of Drexel & Pittman payments, a city contract with Mayor Calder's initials, a memo from the Chief of Staff with a "confidential—destroy after reading" watermark.

"How did you acquire this document?" the prosecutor asks.

I answer straight: "Legally. Through a discovery subpoena after the audit revealed discrepancies." I leave out the part where I used Mark's badge to get into the archive. It's not a lie. It's just better for everyone if that detail stays in the dark.

The prosecutor runs through my highlights, then hands it off to the defense.

The defense attorney stands, all dazzling teeth and fake warmth, and launches straight into character assassination.

"Ms. Maddox, you have a history of, let's say, bending the rules in your investigative work, correct?"

"I follow the evidence," I say, as calm as I can.

He leans in, as if he's trying to hypnotize me. "But you admit to using questionable methods—covert recording, accessing private emails without explicit permission, entering restricted areas?"

"Sometimes the truth doesn't wait for a court order."

There's a little stir in the gallery. He sees it and goes in for the kill.

"And it's true, isn't it, that your own uncle was the subject of a criminal investigation—one that ultimately resulted in his conviction?"

My heart does a slow backflip, but I keep my face still.

"That's correct," I say.

"Do you harbor any resentment against your uncle? Or against other city officials?"

I force myself not to flinch. "I harbor resentment against corruption. Not people."

He smiles, and it's not a pleasant smile. "So you say. But what about your father? He was involved in an internal affairs investigation, wasn't he? Years ago?"

The line lands, but not how he wants it to. Two jurors shift, faces hardening. I don't break.

"My father has been nothing but honest. If you're suggesting my testimony is about family revenge, you're wrong."

He drops the pretense. "So when you provided these documents, when you accused the Mayor, you were acting—what, as an agent of the public good?"

"Yes," I say, simple as air.

He shakes his head, acting disappointed. "Isn't it true that, in some circles, you're being called the 'Maddox turncoat?' That people think you only did this to boost your own career, or maybe to get back at your uncle?"

The words sting because they're true. But in the crowd, Rafi's eyes lock onto mine, and I find the backbone I didn't know I had.

"Justice matters more than blood," I say, loud enough for the entire room can hear.

The defense sits down, the judge thanks me, and I step off the stand with my pulse racing so loud I can barely hear the next witness.

The rest of the hearing is a blur of closing statements, witness rebuttal, and legal posturing. But I don't hear most of it. I sit in the witness waiting room, staring at the ceiling and counting my breaths, waiting for the verdict. After an hour, the assistant DA pops her head in.

"They want a comment," she says. "The press."

I shake my head. "No, thanks."

Outside, they close ranks. Microphones hover inches from my face, notepads already moving, everyone hunting for the one line they can strip of context and run tonight.

"Cassie! Did you really bring down the Mayor?"

"Do you regret testifying against your own family?"

"Are you the next Erin Brockovich?"

I duck the questions, shielding my face. One of them, a woman with a voice like a chainsaw, shouts: "She's the niece turned hero!" and the phrase catches, ricocheting off the others until everyone is yelling it.

I find Rafi, waiting in the car, engine running. He gives me a lopsided grin and holds up a bottle of orange soda.

"You did it," he says, as if it's that easy.

I close the door and let the noise fade behind me.

We drive, neither of us talking, until the courthouse is just a memory in the rearview. The city is quiet in a way I've never heard before, and for the first time, I believe it might actually stay that way.

I take a long pull from the soda, let the bubbles burn my throat, and let myself hope for a world where maybe the truth gets to win every once in a while.

* * *

By Friday, my phone is a weapon of psychological warfare. The notifications never stop: reporters, lawyers, internet randos, even an old elementary school teacher who wants to know if I'll do a podcast. Rafi disables the location on all my devices, but it's too late. There are news vans outside the pharmacy by dawn, and two more parked half a block from my apartment, just waiting for the "Lenape Whistleblower" to step outside and maybe cry for the cameras.

Inside, the TV won't settle. Channels blur, voices overlap, and my name keeps resurfacing—trimmed, reframed, repurposed.

On one channel, they run the same blurry photo of me from high school, hair flat and eyeliner smudged, next to a shot of Mayor Calder in handcuffs. It's so ridiculous I almost laugh until the next segment scrolls up a screen full of angry tweets calling me everything from "saint" to "sellout."

Lila texts every hour; her messages a blend of memes and soft threats to come rescue me if I don't "log off and take a nap." The Musketeers— Mel, Janice, Marcus, and Alissa—form a group chat called "Maddox Defense Squad." I get a hundred notifications in two days, all of them reassuring, all of them spelling my name wrong.

Dad calls twice, both times on burner numbers he claims to have gotten from "contacts in Harrisburg." He tells me to consider doing the morning shows: "Control the narrative," he says, like the world is just a story you can edit if you use the right words. I say no, because I'm not ready for the public to see what the private has already eaten away.

Rafi cooks me breakfast, lunch, and dinner, and insists on "media blackout" after six pm, but I catch him watching the news from his phone in the bathroom. He doesn't know that I know. We both pretend it's fine.

By Saturday, the worst of the storm passes, but the calls don't stop. A package arrives at Rafi's house: flowers, from "a fan." He throws them out without reading the card. That night, we eat instant ramen at his kitchen table, rain hammering the windows. Our knees touch underneath. Neither of us moves away. We talk about movies we watched as kids, books we never finished, places we've never been.

"You want to get out of town?" Rafi asks, his voice lower than usual. His fingers brush mine as he reaches for the soy sauce. "Go somewhere nobody knows your name?"

I shift closer, noticing as though for the first time the blue shadows under his eyes and the curve of his mouth. "Where would we go?"

He grins, leaning closer until I can smell his aftershave. "Doesn't matter. Just you and me, somewhere they've never heard of spreadsheets or mayors or whistleblowers."

His hand covers mine on the table. I almost say yes, right there. But the mess we're leaving behind rises up between us—Alfred. Calder.

"I'm not running away," I say, but I don't pull my hand back.

He nods, his thumb tracing circles on my wrist. "I know. But you're allowed to leave, Cass. You're allowed to want things for yourself."

The next morning, I wake up to a sky so bright and clean it's like a reset button. Rafi has already packed a bag and left a note on the counter: "Pick you up at noon. Don't make me break down your door." His handwriting curves at the edges, softer than his usual sharp scrawl.

I stand in the window and watch the street, watching the news vans drive away, one by one, until it's just the city, quiet and new. My phone buzzes with a text from him: *Wear that blue sweater I like.*

I change into clean jeans, the blue sweater, and lace up my boots. The fabric feels steadier than I do, like armor softened by familiarity.

In the mirror, the woman staring back isn't fearless, but she isn't hiding either. There's color in her cheeks. There's a steadiness in her shoulders. Someone who might deserve the way Rafi watched her across the kitchen table last night—his fingers warm against mine, his gaze unguarded in a way I hadn't earned before.

When I step outside, he's already waiting, leaning against his car, breath clouding in the cold. He straightens when he sees me. The smile that finds his face isn't playful this time. It's certain.

My pulse stumbles, then settles into something stronger. Not panic. Not doubt. Something like belonging.

It's cold, the air sharp against my lungs, but the world feels open in a way it hasn't in a long time.

He's there.

Waiting.

And for once, I don't feel like I'm about to outrun it.

23

Crossroads

After the trial, after the interviews and the sopping gray parade of news vans, after the last text from my mother—just "Let us know when you're safe, love you"—I sit at my dining table, unmoving, as if the plastic chair might let me sink through the floor and all the way into the crawlspace beneath the building.

It's so quiet, I can hear the fridge rattling every time the compressor kicks on. Remaining file cases lay scattered on the floor in a neat fan: final disposition, sentencing memo, my uncle's signature on a battered consent decree. I tell myself to put it all away, to sweep the papers and half-empty cup off the table, but a weight I can't name buries any urge to move.

I stare at the edges of the manila folder, the exacting geometry of legal process, and wait for the memories to soften, but they don't. There's nothing soft about what comes next.

People say "closure" like it's a plastic lid you can snap on a bin, but the thing with family is, you never actually get to seal it. Not the way you want.

I try to conjure a single warm memory of Alfred Maddox, but none float up. No fishing trips, no illegal firecrackers, not even a birthday card. If anything, he was a rumor—an expensive ghost who showed up at Thanksgiving in a suit, smiled like a TV anchor, and left without ever eating pie. When he walked into a room, you felt the temperature change, like the A/C kicked on too high or the windows snapped shut.

He never ruffled my hair. Never called me by a nickname, not even the "Cass" that everyone else used as shorthand. He'd set his leather briefcase on the kitchen counter, and the smell of it—expensive, foreign—would snake into the roast turkey and masking-tape school projects, making everything less real and more like a stage set.

My father always stood when Alfred entered. I noticed this even when I was eight. Dad never stood for anyone. If he was at the table, he stayed there, unless Alfred showed up—then he'd push back his chair, roll his shoulders, and put himself between my mother and the entryway. He never met Alfred's eyes when he did this, but I could see his jaw working, grinding up something hard and bitter.

My mother would immediately start cleaning. She'd rinse dishes that were already clean, reset the napkins, wipe crumbs from the counter with perfect precision. Sometimes, she'd make eye contact with me, and there would be a kind of warning in it, a "don't make this worse" broadcast that hummed louder than the fridge. I learned young that the best way to survive a visit from Alfred was to leave as little evidence as possible that you'd ever been in the house.

If he spoke to me, it was to correct something. My posture, my math homework, the way I held a fork. He'd say, "Discipline is a habit," and my mother would say, "She's a good student, Al," but his eyes never left me. As if he could see every flaw in my wiring and wanted to tally them, like a forensic accountant doing a silent audit.

Once, he tried to teach me chess. Not in a fun, "let's play a game" way, but as a tactical exercise. He didn't let me move my own pieces—he directed my hands, forced me to replay the same opening a dozen times until I "got it." When I finally made a move he liked, he smiled, but it felt less like approval and more like he'd just confirmed a hypothesis about my limitations.

Afterward, I told my father I never wanted to play chess again. He didn't try to talk me out of it.

Even now, as an adult, my entire career as a private investigator feels like an elaborate attempt to unlearn the rules of Alfred's game.

I drink the coffee, cold and bitter, and watch the clouded glass of my apartment window. The news has already forgotten Alfred Maddox; the mayor's story has eclipsed everything. But the shape of his presence lingers in every conversation with my parents, every old family photo where he stands apart from us, hands tucked into his pockets, smile razor-sharp.

The apartment is still. Rafi has gone home, promising to call, and I know he will. But there's something I need to finish before I let anyone else in.

I walk to the corkboard where I mapped out the entire case: red string, yellow post-its, printouts of emails in nine-point font. I thought when I finished the investigation, I'd get closure. Instead, all that remains is the string doesn't end—it just loops back to where it started. Me, in a room, searching for an answer nobody wants to hear.

My uncle's legacy isn't a wound. It's a shadow. A low-frequency pressure that follows me from case to case, from sleepless night to sleepless night. And I've spent my whole life trying to prove that I can step out of it, that I can define myself in terms other than what he left behind.

I step back, taking in the corkboard, and pull out the first pin—top left, the origin of it all. The string goes slack, then I pull the next, and the next, until every lead, every question, every chain of evidence lies limp on the floor.

I remember what my father said after the verdict: "Sometimes, the only thing left to do is sweep up and move on."

My mother still sets an extra place at Thanksgiving. Alfred will never sit at her table again.

I gather the string in my hands. It's softer than I expect, almost warm.

I drop it in the trash.

When I return to the table, I slide the manila folder into a drawer and wipe the surface clean.

I stare out the window at a city that has never quite belonged to me, but now sits a fraction closer. The phone rings. I answer it on the first try.

"I'm downstairs," Rafi says. "Ready for Sunday dinner at Julia's house?"

My stomach doesn't clench the way it usually does at the thought of my mother's dining room table. Instead, I smile at my reflection in the glass.

"Be right down," I tell him, and for once, I mean it.

* * *

I recognize the smell of home before I ever see it: rosemary chicken, lemon broth, and the faint ghost of dryer sheets drifting out the open kitchen window, despite the damp March air. For a second, I'm thirteen again, standing outside after track practice, steeling myself for whatever mood waited on the other side of the door. Only this time, Rafi is with me, and he's wearing a shirt with real buttons while panic flickers across his face.

"Relax," I tell him. "My parents aren't going to frisk you."

He grins, but his knuckles are white on the bag of bakery cookies he insisted on bringing. "I'd prefer the frisking. At least I know how to handle that."

Terracotta planters litter the front porch, just as they have since before I could walk. My mother's superstition—plant basil by the steps, and evil spirits stay out.

Sometimes the spirits live inside.

The door opens before we even ring. My mother stands in the frame, apron over a dress I'm certain she bought just for tonight, hair pinned back and eyes bright. She beams at me, then at Rafi, and pulls us both into a hug that is more of a surprise attack than an embrace.

"You're early! I love you. Come in, come in, take your shoes off, the floor's just been cleaned."

She releases us and disappears, her voice trailing into the kitchen like a heat-seeking missile: "Dinner's almost ready, just getting the sauce thickened!"

Rafi tracks her movement down the hall, shoulders squaring without him meaning to. He leans in, lowering his voice. "I've been interrogated by better."

I nudge his arm with my elbow. My fingers catch briefly at his sleeve before I let go. "Don't get cocky," I say. "She likes you. That's the problem."

We step inside. The house is exactly as I left it just a few months ago—photos on the wall in chronological order, piano covered in sheet music I never played, the old sofa that dips in the middle where Dad used to nap after shift before the divorce. Nothing ever changes here, even when everything else has.

Mom has set the table with the good plates, the white porcelain with the silver trim my mother kept in a box labeled "For Best." Each place setting has a folded napkin, a glass of sparkling water, and a handwritten name card. Mine says "Cassie" in blue ink, with a tiny heart dotting the *i*.

I can already tell what kind of night this will be.

My father stands in the living room, as if guarding the space between the kitchen and the front door. He appears older than I remember, hair grayer at the temples. I didn't notice when that happened because I just never stopped long enough to see it, but his posture is pure cop—alert and ready, yet inviting. He waits until I cross the rug before speaking.

"Cass." He nods at me, then at Rafi. "You made it."

Rafi grins. "Figured I should show my face."

Dad pauses, then offers his hand—not the grip he uses at the precinct, but something steadier. "Dylan," he says. "Tonight, we eat first."

Julia pops her head out of the kitchen, apron splattered with something that smells like garlic and heaven. "Everyone to the table, please! Before the rolls go cold!"

We sit. My mother serves first—she always does—heaping plates with chicken, potatoes, and vegetables arranged in little towers. She pours the broth into wide bowls, and the smell floods the room. When she slides the dish in front of me, she squeezes my shoulder, not quite letting go.

"Eat," she orders. "You both look like you haven't seen a vegetable in a year."

I sneak a glance at Rafi, who is already halfway through his first bite and visibly melting. "This is incredible," he says, mouth full.

The meal unfolds in slow layers. My mother tells stories about the bakery—how the new girl botched an order for "Happy Bar Mitzvah, Logan" and wrote it in purple icing on the wrong cake.

My father spears a potato and asks, "Any big cases on the horizon?" His eyes flick up, then back to his plate. It's his way of showing interest without crossing the line—he knows I can't share specifics, and he's careful not to put me in the position of having to refuse him.

He does, however, probe Rafi with what I recognize as a cross-examination, only it's weirdly gentle.

"So, Rafi," he says over the salad course, "any chance my daughter's planning to promote you from tech wizard to partner?"

Rafi's fork freezes halfway to his mouth. His ears redden first, then the flush spreads. "I, uh—that's really up to Cassie."

"That's not what I heard," my father says, and I brace for the punchline. Instead, he adds, "She's lucky to have you."

The words hang for a moment, and my mother jumps in to shatter the awkward. "He is, isn't he? And smart, too. Cassie needs someone to remind her to sleep now and then."

I want to object, to push back, but I let it go.

We talk about nothing for a while—sports, the weather, whether the city will finally fix the potholes on our street. There are gaps in the conversation, but they're not sharp; they're soft, like the quiet between rainstorms.

By the time my mother brings out the lemon pie (homemade, crust perfect), nobody has mentioned Alfred. Not the trial, not the fallout, not the way this family learned to carry something heavy without passing it around.

The silence isn't denial. It's care.

* * *

After dinner, Julia traps Rafi in the kitchen under a pretext—Tupperware logistics, maybe, or some quiet motherly assessment of the boy who's suddenly crossed from familiar to important. The screen door closes behind them, leaving me and my father standing on the back porch, the hush of the evening settling around us like insulation.

The old wooden step still creaks when I shift my weight, even though I've grown into shoes big enough to flatten it. Dad doesn't speak right away; he leans on the railing, watching the sodium lamps click on along the street, the spill of yellow light pooling on cracked concrete. The neighborhood is quiet except for the occasional shudder of a passing car and the distant sound of someone's TV stuck on the news.

"I never liked this porch," Dad says finally. "Always thought it faced the wrong way. Too much of a view."

I almost laugh, because for a man who's spent his life wanting to see trouble before it arrives, it's a strange complaint. But I let him have it.

We stand there in the dark, neither of us meeting the other's eyes.

"You did good, kiddo," he says, voice so low it almost gets lost in the night. "Better than I ever taught you. Better than I could've done."

I wait for the qualifier, the lesson, the "but," but it never comes. It's the first time in my life he's said it that plainly.

For a minute, we say nothing else.

His profile is familiar—the slope of his nose, the way his ears stick out just enough to keep him perpetually alert. He's still fit, but there's a heaviness to him now, like exhaustion has settled into the lines he never used to have to think about. The stubbornness is still there, though. That hasn't gone anywhere.

"Did you know?" I ask, not even sure what I mean. *About Alfred? About me? About how all the stories we grew up on turned out to be just that—stories?*

He sighs, a long exhale that carries more history than air.. "I knew your uncle was into things I wouldn't want in my report. Always suspected. Never thought he'd sink the whole ship just to stay afloat."

His expression droops with regret , but not the self-pitying kind. "I'm sorry you had to be the one to pull the plug. That's not the job I wanted for you."

I shrug. "You raised me to run toward the fire, Dad."

He half-smiles. "Yeah. Guess I did. Didn't think you'd torch the whole building."

I smile, then study my hands. "I was scared. Not just of what I'd find, but of being the one to find it. If it had been anyone else—"

"It was always going to be you," he says. "You're the only one who gets to finish the story."

We watch the street for a while, the rhythm of old houses breathing in and out as lights flick on and off. Somewhere, a dog barks. A neighbor takes out the trash. The world keeps rolling, as if nothing under its surface has changed.

I think of Alfred, how he always stood apart in family photos, how his presence possessed even the air around him. We tried to ignore the rot, and every Christmas and Fourth of July became an exercise in avoidance.

I say, "I don't know if I can do this again. Another case, another—"

He stops me with a hand on my shoulder. It's steady, warm, heavier than I remember.

"We move forward," he says. "Together. And Rafi, if you'll have him."

The words hit differently coming from him. For a second, I want to argue, to push back, but there's nothing left to fight. The old porch, the street, the glow of the kitchen window behind us—it's all the same, and it's all new.

From inside, I hear Julia laugh at something Rafi says. It's a big, brassy sound I haven't heard it in months.

Dad squeezes my shoulder, then lets go. "This isn't the end, Cass. Just the end of his chapter. We've got more work ahead."

He doesn't need me to say it. I already know where that work leads.

We stand together a little longer, saying nothing, letting the night do what it does best—wrap the ugly things in quiet and wait for the morning to burn them off.

Inside, Rafi and Julia wash dishes side by side, voices soft and conspiratorial, their heads bent together over a mountain of soap and silverware.

Dad sits down on the step next to me, the wood groaning but holding. He leans forward, elbows on his knees.

"World's a mess," he says, "but you're making it better."

I want to believe him.

Maybe I do.

When we finally go back inside, the house smells like lemon and comfort. Rafi smiles, just for me, and my mother wipes her hands on a towel before pulling me into a hug that's all bones and strength.

The four of us sit in the kitchen, drinking tea, saying nothing important, but saying it together.

For the first time, I let myself imagine a future that isn't defined by the wreckage of the past. But one that is defined by family, warm and whole.

24

Back to Business

The morning sun slants in sharp and clean, slicing through the blinds of Maddox Investigative Services and painting the conference table with stripes like a prison uniform. I've never been a "bright and early" person—my best hours happen after dark, after the city's lost its edge and nobody expects you to smile—but lately I keep showing up before Rafi, sometimes even before the coffee. Maybe it's because the office is emptier now, the wall where our string-and-pin board once hung conspicuously bare, a ghost rectangle against the fresh coat of paint.

There's a stack of intake folders on the desk, organized in order of urgency and expected payout. I thumb through the top one: a car insurance fraud with surveillance video so grainy you could swap the sedan for a small bear and nobody would notice. Next is a corporate theft, then a missing person with a hand-written sticky note: "Low budget, high drama." We're supposed to do a triage on the new cases before noon, but I've already cracked three files and made a cheat sheet on a yellow legal pad, just to make Rafi's life easier.

The door opens at 8:17. He's in a puffer vest and Henley, hair still wet from a shower, which means he got out of bed twenty minutes ago. He brings with him the smell of gas station cinnamon rolls and a blast of March air so cold my hands go white on the file folder.

"Morning, boss," he says, dropping his messenger bag and heading straight for the Keurig. "You see the inbox? We're celebrities. Channel

8 wants to do a follow-up."

"If they bring doughnuts, maybe I'll talk," I say, not looking up from the intake. "Otherwise, we bill our standard rate for media engagement."

He laughs, but it's only half a joke. After the trial, the city decided I was a kind of local heroine, at least for the two news cycles it took for the story to be replaced by a dog rescue and a scandal about the mayor's yacht. I'm not proud of the attention, but I'd be lying if I said I didn't like the sound of my name when it's spoken with respect.

Rafi sits, cracks open his laptop, and gets to work on the digital forensics for a case so routine I could solve it with my eyes shut. He still makes it look fun: fingers flying over the keyboard, a running commentary on the idiocy of the password "1234" and the predictable sequence of most employee logins. He finds the first breach before I finish my second cup of coffee.

"You know, after the Scott-Calder case, all this seems so... tame," he says, spinning the monitor toward me. "The worst thing about this guy is his taste in wallpaper."

I squint at the desktop background: a pyramid of cats in pirate hats, all cross-eyed. "I'm actually impressed. Takes a certain kind of chaos to pick that image on purpose."

"Nothing says 'I'm not embezzling' like a JPEG called 'MeowtyCrew.jpg'."

We work in companionable silence for a while, the kind that comes from surviving something together. Outside, the city is waking up: garbage trucks reversing, the shriek of a bus's air brakes, a delivery van double-parked in front of the dry cleaner. I can see our reflection in the window—the shape of Rafi's hunched shoulders, the flash of his grin when he cracks a new password, the way I keep tapping my pen even though I've already written all the notes I need.

At 9:02, the intercom buzzes. Our first client of the day: a couple in their fifties, both dressed as if they're headed for a regional airport after a convention, hands clutching the same battered accordion folder. I recognize the woman's shoes before I recognize her face—pointed flats with a gold bow, the kind that only show up in mall stores or the "big and tall" catalogue pages.

I rise and open the door, doing my best imitation of professional courtesy. "Good morning, I'm Cassandra Maddox. This is my associate, Rafi Alvi."

The woman smiles, a thin line. "Glad to meet you. We're the Duncans. We spoke with you last week about our claim?"

"We have all your records," I say, gesturing them to the table. "Please, have a seat."

They do, arranging themselves with the precision of people who have spent most of their marriage balancing the same invisible checkbook. The man hands over their folder, then folds his hands tight in his lap, knuckles pale.

"We just want to get this over with," the woman says, already bracing for bad news.

I run through the summary: their car was stolen. The insurance company denied the payout because of "evidence of owner negligence," which is code for "we don't believe you, prove it." Rafi brings up the spreadsheet he made of all similar cases in the past year, and I walk the Duncans through how the company's claims department uses software to flag likely frauds. The entire time, the man barely speaks, except to grunt in agreement or clarify the color of the missing Honda.

It's over in twenty minutes. We tell them exactly what to expect, exactly what it will cost, and exactly how long it will take. The woman seems relieved. The man stands and offers his hand, his grip weak with defeat.

Outside the office, as the Duncans leave, huddling under the same tiny umbrella, their heads bowed against the wind. A twinge hits—sympathy, maybe, or just the echo of all the times my own parents did the same thing, side by side but never together.

When I turn back, Rafi is watching me. His expression doesn't soften, doesn't harden—but he doesn't look away either. He holds my gaze like he's already taken stock and decided to stay.

"They noticed," he says. "That you didn't treat them like a case number."

I shrug, not sure how to accept the compliment. "I'm getting better at the people part."

He nods, then gathers the intake forms, arranging them in a stack with meticulous care. When he reaches for the next file, our hands brush—skin on skin, a shock of warmth in the cold office.

Neither of us pulls away right away.

The moment hangs between us, charged with the promise of something I don't have the language for. My heart skips, then resets. It's not like a movie. There's no swelling music, no sudden realization. Just the weight of what we've been through together, and the possibility that maybe, this time, I'm allowed to let something good happen.

Then my phone buzzes, shattering the spell.

Lila, of course: "Dinner at home? I'm picking up breadsticks. No excuses, Cass."

I show the text to Rafi, and he grins, the tension dissolving into laughter.

"Guess you're booked," he says, but his eyes linger on mine.

"I'll save you a breadstick," I say, and I mean it.

We get back to work. There are calls to make, statements to follow up, and another client at 11. The morning passes in a blur, but the warmth from that brief touch lingers long after.

By noon, the sun is higher, the city is louder, and the world outside seems less sharp than it did before. I take a breath and let it fill my lungs. For the first time, I'm not chasing something just out of reach. I'm here, in the moment, with people who matter.

Maybe "boring" is normal. Maybe it's happiness, too.

25

The People Who Stay

I forget how much I miss the smell of a real kitchen until I'm standing in ours, apron over jeans, both hands wrist-deep in ricotta and basil, and the entire apartment filled with a garlic-fog that should be bottled and sold as an antidepressant. The oven's ancient and the fridge groans when you open it too fast, but for the first time since the start of the trial, the place is alive instead of like a crime scene waiting for a cleanup crew.

I've had my mother's lasagna recipe folded in my wallet since high school, back when she wrote it on a grocery receipt and made me promise not to substitute "grocery store cardboard" for the "good cheese." I'm using the real stuff tonight, and not just because Lila deserves it—though she does, probably more than anyone in Lenape. Mostly, it's because I'm terrified to have an actual conversation with my best friend and need the muscle memory of kitchen work to keep my hands from shaking.

Lila texts at 6:04: "Leaving in five. Should I bring wine, or did you already drink the entire city's supply?"

I text back: "Surprise me. And no pinot. Please."

Her typing bubbles go for a few seconds, then she sends: "You only say please when you're up to something. Don't poison me."

I laugh, set my phone down, and return to layering the noodles with a focus I usually reserve for red-lining an affidavit. By the time the door rattles open, the kitchen is a disaster—tomato stains on the counter, three wooden spoons in the sink, and half a baguette missing because I got hungry during the forty-minute bake. The table's set, though. I even found candles and set them out in a careful line.

Lila's boots thud against the entryway wall as she kicks them off. She's talking to herself, words clipped and rhythmic, like she's running through her day in bullet points. When she rounds the corner, she stops, puts her bag down, and sniffs the air.

"It's either lasagna," she says, nodding at the baking dish, "or you murdered the tomato guy from the farmers' market."

"Check the fridge," I say. "He's in there with the wine."

She does, and comes back with two bottles—one from her bag, one from the fridge. She weighs them for half a second, then sets my bottle on the counter and tucks hers into the refrigerator. Her eyes flick to me, amused approval with a raised eyebrow, before she digs through the junk drawer for the opener.

"Want to talk about your day?" she asks, voice casual.

I shake my head. "Only if you want to hear about the world's most boring insurance scam."

She grins. "Honestly, yes. After my shift, I'd take a five-hour story about someone switching their health plan just to score free acupuncture."

I ladle out salad, plate the lasagna, and try not to overthink the next ninety minutes. We sit at the table, clink glasses, and start with gossip: office drama, Rafi's latest theory about our building's unreliable Wi-Fi, the parade of weirdo clients who have called this week convinced their neighbor is spying on them via Amazon delivery. I keep the banter moving, hoping the comfort will settle in like a weighted blanket.

Lila doesn't let it. After her second glass, she leans in, elbows on the table, and says, "You know this isn't normal, right?"

"Lasagna?" I ask.

She rolls her eyes. "You, making dinner. You, not buried in a case file or three cups of gas-station coffee. You, not pretending everything is fine."

I'm quiet. The only sound is the tick of the oven cooling down, and outside, the faint buzz of streetlights.

She takes a breath, then says it: "I was scared, Cass. Like, actually scared. You were getting—" She circles her finger in the air, searching for the right word. "Dark. You didn't let anyone in. Not even me."

I push a strand of cheese back onto my plate, studying it like it requires analysis. "I know. I did that on purpose."

She waits, not letting me off the hook.

"I thought I was protecting you," I say. "Or at least protecting myself from making things worse."

"Did you ever think I wanted to be there for you? That's what friends do. Family, too."

The word lands harder than I expect. I haven't thought of us as family for a long time, not since I started seeing Lila as collateral damage in my ongoing crusade against everything broken in Lenape City.

She continues, softer this time. "You always say you don't care what people think, but you care a lot. Especially about what I think. So when you go off the grid, it makes me wonder if you're trying to fix something I can't help with—or if you're just scared to let me see how bad it is."

"I was scared," I admit. "But not of you. Of what I'd find. Of what it would do to us."

She leans back, crossing her arms. "So, what now?"

"I guess... I try to fix it," I say. "Starting with this lasagna."

It's a weak joke, but she laughs anyway. She always does.

We eat in silence for a bit, the tension winding down. I pour more wine, and when I reach for the bottle, my hand shakes. Lila notices, but instead of saying anything, she pours for me, filling my glass to the brim.

She raises hers. "To family," she says. "The kind you choose."

"And the kind that drives you nuts," I add.

We clink. The sound is small, but it breaks through the last layer of awkward.

After dinner, we leave the plates for tomorrow and sprawl on the sofa, feet tangled together, watching a reality show so bad it might actually be brilliant. Lila falls asleep first, her head on my shoulder, and I let myself drift, too. For the first time in months, I don't dream about evidence folders or courtrooms or the sound of a judge reading out a verdict.

I just dream of this: warmth, comfort, the smell of garlic in the air, and the simple, unremarkable fact of not being alone.

When I wake, it's nearly midnight. I cover Lila with a throw blanket and clean up the kitchen in the quiet. The apartment is dark, but isn't empty.

Before I go to bed, I text Rafi: "She forgave me. More or less."

He replies, "Of course she did. You're not that hard to love, you know."

I stare at the screen, a smile creeping in despite myself.

I turn off the lights and let the silence settle. There's nothing left to say.

Tomorrow is another day, but for once, I'm not afraid of what it brings.

* * *

The next day, at exactly 12:02 p.m., I walk into Slice's and find the Four Musketeers crammed into their usual corner booth, surrounded by a half-dozen empty soda cups and three pizza boxes in varying stages of disintegration. The restaurant is pure chaos: middle-schoolers on the loose, parents corralling toddlers, the flat-screen above the soda fountain blaring a muted rerun of some dating show. It's everything I used to hate about public eating, but today, it's background noise. Today, I'm just glad to be here.

Nate spots me first. He does a finger-gun salute and slides over to make room, his broad shoulders making the move clumsier than intended, nearly knocking Janice's Coke into her lap. "Cassie! You made it," he shouts over the din. "We thought you'd bail for, like, work or something."

I slide in next to Alissa, who immediately plops a napkin in my lap and gestures at the half-eaten pizza. "We saved you a slice. Don't say we never did anything for you."

Janice leans in, eyes wide and conspiratorial. "You missed the big announcement. Mel's not going to Penamore after all."

Mel straightens, blonde hair pulled back, expression easing into a rare smile. "Thank God for that," she says, reaching for a breadstick. "Turns out, I can go anywhere as long as I keep my grades and avoid criminal charges. Thanks for the rec letter, by the way."

"Anytime," I say. "You're not the only one who hates Penamore."

Marcus, who's spent the first five minutes pushing olives off his slice with surgical precision, glances up. "She got into Oberlin. Full ride."

There's a chorus of mock applause. Alissa pretends to cry. "Now you're going to be too cool for us."

Mel elbows her. "I was already too cool for you, Al."

It goes like that for a while—banter, inside jokes, and a surprising lack of trauma for a group of teens who were, until last month, tangled up in a high-profile city corruption case. Maybe they process faster than adults. Or maybe, after all they've been through, nothing can phase them.

I eat my slice and watch them. For all the ways I tried to keep my distance, they found their way under my skin: Marcus with his methodical calm, Alissa's zero-tolerance for bullshit, Janice's flair for drama, Nate's goofball optimism, and Mel's ability to play every room like it's her home turf. They're a weird family, the kind you build when the real one's not enough.

"Okay," Janice says, raising her voice over the clatter of a dropped tray. "Now that we're all here, what's next? Do we finally tell Cassie about the time Nate spray-painted 'DECAF FOR LIFE' on the principal's car?"

Nate blushes, which is impressive given his skin tone. "It was a social protest. And I got caught, so it doesn't even count as a crime."

"You're all going to jail," I say, deadpan.

Alissa snorts. "Not unless you're the one testifying."

"Never," I promise.

We run through the group's future plans, or at least the early outlines of them. Marcus is talking about computer science at Rutgers; Alissa's circling pre-law at Penn State; Janice has her eye on a journalism scholarship and keeps half-joking about staging her first campus coup someday. Nate mentions he's considering a summer internship with the LCPD, something in digital forensics—pulling data apart, rebuilding timelines. He says it like it's no big deal. They talk about it all with the nonchalance of people who've just survived a tornado and are still counting the shingles on the roof.

At some point, Mel turns to me, serious for the first time. "Do you ever miss it? Being our age?"

"Not a single day," I say, and it's the truth.

She smiles, satisfied, then returns to the pizza.

The conversation turns, as it always does, to what comes next. Not in the "what are you going to do with your life" sense, but in the literal: Where do we go after Slice's? Is there gelato left at Cafe Stella? Should we hit up the thrift store for "retro blazers" and see if the lady at the counter will let them try on the hats again?

I let them argue about it, a weirdly affectionate chaperone. When the last slice disappears and we pay the check (Nate foots it, a rare gesture that nearly makes Janice cry), I gather my things. But Janice stops me with a hand on my wrist.

"You know, we could totally solve another case together sometime," she says, half-joking, half-daring me.

I shake my head. "I've had enough excitement for a while."

"Liar," says Alissa.

I smile because she's right. I'll always say yes if they need me.

The others file out, chasing Mel to the parking lot where she's already started the engine on her borrowed Subaru. Marcus lingers behind. He fidgets with the sleeve of his hoodie, then lifts his head, jaw set.

"Thanks for everything, Cassie," he says. "You showed us that doing the right thing matters. Even when it costs you."

I want to say something profound, but all I can manage is, "You did most of it yourself, Marcus."

He shrugs, a little embarrassed. "Maybe. But I wouldn't have tried if you hadn't made it seem possible."

He heads out after the others, and they pile into the jeep, laughing and shoving, the way kids do when the world hasn't beaten it out of them yet.

For the first time, it holds—not just the release after a long fight, but something deeper. The kind that settles in the bones and doesn't shake loose, no matter what comes next.

I leave Slice's a little lighter than when I walked in, and a lot hungrier for whatever comes after.

<h1 style="text-align:center">26</h1>

Proof Enough

There's nothing romantic about the Lenape City Police Precinct. The main entrance is all bulletproof glass and busted tile, but it's the side door that tells the real story. There's a back porch, poured concrete gone uneven with time, a metal railing scarred by generations of nervous palms. The steps are studded with gum wads and cigarette burns— two decades' worth of bored officers ignoring the "No Smoking" signs. When I show up at shift change, my father is exactly where I expect him: slouched on the second step, coffee cup in one hand, phone in the other, eyes somewhere far past the edges of the lot.

He stays bent over the file as I approach, but I know he clocks my footsteps anyway. He's always had a sixth sense for movement, probably from years of waiting for it to go wrong.

I ease onto the step above him, the way I did as a kid when I didn't want to block his line of sight. He sips his coffee, says nothing.

It's cold, but not the cold that makes you rush. It's the cold that sharpens the air and makes every sound travel. A garbage truck reverses two blocks over; a city bus gasps at a red light.

We sit like that for a minute, maybe more.

Finally, I say, "You know you can smoke out here. Nobody's going to rat you out."

He snorts, but the smile is real. "Quit three years ago. Coffee's my last vice."

"Liar."

"Yeah," he admits. "You caught me."

I pick at the peeling paint on the railing. "I'm not here to fight, Dad. I just want to talk."

"About Alfred?"

"About you and me. But yeah, Alfred too."

He sets the cup down, turning it between his palms. "Say what you need to, Cass."

"I don't need your approval anymore," I say, and my voice doesn't even shake. "Just your honesty. About what you knew. About why you never stopped him."

He's silent for a long time. I expect him to dodge, but instead he sighs and leans forward, elbows on his knees.

"I always knew your uncle cut corners. Everyone did. That's how he got ahead. But I never thought he'd go full-on criminal. I figured he'd get his hands dirty, take the shortcuts, then get out before he drowned." His gaze drops to his hands. "I was wrong."

"You enabled him," I say. "You let him be family first."

He nods, slow. "I did. And I pushed you away when you started asking the right questions. Because it scared the hell out of me to think you'd go down the same road. Or that you'd end up on the other side of it."

I let the words sink in. It's not an apology, exactly, but it's closer than we've ever come.

"I'm not him, Dad," I say.

He glances up, and there's a kind of sadness in his eyes I haven't seen before. "No," he says. "You're not."

He meets my gaze again, and this time it's different—respect, maybe even pride.

"You're better than both of us. You've got his determination but none of his greed. My stubbornness but none of my blindness. And you've got something neither of us ever had—the courage to stand alone when it matters."

We sit there, the cold working its way through the denim and into my bones.

It's not comfortable, but it's honest.

After a while, I ask, "What happens now?"

He shrugs, the gesture pure Maddox. "We keep working. We try not to repeat the same mistakes. We do better."

I can live with that.

He stands, stretches his back, then turns to me with a half-smile. "Want to grab a burger? I know you skipped lunch."

I shake my head. "I'm good. I just wanted to clear the air."

He hesitates, then sticks out his hand like we're sealing a deal. I take it, and he pulls me in for a quick, awkward hug. It lasts less than a second. The echo doesn't.

"You're a damn good investigator, Cassie," he says, voice gruff. "Better than I was at your age."

"Low bar," I shoot back, and he laughs.

I head out, leaving him on the step, staring out at the city. The air lighter, the day a little less heavy.

When I hit the sidewalk, I'm not carrying any of the old weight. Not today.

Maybe not ever again.

* * *

After dark, the office is a different animal—quieter, the city's white noise filtered down to a gentle hum through the cinderblock walls. The new cleaning crew leaves at six, which means I have two hours alone, just me and the glow of the monitor and the faint tang of Pine-Sol.

I stand in front of the wall where my investigation board used to be, hands in my pockets. The fresh paint is still clean, no thumbtack scars or masking tape ghosts. In its place, I've hung a single framed photo: me, Lila, Rafi, and the teens, snapped outside Slice's the day after the verdict. We're all elbows and inside jokes, but there's something in the way our shoulders are touching—a kind of accidental family portrait.

I trace the edge of the frame with my finger. For years, I thought the work was the only thing that made me worth something. That if I solved enough cases, if I stacked enough evidence, I'd outrun the past. But now, with nothing left to pin to the wall, it's clear I was just chasing proof that I belonged somewhere.

The photo is proof enough.

Behind me, the elevator dings. Rafi appears in the doorway, messenger bag slung over one shoulder, hair damp from a post-gym shower. He sees me by the wall and grins.

"Staring contest with the paint again?" he asks.

"Lost," I say. "It's got a killer poker face."

He shrugs, zips his jacket. "Dinner?"

I don't move right away. There's one last thing to do.

I grab my coat and flick off the light, the office fading to blue in the dark. The last thing visible is the photo on the wall—team, family, whatever you want to call it. It's all the same.

We walk out together. In the elevator, Rafi's fingers brush against mine, tentative at first, then deliberate. His palm is warm against my cold skin as our fingers interlock.

The night air hits crisp and new.

27

What We Keep

It's been two weeks since my mother's lemon pie and the first time Rafi and I sat at the Maddox table pretending we weren't a couple.

Long enough for the polite smiles to stop being placeholders. Long enough for the tight knots in my chest to loosen.

Long enough for me to believe I can do something as ordinary as cook a real dinner—not a rushed bowl of pasta, not takeout eaten over case files, but something that requires planning, multiple ingredients, and a recipe I've never attempted before.

The surprise isn't that I want to do this.

It's that I'm not trying to earn forgiveness.

At 5:17 p.m., I'm standing in our kitchen with a mountain of cremini mushrooms and a pack of chicken thighs that still smell faintly of the grocery store, rereading an online recipe like it might betray me if I don't keep an eye on it.

Chicken Marsala. Garlic mashed potatoes. Lila's favorite—provided the potatoes have real butter and the chicken isn't dry. I hover over the stove top like a detective waiting on a wiretap, refusing to leave even when the oven timer insists I check the rolls. The counter is chaos—flour dusted everywhere, three cutting boards in play, a damp hand towel doing triage on my mistakes. Lila's "good mood" playlist hums through the apartment: eighties power ballads, Sondheim, something embarrassingly earnest drifting into the living room.

I glance up, checking the other half of the plan.

The investigation board is gone. Not covered. Not relocated. Gone. No tape ghosts. No thumbtack scars.

In its place is a line of photos in cheap black frames I bought at the grocery store while grabbing mushrooms and Marsala wine. Four years' worth of us — graduations, bad haircuts, road trips, sunburns, half-caught laughter. In two photos, Lila's flipping off the camera. In one, I'm giving her a piggyback ride across a muddy field, both of us mid-howl.

It was supposed to be ironic. A joke. A parody of the suburban memory wall.

As I straighten the frames for the fourth time, honesty is all that's left.

The pan sizzles. I flip the chicken and splatter sauce on my wrist. It stings, but I don't swear. Not because I'm trying to keep the mood light — just because I'm intentionally not breaking anything tonight. The potatoes are done, and I stare at them longer than necessary. The recipe says whip until smooth. Lila prefers lumps. Visible skin. Evidence of effort.

Love, I decide, probably tolerates a few imperfections.

By the time I set the table — mismatched plates, a candle I found under the sink that smells faintly of pine — my shirt smells like chicken and my sleeve is dusted with flour. I wipe the counter again, then stop myself. It doesn't need to be perfect. It just needs to be real.

At 6:01, the lock clicks.

"Cassie?" Lila calls. "It smells like an Olive Garden in here. Should I be suspicious?"

She rounds the corner and stops.

Her eyes move from the table to the wall to me. She's in black jeans and boots, a striped shirt she stole from my closet last fall. Her hair is still damp at the ends from a rushed shower. Eyeliner perfect — meaning she had a meeting that mattered.

She blinks. "Okay," she says. "What did you do?"

"Cooked," I say. "On purpose."

She approaches the table like it might be a trap, inspecting the fork for wires. "Is this... chicken Marsala?"

"With extra garlic. And real butter."

Her mouth curves. Her gaze drifts to the wall, then returns to me. Tension slips loose from her shoulders.

"This is either a date," she says, "or you're trying to distract me from something."

"Could be both," I say. "But mostly I just wanted dinner."

She studies me for a beat, then steps in and hugs me. Tight. Familiar. Vanilla lotion and rain. She lets go before it gets weird.

"I like dinner," she says.

We sit.

The food is good. Not perfect—but good. The sauce is rich. The potatoes are exactly right. Lila goes back for seconds, and a ridiculous, quiet pride settles in my chest.

Billy Joel plays in the background; the apartment less like a staging ground and more like home.

"You know," she says, pointing her fork at the wall, "you're in more of those photos than I am."

"Composition," I say. "Otherwise it looks like I'm obsessed with you."

She laughs. "You are."

"Fair."

After we eat, we clean up together, bumping elbows and arguing about who left the water running. Lila steals a bite of cold chicken, pretends it's awful, eats the rest anyway.

She lingers by the photos afterward, taking her time this pass. Stops at our graduation picture. Her arm slung around my shoulders. Both of us laughing at something I can't remember.

"Thanks for this," she says. "I didn't know I needed it."

"Neither did I," I admit.

We end up on the couch, city lights flickering through the window, the playlist looping back to the start. She leans her head on my shoulder. I let her. The silence earned.

The next night, she suggests wine.

"Let's toast to not being total train wrecks," she says, already grabbing glasses.

She disappears into her room and comes back with a blanket and an old photo album, the kind with peeling corners and pages that stick.

We take it out to the balcony. Five feet of concrete. Plastic chairs. The auto-body shop across the street glowing amber. March air brushes against us, warm enough to stay.

We flip through the album slowly. High school. College. Bad costumes. Worse decisions.

Halfway through, she goes quiet.

"I have news," she says.

I don't brace. I just meet her eyes.

"Peterson Group wants to promote me. Senior accounts." She exhales. "Boston."

"That's huge," I say. "I'm proud of you."

Her gaze lingers, searching. "You're not mad?"

"No," I say. "I'm... glad you told me."

She lets out a breath. "I was worried."

"I know," I say. "But we're not fragile."

She smiles, soft and relieved. "That's growth."

"I'm still annoying," I say. "Just less dramatic about it."

We toast. Plastic cups. Hollow sound. Hopeful.

"Promise we'll still do Sunday dinner?" she asks.

"I'll drive to Boston if I have to," I say. "We'll make it work."

She nods, satisfied.

At midnight, she insists on one last photo. "For the wall."

We lean in, pull faces, laugh mid-snap. She sends it to me before we go to bed.

Two girls. Older. Messy. Still us.

Underneath, she types: *Don't forget. Not ever.*

I don't.

The future is still coming fast and uneven.

But I'm staying.

I'm choosing.

I'm letting the people I love walk beside me—even when the road bends.

And tonight, that's enough.

28

The Shape of the Work Ahead

My office has the forced calm of someone fresh out of rehab and determined to keep it together this time. Everything is clean, every binder standing upright, the file folders lined up on my desk in a color-coordinated fan. I come in early—earlier than usual, because I have an uneasy relationship with the idea of free time—and for five whole minutes I don't check my phone or open my email. I just breathe the quiet, let the morning sunlight do its work. The light bounces off the sidewalk and through the big plate window, etching pale lines onto the faux wood of my desktop.

The wall to my right used to be a fever dream of string, sticky notes, and thumbtacks. Now it's blank, freshly painted, and the only thing left is a single framed photo: me, Rafi, Lila, and the four teenagers who, depending on your source, either saved the city or almost destroyed it. Mel has her arm around Janice, both of them flashing double peace signs. Nate is in the background, mid-sneeze, and Marcus is squinting like the sun owes him an apology. Rafi's got his eyes closed, as usual, and I'm dead center, hunched forward with a half-smile, caught in the act of explaining something to no one in particular. I never meant to hang the photo. Lila put it there after the verdict, and it's the only thing that stuck.

I take the folders from my inbox and arrange them by case type, for the sake

217

of control. Insurance fraud. Corporate embezzlement. Pet custody dispute.

I like the smallness of it—the way every problem has a perimeter, a known number of moving parts.

It's almost possible to forget that three weeks ago my world was a minefield and my own last name was trending on X.

When I open my laptop, the homepage loads to the Lenape City Chronicle, because I am a masochist and because I need to know what's coming before it hits my phone. The headline is in sixty-point type: "PRIVATE EYE, PUBLIC GOOD—THE WOMAN WHO SHUT DOWN LENAPE'S OLDEST SECRET." Subtle. The byline is a junior reporter I've never met. They must have called Rafi or Lila for quotes, because the pull-quote halfway down the article says, "She's the PI who brought down a dynasty—without seeking the spotlight."

The article is pure flattery, probably run through an AI to scrub out the facts. It retells the story of my uncle's downfall in neat paragraphs, skipping the nights spent panicking in my car and the months I spent piecing together bank records with a magnifying glass. They make me sound like a cross between Sherlock Holmes and Erin Brockovich. The truth is, I just noticed the lies that were a little too loud to be accidental.

I scroll until I find the paragraph about the "aftermath"—the city's scramble to rebuild after Mayor Scott-Calder went down with half the old guard. There's a line about "civic healing," another about how the youth of Lenape can look to a brighter, cleaner future. No mention of the sleepless weeks or the gut-clenching worry that someone, somewhere, is already starting over with a new scheme and a better digital trail.

Halfway through the article, my phone buzzes—a number I don't recognize, but with a "City of Lenape" caller ID. I let it ring out. Five seconds later, I get a voicemail notification.

I don't want to listen, but I do.

"Ms. Maddox," says the voice, tight and well-practiced. "I'm calling on behalf of the mayor's transition team to thank you for your diligence and discretion in recent city business. Please know that your efforts to protect the students named in the admissions review have not gone unnoticed, and the city is grateful for your... stewardship. If you ever need anything—" The voice tapers off, as if embarrassed to offer anything tangible. "Thank you, and good luck in your future endeavors."

I put my phone face down and let the quiet fill up again. The sunlight's shifted, picking out dust motes floating in the air like tiny, indifferent spies.

There's something in my chest I haven't cataloged yet. Not relief. Not victory. Maybe just the absence of dread.

The photo on the wall—arms, faces, hope—sits where it always has.

I don't linger. I straighten my shoulders, close the *Chronicle* tab, and open the first real case file of the day: a missing poodle and a neighbor feud old enough to have its own lawyer.

I fill out the intake forms, one at a time, careful and methodical. I line up the paperclips and tap the edges until they're even. The city outside my window is waking up, and for the first time since all this began, I don't have to chase it.

I just have to keep going.

* * *

At exactly 8:41, a second key scratches at the lock. Rafi enters with a cardboard tray of coffees and a bakery bag clamped in his teeth. He nods in greeting, kicking the door closed with his heel before setting the coffee down on the intake desk.

"You already started?" he says. "What happened to 'never before nine'?"

"I was bored," I say. "And you're late."

He glances at the wall clock, shakes his head. "It's only late if you're measuring time in human units, not in 'Cassie increments.'" He pulls out his phone and makes a big show of syncing it with the wall clock, then sets the phone on the desk. "There. Official time. Also, I got your favorite." He pushes a tall cup toward me, the sleeve covered in hearts and a cartoon of a detective's hat.

I take the cup and breathe in the caffeine. "Thanks, but you didn't have to.

It's not even a case day."

He raises an eyebrow. "Every day is a case day here."

He opens the bakery bag, removes two croissants, and divides them neatly on a napkin. He handles the food with precision, as if he's afraid of breaking something delicate. He hands me one, then wipes his fingers on the napkin before logging in at the workstation beside me.

For a while, we don't talk. The office is warm, the hum of the old radiators and the clatter of keyboards the only music. We work through the backlog, alternating between printouts and email, clearing out a week's worth of cold calls and "can you find my ex?" requests.

I slide the next folder across, the edges sharp and new. He picks it up, eyes scanning the header.

"Divorce asset search," he says. "These are getting more common."

"They're safe," I say. "Low exposure."

He gives me a sidelong glance. "You're still in self-care mode, huh?"

I shrug, biting into my croissant. "I don't mind. I like it when the worst thing I have to do is track down a hidden bank account."

"You know, most people would have taken a vacation after what you pulled," he says, keeping his voice low. "Or at least pretended to take one, so their partner would stop worrying."

I glance at him. "You're worrying enough for two people," I say. "I don't need to give you more material."

The corner of his mouth lifts—not quite a smile, but something close. He doesn't argue. Just nods once, like he's filing the answer away.

"You don't have to save the whole city in one go," he says instead. "It's okay to take the easy jobs for a while."

I want to argue, but he's not wrong. My left wrist still aches if I type too long, and some nights I wake up convinced someone is trying to burn down the building. I've gotten good at hiding it—better than I was at hiding anything else—but I'm not about to fool Rafi.

"I'll go on vacation," I say, "when you do."

He smiles then—not the smirky one, but real and effortless. "Deal. But it has to be somewhere without Wi-Fi. Or murder."

I picture us on a beach, both of us bored out of our minds. "I'll bring board games."

"Only if you let me win at Scrabble for once."

"Never," I say. He knows it's true.

We cycle through the case files, a rhythm easy as breathing. Sometimes our hands brush as we pass papers, sometimes our knees knock under the table. He's rearranged the digital folder tree exactly how I like it—alphabetized, with color labels for active, pending, and closed cases—but I pretend not to notice. The old version of me would have said something sarcastic, turned it into a joke. Now I just let it be.

After an hour, the office is a mess of empty cups, half-eaten pastry, and case files stacked like playing cards in a losing game of Solitaire. I stretch my arms overhead and the muscles in my back pop, one by one.

Rafi closes his laptop. "You want to take a walk?" he asks. "Fresh air, minimal risk. We can pick up lunch or just people-watch."

I consider it. "In a minute. I have to finish this."

He's always been like that—never in a hurry, never careless. Maybe that's why we work so well together. Or maybe it's because neither of us is afraid of silence.

When he returns, I've already forgotten what I was doing. The city outside the window is waking up fast: foot traffic on the sidewalk, a cop car idling at the intersection, the rumble of a bus as it lumbers past the coffee shop. There's a weird comfort in knowing it's all still there, unbroken.

Rafi drops into the chair across from me. "You finished your croissant," he says, mock surprise.

"I'm a growing girl," I say.

He laughs. "You want to look at the Duncan file? The insurance rep's been calling every hour, says the claim is urgent."

I pass him the folder, and our fingers brush, just for a second. I don't pull away. Neither does he.

He reads the first page, then lifts his head. "You know," he says, quieter now, "I really am proud of you."

The words catch me off guard. I blink and drop my gaze to the mess of papers in front of me. "For eating a croissant?"

"For surviving," he says. "For knowing when to stop pushing. I don't know how you do it."

I want to tell him I don't, not really. That most days I fake it and hope the muscle memory kicks in. But I just nod.

We spend the next hour working in silence, but the atmosphere is different, lighter, as if an important matter had been recognized without explicit mention.

When the phone rings, I pick it up before the third ring. The client is nervous, wants an update on their "situation," but I handle it calmly, typing notes as I listen. When I hang up, Rafi is already waiting with the next case, highlighted and ready for my review.

We move through the day like that, each doing our part, each leaving space for the other. By lunch, the stack of urgent files is gone, replaced by a single to-do list taped to the monitor.

"You know," I say, looking at the list, "maybe we are getting good at this."

He grins, and this time I let myself enjoy it.

We grab our jackets and step outside. The city air is cold and clean, and for the first time in a while, I let myself imagine a future that isn't just damage control.

We walk side by side down the block, and our hands almost touch.

Almost.

29

The Wrong Kind of Thank You

The apartment is in that awkward state between old life and new: half the kitchen cupboards empty, cardboard boxes forming a miniature skyline by the hall closet, and the living room rug rolled up and plastic-wrapped like a body in a procedural. I find Lila perched on a step stool, taping a label onto a box that says **BOSTON—MISC.** in her swirly, Broadway Playbill handwriting. She grins as I drop my bag by the door.

"Hey," she says, voice cheerful but tired. "Dinner in twenty. You're on garlic bread duty."

I salute and head for the kitchen, where the counters are a disaster zone of pots, sauce packets, and measuring cups. A half-chopped bundle of basil wilts beside the sink, surrendering to the steam rolling off a pot of pasta. Lila hums as she moves between stove and pantry, every so often holding something up and calling, "Keep or pack?"

"Keep," I say. I'm not ready for the couch to disappear. Or the *Big* poster that's been above our TV since sophomore year.

She tosses an oven mitt with a coffee stain onto the keep pile and goes back to stirring sauce. "How was work?"

"Low stakes," I say. "Productive."

"Rafi still babying you?"

I glance at her, then at the window, where dusk paints the city in bruised gold and blue. "Not babying. More like... reminding me I don't have to treat recovery like a solo sport."

She hums. "That man is criminally patient."

"He offered to take a vacation," I add, focusing on slicing the bread. "Somewhere without Wi-Fi. Or murder."

Lila stops stirring. Slowly turns. "Excuse me—*what?*"

"Don't get excited. It was theoretical."

She hops off the stool. "Cassie. He offered you a vacation. That is not theoretical. That is a man putting out a flare."

I line the bread slices up like dominoes. Butter. Garlic. Control. "I know."

"And?" she presses.

"And I didn't run," I say. "Which feels... new."

She studies me, then nods once. "Good. Because he's not just your business partner, and he's definitely not me. You don't get to treat him like an optional attachment."

"I'm not," I say, maybe too quickly. "I'm just... getting used to the idea that having a partner doesn't mean losing my footing. Or my identity."

She smiles, softer now. "Welcome to growth. It's annoying."

She goes back to the stove. "Are you sleeping any better?"

"Yeah," I lie.

She snorts. "You're a terrible liar."

I don't argue. I anchor myself in the ritual—sprinkle, arrange, slide the tray into the oven.

"I got the final confirmation today," she says, unloading the dishwasher with her usual surgical precision. "Orientation's the second week of April. Payroll by the first."

"That's fast."

"Fast is good," she says. "Less time to panic."

We move around each other in the kitchen, an old choreography—her to the stove, me to the oven. She brushes my shoulder reaching for the salt, and the contact lands heavier than it should.

"You okay?" she asks.

"Mostly. I keep waiting for the next shoe to drop."

She sets the salt down. "Talk to me."

I exhale. "I know we closed the loop. I know Alfred's accounts are frozen, the Genesee mess is public record, and the Penamore thread went nowhere." I hesitate. "But it bothers me that it went *nowhere*."

Her brow creases. "Because?"

"Because Penamore was clean on paper," I say. "Too clean. The Genesee–Penamore Action Fund checked out. Legal. Boring. And yet somehow kids with no financial footprint were getting scholarships like party favors."

"Alfred said it was donor discretion," she says.

"He said a lot of things," I reply.

Dinner lands between us, steam curling up like a ceasefire, as if nothing ever broke.

"So," Lila says, twirling her fork. "What's next for Lenape's most unwilling celebrity?"

"Insurance case," I say. "Possibly a missing cat."

"Promise me you'll take it easy."

"I promise."

She smirks. "And promise me you won't keep Rafi at arm's length just because it's safer."

I meet her eyes. "I'm trying."

"That's all I want," she says.

At midnight, the apartment is half-empty but not hollow. Lila's already asleep, curled on the bare mattress. I check my email out of habit more than expectation.

At the top of the inbox:

Dean Harold Stratford

Office of the President

Penamore College

That gets my attention.

The message is stiff, ceremonial—gratitude for my "professionalism," thanks for my "care with sensitive student matters." An offer of future assistance.

I sit back.

Penamore College. I know Penamore. I know where they were in Alfred's files—adjacent, insulated, legally pristine. I know Dean Stratford's name because it showed up more than once, always just outside the blast radius.

Nothing actionable. Nothing illegal. Nothing that ever stuck.

Which makes this... strange.

I close the email without replying and stare at the ceiling.

Tomorrow, I'll call my dad.

Tomorrow, I'll ask Rafi what he knows about Stratford.

Tonight, I let the quiet hold.

* * *

The next afternoon, the office is glazed with that honey-colored light that only shows up in the last hour before sunset. The city beyond the window is quieter than usual, a faint haze softening the angles of every building. I finish my last intake call and lean back in the chair, letting the sun stripe my arms and the desk. There's a deliberate stillness to the moment, as if the universe is daring me to disturb it.

The photo hangs on the wall. Dust catches in the light, haloing every head in the frame—Mel and Janice forever mid-joke, Marcus half a smile, Lila bright-eyed and unconstrained. Rafi seems to have wandered into the shot by accident, shirt untucked, grin crooked, as if the camera caught him mid-thought. My face is harder to read, caught between laughter and argument, an expression I've never quite mastered.

I linger a moment too long, then straighten my shoulders and turn away.

On my monitor, the email from Penamore College is still sitting at the top of the inbox. Unread. The subject line glows like a warning light.

I don't open it.

Instead, I pick up my phone and scroll until I find my dad's name. I hesitate just long enough to annoy myself, then hit call.

He answers on the third ring. "Everything okay?"

That's his way—straight to the point, no warm-up.

"I think so," I say. "I just... needed your advice."

There's a pause, the soft clink of something in the background. A mug, maybe. He's home, which helps.

"Trust your instincts," he says without hesitation. "They didn't fail you last time."

"I keep thinking maybe I'm overreacting."

"Careful doesn't mean paranoid," he says. "It just means you don't run headfirst into something you don't understand yet."

I close my eyes. "You think I should let it go?"

"You should tread carefully," he replies. "Keep your friends close. And know this—if you need backup, I'm in your corner. No questions asked."

The words land heavier than he probably intends. "Thanks, Dad."

"Anytime," he says. "Call before you do something reckless."

"I always do."

"That's debatable," he says, and hangs up before I can argue.

I set the phone down and stare at it for a second longer than necessary, then turn back to my desk.

Rafi is at the other workstation, half-lit by the window, reviewing a file with the kind of focus that makes everything else fade. I clear my throat.

"Hey," I say. "Quick question."

He swivels his chair. "Shoot."

"What do we have on Dean Harold Stratford?"

His brow furrows—not confusion, recognition. He leans back, thinking. "Stratford's... polished. MBA from Wharton. PhD in Applied Leadership. Sits on a handful of S-Corp boards—education, finance, a couple nonprofit foundations. Big on entrepreneurship, big on philanthropy."

"That's a lot," I say.

"Impressive resume," he agrees. "Almost aggressively so."

"Did his name ever come up in our investigation—Alfred or Scott-Calder?"

"At the beginning," he says. "Genesee–Penamore Action Fund. But it led to a dead end."

He leans back slightly. "He's the kind of guy who makes sure there's nothing to dig up."

His eyes linger on my face. "Why?"

I hesitate, then decide honesty—with limits—is the right move. "It's probably nothing. Just... a lead."

"A lead," he repeats carefully.

"For now," I add. "I'll fill you in when I have more."

He doesn't push. Just nods once. "Okay. But if it turns into something else, you don't carry it alone."

I meet his eyes. "I know."

The office settles back into quiet. Outside, a police cruiser rolls past with its lights off, the reflection streaking red and blue across the far wall. Somewhere down the block, a couple argues about groceries. The trolley shrieks as it rounds the corner on Spruce. The city is still moving—but it's moving with me.

I glance once more at the Penamore email, then close the inbox. The screen goes blank. I stand, stretching until my spine cracks back into place.

The wall is bare except for the photo and a single yellow post-it—*Trust your instincts*—in my handwriting. I touch the edge of the frame, then let my hand fall to my side.

I don't know what's waiting at Penamore. I don't know if I'll open that email tomorrow, or if I'll spend the rest of the week dodging it like an overdue bill.

But right now, in the quiet gold of late afternoon, I let myself enjoy the stillness.

Outside, the city exhales.

Inside, I do the same.

30

The Call Forward

The sunlight is different in this office now. Not softer—Lenape City mornings don't do soft—but honest, sharp at the edges, filtered through the new white blinds I installed after the trial ended and the world stopped watching. The windows are so clean you can see the little scratches in the glass, the ones that catch light and scatter it in tiny, blinding points across my desk. I like them. They're proof that nothing here is too perfect.

It's been a month since Alfred Maddox was led out of the courthouse in handcuffs, and the city decided, in a fit of collective optimism, that the air was safe to breathe again. I celebrated by painting the office walls and putting up a single framed photo, centered over the now-empty space where my stringboard lived. Lila is in the picture, mouth wide with laughter. Rafi has an arm slung around my shoulders. I'm at the front, squinting at the camera like it owes me money.

The only other décor is a yellow post-it stuck next to the light switch: **Trust your instincts.**

My handwriting. Equal parts mantra and dare.

My coffee is half-empty. My inbox is half-full. I tell myself this is progress.

I've sworn off dangerous cases—for now. I promised Rafi, then Lila, then myself, so it counts three times over. The files on my desk are deliberate, low-calorie: the Duncan insurance dispute, a missing Persian cat, a pizza oven theft that somehow made it to small claims. Work that keeps my brain from rusting without risking another headline.

After thirty minutes of cross-referencing receipts and security footage, I'm drumming my fingers hard enough to make the paperclips dance. I check the clock. The street. My phone. Each time I find nothing, and I keep waiting for the stillness to turn into relief.

It doesn't.

It's more like a waiting room.

The door opens at 8:12.

Rafi walks in with two coffees and a wax-paper bakery bag, the warmth of his arrival immediate and grounding. He's wearing a soft blue shirt, sleeves rolled to the elbow—something I notice without letting myself unpack it. He sets the bag on my desk, pulls out a pastry, and hands it over.

"They ran out of almond," he says. "I got poppy."

"Poppy's fine," I say. "You're early."

He shrugs. "You were typing loud enough to hear from the elevator."

I gesture to the folder. "I might crack the Percy's Pizza Oven mystery."

He sits across from me, amused. "I give it two weeks before you're back on city-wide racketeering."

"Not happening," I say. Too quickly.

He smiles, then lowers his voice. "Or—we could take the day off. Go to the track."

"I can't," I say. "I've got a date with a three-year-old arson report and a lost cat."

He doesn't push. Just opens his laptop and starts working beside me, the rhythm settling into something familiar and easy.

The itch starts anyway. A question. A thread.

At **9:06**, my email dings.

The sound is sharper than usual, or maybe the office is just quiet enough for it to matter. I glance at the screen—and freeze.

Dean Stratford, Office of the President, Penamore College.

I click it open, expecting boilerplate.

Instead, the language is careful. Too careful.

Ms. Maddox,

 I am writing in confidence regarding a matter of great sensitivity...

I don't finish reading before the word *reputation* hooks under my ribs.

The last time someone flattered me like that, I broke into a city archive at two in the morning and slept in my car for three days.

Rafi notices immediately. "What's up?"

I turn the monitor toward him.

He reads it once. Then again. "You know him?"

"Not personally," I say. "But this is the second Penamore message this week. The first was benign. Ethics talk. Student group."

"And this," he says, tapping the screen, "is not that."

"No."

He leans back. "Do you want to respond?"

"I want to understand why he thinks I'm the right call," I say.

He circles behind me, rests a hand on my shoulder—warm, steady. "I can scan for anything breaking."

"I know."

"And before you say it," he adds, "low-stakes. We agreed."

"I'm not walking away," I say. "But I'm not turning this into a crusade."

"A lead," he says.

"Exactly."

He nods.

I reread the email. *Discretion. Absolute confidentiality.*

I don't like either phrase.

Rafi shifts. "Before we go further—about the vacation. If this gets bigger..."

Lila's voice cuts through my head, clear as a bell:

Cassie. He offered you a vacation. That is not theoretical. That is a man putting out a flare.

"No," I say.

He blinks. "No?"

"We're doing it," I say. "Charleston. Two weeks. End of the week after next. No work. No exceptions."

He studies me, genuinely surprised. "You're serious."

"Yes. I want this on the calendar. I want something that doesn't disappear the moment things get complicated."

A beat—then his smile, slow and unguarded.

"Okay," he says. "I'll book it."

"Good," I say. "Before I find an excuse."

The office settles again, quieter somehow. The city moves outside—sirens muted, trolley shrieking at the corner—but it isn't pulling me along anymore.

I settle on the email. "Help me write this."

He pulls his chair closer. "What do you want to say?"

I take a moment. Then I start typing, and he reads over my shoulder, offering a word here, cutting a phrase there.

> Dean Dean Stratford,
>
> I am available for an initial meeting early next week. Please propose a day and time.
>
> Please note that I will be out of town the following week and unavailable during that period.
>
> —Cassandra Maddox

I hover over send.

"Clear," Rafi says. "Professional. Boundaries intact."

I click it.

The inbox goes quiet.

I stand and stretch, my spine cracking back into place. The wall is bare except for the photo and the yellow post-it. I touch the frame, then let my hand fall.

I don't know what's waiting at Penamore.

I don't know if I'll open that email tomorrow, or let it sit while I finish closing out the week.

But I do know this:

Whatever comes next, we'll face it together.

And for now, Charleston is waiting.

Outside, the city exhales.

Inside, I do the same.

About the Author

Tim, a seasoned educator with over 15 years of teaching experience across multiple grade levels in English and Drama, has established himself as a dedicated writer with a diverse academic background. He holds a B.S. in Theatre from Towson University, an M.A.T. from Notre Dame of Maryland University, and an M.A. in Creative Writing and Literature from Fairleigh Dickinson University.

Originally from Syracuse, New York, Tim currently resides in Maryland, where he imparts his passion for English, Creative Writing, Film, and Theatre to high school students. His journey into writing began earnestly in 2014, spurred by the encouragement of his own students.

Tim's love for storytelling stems from his upbringing, where his mother's dedication to reading to him and his siblings laid the foundation for his literary pursuits. Tim embarked on his writing endeavors, influenced by authors such as C. S. Lewis, J. R. R. Tolkien, Piers Anthony, and others in the mystery, thriller, and fantasy genres.

Since his debut publication in 2019, Tim has rapidly expanded his literary footprint, amassing a wealth of published works. Beyond writing, Tim enjoys indulging in his diverse interests, including reading, teaching, camping, savoring cigars, shooting, and attending live music concerts.

Tim is also grateful for the support he's received from the editors, authors, and publisher at Indies United Publishing House. So, if you're looking for your next great read—or a vibrant community where authors and readers connect—visit Indies United Publishing House. It's where diverse voices, fresh stories, and passionate indie authors come together to celebrate creativity in every genre.

You can connect with me on:
- https://linktr.ee/timothyrbaldwin
- http://www.x.com/timothyrbaldwin
- https://facebook.com/timothyrbaldwin

Subscribe to my newsletter:
- https://books2read.com/r/B-A-PUHJ-RLPCJ